About the author

BORN IN LONDON in 1978, Mary Karras is the daughter of Greek Cypriot emigres. Her parents separately fled Cyprus in the sixties and seventies, seeking a new life free of the turbulent politics of their native island, settling in north London where they met and married. As a child, Mary and her sisters would visit their grandparents in Harringay, spending time in the Greek Cypriot grocery shops and bakeries that flourished on Green Lanes at that time. Growing up, she developed a keen interest in the concepts of community, cultural dissonance, language and belonging, leading her to pursue a degree in English Literature and Language at King's College London. She lives in north London, and *Mrs Petrakis* is her first novel.

Mary Karras

THE MAKING OF MRS PETRAKIS

First published in Great Britain in 2021 by Two Roads
An Imprint of John Murray Press
An Hachette UK company

This paperback edition published in 2022

3
Paperback ISBN 978 1 529 34495 0
eBook ISBN 978 1 529 34559 9

Typeset in Albertina MT by
Palimpsest Book Production Ltd, Falkirk, Stirlingshire

Printed and bound in Great Britain by Clays Ltd, Elcograf S.p.A.

John Murray policy is to use papers that are natural, renewable and
recyclable products and made from wood grown in sustainable forests.
The logging and manufacturing processes are expected to conform
to the environmental regulations of the country of origin.

Two Roads
Carmelite House
50 Victoria Embankment
London EC4Y 0DZ

www.tworoadsbooks.com

For Jim and our Ls

Chapter 1

London – 1988

IT'S GROWING LATE when she walks into the police station and outside, the red rays of the retreating sun streak the sky like flames. She's distraught. The policeman behind the glass looks up at her as she makes her way towards him. Her hands are shaking and she grips the counter to steady herself. Her whispered voice is filled with urgency and panic.

Please. I've lost my son.

The policeman sits bolt upright, galvanised by the information. He's caught off guard. He wasn't envisaging. Not this evening.

Your son? When did you last see him?

She is small and pale and her large dark eyes are wide and watery. Two muddied pools. She's disorientated. A shadow of a lost self. She hugs her clothes tightly around her chest and disappears into her embrace.

This morning. He went out to play football in the schoolyard with his friend and he didn't come home.

The policeman grabs a pen, opens his notebook.

Can I take some details? How old is he?

He's eight.

Eight? And what's his name?

The woman hesitates. Her breath mists the glass in front of the policeman's face and she raises her finger hesitantly and draws five letters in it.

Chapter 2

London – 1974

PETRAKIS BAKERY SITS in the heart of the London Greek Cypriot community, ensconced snugly between Themis Continental Supermarket and George Groceries on Green Lanes in Harringay. The warm, mouth-watering scents of rose water, cinnamon and sugar waft around the little shop and sticky pastries glisten behind half-steamed windows, delighting hungry locals. Maria Petrakis is proud of her bakery, and of her delicious shamali in particular. Green Lanes may be no stranger to a Cypriot bakali selling overripe watermelons and garlic olives and even the odd stale galatoboureko, but nobody's syrup and semolina cakes taste quite like hers. The customers agree, and the till rings all day long as baklava and pastitsia fly off the shelves. Ting ting! The sound, Maria thinks, of satisfied bellies and a successful business.

At the end of a long hard day behind the counters, she will carefully arrange some of the leftover pastries into a cardboard box and make her way slowly up the stairs to Costa, who'll sprawl out on his favourite orange sofa and finish them in front of the telly.

You're making me fat, Mamma!

You don't need to eat them all at once, hah?

Costa, her only child – her beautiful Katerina, may God rest her soul, died when she was little – is twenty-five and still living in the small two-bedroomed flat above the bakery with her. It's true that he is getting fat, but it's also true that he should have married years ago and be raising a houseful of children by now. Instead, he follows her around the kitchen like a bored, hungry cat looking for food.

Maria is certainly not oblivious to her son's short-comings but everybody knows that a lack of facial symmetry doesn't stop a man from getting married. A woman perhaps, but not a man. It didn't do Themis of Themis Continental any harm. Or George on the other side, although judging by his years and the size of his wife's bosoms, she suspects money was the allure in their union. Costa is lazy and that is the fact of the matter. Lazy and insolent.

Maria decides it's time to take matters into her own hands while firing up her ovens in the back room of her shop early one morning. The day has barely begun, but enough is enough. Besides being sick to the back teeth of the insurmountable piles of laundry and insinuating questions from the customers, Maria needs to make sure that Costa doesn't bring an English girl home to her. A xeni, with eyes the colour of ice cubes, who would turn her nose up at their traditions or worse, ridicule them. And God forbid she drag her Costa away to a tired old town in the middle of nowhere so they can live alone like hermits, miles away from the community. This very thing did, in fact, happen to her favourite customer, Mrs Koutsouli, and the poor woman has never got over it.

Her son, such a beautiful boy, a real leventi as they used to say back home, married a woman named Linda and moved to Maidstone. Maidstone, indeed! Imagine that? Maria had never heard of this place and Mrs Koutsouli was practically a broken woman and who could blame her? Such a waste of a perfectly eligible son and years of motherly sacrifice. *And for what?* she'd cry when she came into the shop for her box of bourekia. A quick civil ceremony with no God or priest in sight and a couple of grandkids whose names she couldn't pronounce. Ptu! A kick in the teeth more like. Maria tuts at the memories. She considers herself fair, but she has to draw the line somewhere and this is most certainly it. No, what she needs is a nice Greek girl. From Cyprus, preferably, but Greece would do just as well.

She quickly discovers, however, that finding a nice Greek girl in a bakery selling nice Greek pastries is not as easy as it seemed in her head. Modern girls apparently don't want to be probed about their love lives by a goji-akari who could pass for their grandmother. An ageing lady of sixty with tired, olive-coloured skin and a silver-grey knot for hair. They are not interested in the proxenia of her day where relatives played cupid for blushing couples who would sit coyly across the table from one another while their parents drank kafe and planned their wedding. You could say no of course, if you didn't like the boy, but you couldn't say no forever. Once was acceptable. Expected, even. Twice, maybe. But sooner or later you needed to pick a groom and get on with it. A woman's ovaries wouldn't wait forever.

But times have moved on and girls want to find their own husbands. *Not for me, thea,* the pretty ones giggle when she mentions her son and points to the ceiling above them. Their faces blazing brighter than her upstairs carpets. He's a little short, she'll admit. For a man. A little fat, perhaps, but his heart is made of golden syrup. *I'm in a hurry, another time.* Or sometimes, *I have a boyfriend.* It never did her any good, choosing her own husband. No good at all. *Suit yourselves.* She's not disheartened. There are plenty of opportunities for the patient matchmaker and you only need one of them to say yes.

~

The girl walks into Maria's bakery on a wet Saturday afternoon in September, while Maria Petrakis is remembering her own proxenia to Michali. Ach, Michali. Her parents hadn't liked him, but she had thought him a hero for working at the base in Nicosia and couldn't have cared less for their sentiments. A labourer, he'd told her afterwards. Sweeping the floors and cutting the grass for Mr Styliano. A caretaker really, and not a soldier at all. Not that it would have mattered. She was so far gone with the fairy tale she'd made up in her head in the space of time it had taken for her to eat sweet gliko with his parents and go for a stroll around the neighbourhood with him, that she'd have married him anyway and the outcome, she supposes, would have been just the same.

She could tell her parents didn't approve of him because they were sullen and pensive when they returned home from the proxenia. Her father had gone straight outside to sit in the yard and fiddle with his long black beard and her mother had sighed deeply as she'd tied her apron around her waist and prepared the lunch, the long silver blade of her knife moving adeptly through the flesh of the tomatoes and tapping impatiently on the chopping board as it sliced.

She, in contrast, had been full of expectation. A husband, at long last. A chance at a proper life like Thora's and she'd even thanked God for him that day. Thank you God for sending me Michali! She'd shaken her head and laughed about it afterwards, of course; oh, how she'd laughed. More of a wail than a laugh. Life's cruel tricks. The doctor calling her lucky after her daughter had died. *Lucky? Tell me doctor, how am I lucky?* She was lucky, he'd said, that she could at least sleep and she'd snorted at the absurdity of this declaration. She had a lot to still be thankful for, he'd told her. Her son, her husband. She certainly wasn't thanking God for Michali a few days into their marriage when he'd well and truly wiped the smile off her face and almost sent her flying home to her Pappa.

~

The girl's large umbrella almost engulfs her and she shakes it outside the door so as not to wet the floor and props it carefully against the wall to dry. Her slow, deliberate manner catches Maria's attention and she finds herself back in the present, spying out of the corner of her eye as the girl runs her fingers through her short brown hair and wipes her feet on the doormat. She's polite. The first in a short list of criteria.

Yia sas. Maria nods a hello in return and goes back to arranging kourabiethes into a butter biscuit pyramid for the window display. She's careful not to lose concentration and drop one on top of the other so the whole thing topples over like it did last week. Such a bother and icing sugar everywhere. The perils, she'd said to Costa later. The perils of running a bakery! See what I have to go through?

She walks over to the counter and stares at the pastries lined up in rows and coordinated by size and colour. The browns together, then the golds and then the creams. A little trick she'd learned over the years. People liked rows and people liked categories. You had to know people, and she really did. You couldn't stick a sweet baklava in with a spinach spanakopita and hope for the best.

Are the loukoumades fresh?

The girl taps her wet finger against the glass and it leaves a smudge Maria will have to clean later.

Of course. Rest assured, I get them from a very reputable supplier.

And the shamali?

The shamali I bake myself.

A silent fanfare. Her semolina cakes are unparalleled, she beams proudly. On Green Lanes or anywhere else. *Just ask around and anyone who knows me will agree.* Except for the jealous ones, she thinks. And possibly those thieves, Mr and Mrs Papavasilakis.

The girl walks along the length of the shop, veering from the sweet to the savoury and then back again. She's killing time, Maria thinks. Some of the customers dither like that because they enjoy basking in the warmth of the bakery and the conversation, but today she's glad of the procrastination. It gives her time to study the soft contours of the girl's pale round face and her smooth dainty hands. Her short hair tucked behind her ears like a schoolgirl's. She's still a child, Maria thinks. Barely a woman at all. When she looks up from the pastries, Maria discerns a familiar sadness spilling from her large dark eyes. Perhaps she has been touched by the war or perhaps there's something else.

Have we met?

I don't think so, Kyria.

Madam. The girl calls her Kyria and not thea. Her manners, impeccable. She feels silly. Of course she doesn't know her. Why would she? She's no longer in Kyrenia, where everybody knows everybody else and the neighbour is likely a cousin. At the same time, she can't shake off the feeling that she's seen the girl's face before. A whisper, a shadow. A memory of a well standing in another life.

In a dream, perhaps.

I'm sorry?

By this point her excitement is mounting higher than the biscuits in her precarious pyramid and her mind is almost entirely made up. Further conversation might spoil fate and cause it, and her, to walk out into the English rain, never to be seen again. God forbid she ends up like poor Mrs Koutsouli. She looks at her watch. It's ten to six. Good enough. She walks over to the door and carefully closes it. Then she twists the shop sign around from 'Open' to 'We're Shut!' and clasps her hands together.

~

The girl regards her with suspicion and Maria winks back. A free cup of tea for a compatriot, she assures her. Nothing more and nothing less. Her name is Elena and she is nineteen. Maria's right, she's practically a child. She hails from northern Cyprus. Or did. *It's theirs now.* Her mother sent her to England to live with her sister after the first bout of fighting and when they all still thought President Makarios was dead. *Poor Makarios* and she was glad that the radio stations had got it wrong and that he'd managed to escape in the end. They nod their heads in shared sorrow. He didn't deserve it, what happened to him. Her mother could smell it. The stench of rotting meat, she'd said, seeping through a stalemate bolstered with promises nobody intended to keep. Empty words. The blood of young men, boys even. A terrible thing, war.

They sip hot tea and eat warm honey doughnuts at the little wooden table next to the till, where customers stop for a pastry and a gossip when they've nowhere else to be. Tea and conversation, who can resist? The girl's shoulders relax. She bites into the fluffy pastry ball and golden honey oozes out of the bottom and runs down her chin. Maria chuckles to herself as she licks her fingers one by one. An excited child who can't sit still in her chair.

You're right. These are delicious!

She kicks her feet against the legs of the table and it reminds Maria of a young Costa. Rubbing his belly and waiting for dessert.

Eat! Eat! You're far too thin!

An attempt at humour rather than a reproach.

Elena's sister and the husband were nice to her at first and Valentina had even been happy to see her. A tentative calm had persisted at the start of August when it looked like the war might have been a storm in a cup of chai. All that worry for nothing, they'd thought, and she could practically see her mother kissing the cross around her neck in gratitude and raising her hands to the sky. Her neighbour, Mrs Pavlou, dancing on her porch in delight, the blood of her eldest son spared. But then the Turks invaded for a second time when their backs were turned. A surprise to everyone except, perhaps, her boss, Mr Aleko. People began to lose their livelihoods and then their lives and by the end of August it became clear that there would be nothing left to return home to. Elena could sense her hosts retreating into their dark hollow shells like worried snails. *We're stuck with her now, what are we going to do?* A relative in need, it seemed, was a burden.

Maria nods sympathetically. She leans back in the creaky chair and slurps her tea. She's sorry, she tells her, that there's no cinnamon down here, but she could brew her a proper pot upstairs another time if she'd like. While she pities the girl with the big dark eyes, it's a story she's heard over and over these past weeks. A quarter of the Cypriot population displaced by civil war. Homes in the north lost, people forced south. People from the south forced north. She's sad about it all, of course she is, but she's glad she and Costa are out of it and this doesn't feel like her war. Michali had been right all along. He would be enjoying this, she thinks. His smirk baring his rotten yellow teeth and dividing his face in two. *I told you so. Didn't I tell you so?*

Elena is worried that her mother hasn't called.

Perhaps the phone lines are down?

Yes, that's what I thought.

Perhaps the phone lines are down. Who knows? That's the story Mrs Pantelis is holding on to, at least. Holding on to it like a child clutching a bottle of milk. Her customer, Mrs Pantelis, whose only son was a soldier in the Cypriot army and hadn't called home in a month. A whole month and she was going out of her mind with the worry. Wondering this and that. Whether he'd been captured and whether the Turks were feeding him and if he had a patch of shade to sit in. *His skin is so fair,* she'd say to Maria. *You've never seen such a pale*

Cypriot! I do hope he has a palm tree to shade beneath. Maria would commiserate with her at the back of the shop and stroke her dry leathery hand and tell her whatever it was that she wanted to hear. *Of course he'll have a palm tree. And a hat. And I'm sure he'll you call soon.* It would all be OK.

Maria places her hand over Elena's and squeezes it as if she's Mrs Pantelis. She looks around the bakery at the bare yellow walls above the door and the cake counters, and wonders if she should hang pictures. She'd painted it yellow when she'd first bought it twelve years ago because it reminded her of the sun. A nice cheery colour, yellow. You couldn't go wrong with yellow. It needed paintings, though. Something traditional to remind the customers of home and maybe a tapestry or two. And her girl. She'd brought her with her, the doomed young lady who used to hang over her refrigerator in her old kitchen, although she still couldn't face her. She was in her suitcase, gathering dust, along with her British passport and the dress she'd worn the last time she'd seen *him*.

When Costa had arrived home from school that day, he'd found her in the kitchen, rinsing their plates and crying into her steaming pot of okra. She'd told him that the onions she'd been chopping earlier had stung her eyes and they'd spilled out onto her cheeks. It had been the theme of the past few months, lying to Costa. In reality, she was missing him. He'd only been gone a quarter of an hour and already her chest ached with the heaviness of it. She couldn't imagine living the rest of her life without him. There were other things, too, of course. She pitied the boy and she was afraid, in some measure, of the burden of guilt she'd have to carry around with her. But mostly, her tears were for him.

Elena is still complaining about her sister. Their dingy house stinks of cigarette smoke, but when she opens the windows for some fresh air the noise from the road outside almost pops her eardrums. So many cars, she's never seen so many cars! Like angry wasps buzzing around her. It's a wonder her sister can stand it, but then it's a wonder her sister can stand many things. Like her husband, for a start.

She locks herself in the spare bedroom they've begrudged her and she writes to her mother, although she hates writing letters and by the time she's sealed the envelope and licked the stamp she feels positively sick.

She's been taking the bus from Edmonton to Green Lanes, where at least she recognises familiar names and signs. Valentina told her where to stand and wait for it and to count the stops before she had to get off. She was surprised, at first, to see so many Greek shops in London, of all places. Such a foreign city a million miles away from home. Her friend, Andoni Pavlou, will whistle through his teeth when he comes back home from the war and she tells him about Green Lanes. *A Greek Lane?* he'll tease. She wishes he was here now, to keep her company and make her laugh with his jokes.

She likes to wander aimlessly around the bakalies,

the Greek Cypriot grocers selling pungent cheeses and shiny purple aubergines and garlic salami. She likes the smells and the colours, she tells Maria. The split pink and green watermelons and the baskets full of shiny black and green olives swimming in brine. So many baskets! She likes the way the shopkeepers stand outside the door and twiddle their moustaches and beckon her inside. They remind her of her Pappa and Green Lanes reminds her of home, or what's left of it.

Apart from the weather, of course. The sky, so grey and foreboding. *Is it always like this?* Maria closes her eyes and nods her head in confirmation. But just you wait, she warns, until the winter. You haven't experienced cold until you've spent a winter in England. The chill can cut through your bones. And she can almost see herself, thirteen years earlier, standing in Mrs Iacovou's house, watching the rain splatter against the windows and feeling like her heart would burst with happiness. She took in lodgers for the company, she used to say to Maria. She didn't need the money so much by then. Company and the stories they told. She should hear the stories, she could fill a lifetime of pages with them. Some running away from things and some running towards them and one of them had even murdered his wife, she'd hissed. It's God's honest truth. Maria would sit by the crackling fire in the evening and drink her zivania and nod politely and marvel once again at the bitter irony of it all.

Later, when she'd had enough, she'd walk up Mrs Iacovou's well-worn staircase to her rented room, giddy with the drink but still careful not to place her feet in the centre of the steps to avoid treading the same path as the murderer she'd been told about, and she'd close the door quietly behind her. She'd watch Costa sleep and stroke his curly hair, splayed out on the pillow beneath him, and she'd congratulate herself on her discretion. It's a quality she's come to nurture over the years. Discretion. Far better to be reticent and tight-lipped than like her garrulous customers, noisily blabbing their affairs to all and sundry. She'd undress and crawl into her cold bed and draw the cheap, itchy blankets that caught on her skin up to her chin, and she'd allow herself to think of him. Always him, and the little bakery she was going to buy on Green Lanes. She'd toss and turn in anticipation, excited for her new life to begin and the memory of the old one to disappear. Her real life, she'd say to herself. The life she was meant to lead.

Winter? I hope I'm not still here in winter! Elena wrinkles her nose at the thought of it and Maria's impatience gets the better of her. She's heard enough childish moaning about strange sisters and foreboding skies and salty olives in baskets. *Let me help.* She reaches over and pats the girl's hand. Despite her many great sins, God appears to have smiled on her this evening. She's lucky, and not in the way that Dr Pantazis had meant, either. The situation is perfect. For her and Costa at least, and quite possibly the sister. Besides, when all's been said and done, she likes the girl. She's rather pretty, too. Not in an intimidating way, but in a way the girl in the neighbouring house might be pretty. A pretty that sneaks up on you slowly and taps you on the back. And she's Greek. Maria casts her eyes furtively to the ceiling and thanks God. A nice Greek girl in a nice Greek bakery at long last, and it had only taken a couple of months.

If you want to stay out of your sister's hair for a bit, why don't I ask my son to keep you company, hah?

She'll plan a wedding. Not just any wedding but a huge celebration and she'll post invitations covered in gold and silver glitter to everybody on Green Lanes and all the way up to Finsbury Park. That should cover it. People will be clapping and dancing to the bouzouki while she proudly circulates silver trays stacked high with tasty koubes dressed with lemon, and shamali, of course. *Freshly baked this morning and every bit as good as the ones I sell in my shop!* she'll exclaim.

Costa wants to get married, he just doesn't know it yet. And the customers, overcome with joy they'll be. Her only son, married at last and such a relief for you, Kyria Maria, they'll say. After all these years when she'd nearly consigned him to the sofa with his box of cakes and now here he is, practically a married man.

He can show you around Green Lanes, she ventures respectfully. *Just until you go home, of course, which I'm sure will be soon enough.*

Chapter 3

London – 1981

THROUGHOUT THE FIRST six months of the baby's life, Elena is overcome with a gloom so intense that it takes all her willpower not to be swallowed up by it entirely. All the colour, it seems, has drained out of the world and swirled down a long, dark hole along with all the joy. Where once there were yellows and golds to admire, now there is only grey. So deep is the sorrow that afflicts her soul that she has no energy left to love the poor child who lies in her cot for hours cooing and gurgling and reaching up for her feet, while Elena paces anxiously around her bed and wishes she would vanish into thin air like all the other things which once made her happy.

She misses living with Maria. It's been years since they moved out of her mother-in-law's flat above the bakery on Green Lanes, but she wishes she was there now, curled up on the sofa with Costa in Maria's red and orange front room, her head nestled on his large soft chest, as he ate sticky shamali left over from the shop downstairs. They used to do that a lot when they were first married. Cuddle up together and watch telly while Maria tended to the evening clientele. Costa used to call them the bargain hunters. The tight-fisted stragglers who came in at closing time to pick up a cheap pastry or three. *Well, if they're going begging, Kyria Maria,* they'd chuckle and he'd roll his eyes and sigh when she related her stories. She was becoming a complete pushover.

It's the aromas she misses the most. The way the sugar smelled when it was caramelised and the scent of vanilla and ground almond biscuits wafting around the shop. The smell of hot bread and toasted sesame seeds drifting upstairs into their bedroom at five in the morning when Maria got up to knead the dough and light her ovens. The different fragrances and noises heralding the start of a new day.

She shakes her head at the memory because she can't wait for the day to end now. She counts down the hours and the minutes until it's time to bath the baby and lay her back down into her cot so she can, at least, escape the thought of her for a few hours. Until she wakes for a feed or a nappy change and the day begins again. Time, seemingly interminable.

She'd go and see Maria if she felt braver but the thought of taking the baby on the bus makes her nauseous with anxiety. Riding on the hot, stuffy number 29 with the child sitting on her knee screaming at the top of her lungs. She imagines people staring at her as she tries to squash her cries with her balled fist. Tutting their disapproval at this disruption to their otherwise pleasant journey and Elena nodding in disbelief because what she would give to trade places with them. To have her short journey interrupted instead of her life.

She's almost six months old, darling. Costa points out. *Do you want to try and take her out somewhere by yourself?*

Not really.

It's the crying that gets to her the most. Not the noise of it so much as her body's reaction to it. A bolt of electricity accelerating the beating of her heart and making her feel faint and giddy, like she's about to pass out. All of a sudden, she's in her bedroom back home thinking of Valentina.

Costa is concerned. He tells her this as they sit quietly at the table of their new white kitchen, drinking cinnamon chai brewed the proper way and eating toasted koulouri bread and butter. *I'm concerned about you.* It is the best thing about the place, the kitchen. The rest of the house is shabby and old and needs decorating but the kitchen is brand new. There's even a door leading to the garden, made entirely of glass to let extra light flood in. She basks in it now, picking at her breakfast.

He'd called his old school friend, Johnny, to ask for his medical opinion and whisper behind her back, she supposes. A doctor specialising in women's problems, who lived in a house with seven bedrooms and a garden longer than their street. Elena always wondered what a gynaecologist could have in common with a baker's son. Perhaps he liked Maria's cakes, Costa the convenient conduit.

Elena, are you listening to me?

A conduit for cakes. That has a nice ring to it. She isn't really listening. She knows what he is about to say and she doesn't want to take tablets for her bad mood. She doesn't care what Costa's friend thinks. He can diagnose her over the telephone all he likes but she knows why she's feeling this way, why a sickness has infected the house. Why the light from their new kitchen door has changed from a golden yellow to a steely, ominous grey. It's because of her, Katerina. She's cursed them. Naming the baby after the dead sister at his insistence has brought bad luck on their heads.

She dips her toast into her tea and watches it bloat like a sponge floating in a bath full of warm water. It reminds her of her sweet Pappa soaping her hair and rubbing her back and the sound of laughter echoing around the room. She only laughed when he was there or at least that's how she remembers it. She hates me, she'd whisper to him when they were alone. My Mamma hates me.

Costa says they'll shorten the name. *We'll call her Nina.*

It's the same name, she sulks. *It's the same name and it won't change anything.* He reaches out to stroke her short, brown hair and runs his fingers playfully across her pouting lips to cheer her up.

We've invoked her. Why couldn't we have named the baby something else?

Come on. You know I don't believe this silly superstition. Old wives' tales from the villages. My poor, dead sister is resting in her grave and wishes us nothing but happiness.

She might be dead and buried, Elena thinks, but the

spirit is immortal like Pappa and the cat. Or Valentina's baby, trapped in the place between Heaven and Hell.

She wonders where she's put the censer and olive leaves so she can bless the house with holy incense and drive Katerina's spirit away. It's what her mother used to do when things were going wrong and someone or something was to blame. She'd frantically burn olive leaves and circle the smoke around their heads three times to make everything right again. Then she'd cross herself three times as well and hope that was the end of it but, of course, it never was.

~

It's the first day of December. A cold, crisp winter morning. It's snowed so much overnight that when Elena pads into the kitchen in her dressing gown and slippers to make coffee, the room is illuminated in a light so brilliant that it stuns her eyes. Apart from the time her father took her up to the Troodos Mountains to visit Uncle Pedro and there was ice on the banks by the stream, she's never seen snow. Not like this. Snow so soft and deep that it's as if a duvet has been thrown over the garden to render everything feature-less. Everything, that is, except the apple tree in the middle, which looks a bit like a reluctant bride with her arms outstretched and her head drooping down-wards.

She takes the small metal jisveh pot out of the cupboard and spoons kafe, sugar and water into it, careful to get the quantities of coffee and water right so there's plenty of froth when it's cooked. Her father wouldn't drink it without the froth. *It needs more kaimaki, my darling*, he would say to his wife, as he slid it back towards her. Lenou would tut and curse and roll her eyes at the inconvenience of it all because, of course, she'd have to start all over again and she already had plenty to do as it was. *This is not a kafeneon, Savva*, she'd retort. *Make it yourself next time!*

Her father never went to the kafeneon. The mysterious, smoky coffee shop where idle men drank kafe and played backgammon into the night, boasting, all the while, about their beautiful mistresses. He preferred to be at home with his family. Teaching his daughters things about the world instead of wasting his time talking nonsense with the local good-for-nothings. The dregs at the bottom of the wine barrel, he used to call them. The toothless no-hopers with tiny minds spouting broad, ridiculous statements. The narrower a man's mind, he used to say, the bigger his proclamations. That's why she married him, Lenou would reply. Because he wasn't a man of the kafeneon. And plenty were, he'd better believe it. Plenty were.

She sets the pot on the hob to boil. Her poor Pappa. Long since dead. He passed too soon when she was only nine and she can barely remember his face, although she can still recall how tall he was and the way his arms bulged beneath his tight clothes. Arms inflated by years of hard work. How the time flies. In a few weeks the child will be a year old. Elena claps her hands together as her blood once again begins to flow around her body. A whole year. They should have a party to celebrate her birthday and she could put her in one of those frilly dresses that look like the fancy wedding cakes Maria sometimes displays in her shop window.

She is roused by the hissing and spitting from the pot and she lifts it off the hob by its handle and decants coffee into two small round cups, careful to measure equal amounts of froth into each one. She picks them up and walks over to the back door, drawn to the snow. A red-breasted robin hops cheerfully about on the veranda, leaving a heart-shaped pattern behind. She leans on the door. The thud of her forehead on the cold pane of glass startles it and it flies away. She's sad, for a moment, at the loss. How silly, she thinks. To miss something that was never yours to lose.

There is sound and movement coming from upstairs. The ceiling creaks in excitement. The baby must be awake. Elena turns and walks hurriedly out of the kitchen. The hot cups burn the tips of her fingers and she quickens her pace up the stairs, eager, for the first time in a long while, to see the little girl's smiling face.

～

Maria Petrakis is in the centre of a scrum. Customers push and shove each other out of the way in an effort to buy the biggest, tastiest flaounes before they sell out and the shop shuts for the day. *Eiy, eiy my friend, I was next!* Elena is reminded of piglets on a farm, jostling greedily for their mother's teats. It's the same every Easter. She never bakes enough and people are nervous about going home empty-handed on Holy Saturday, the holiest of days. What would they do, at midnight, when they returned home from church and there were no cheese and raisin scones to break their fast and eat with their boiled eggs? Tradition at threat. The end of the world.

Maria notices Elena hovering nervously in the doorway and tosses her an apron, *here, make yourself useful,* and the pair of them sell flaounes until closing time. Greek Easter is a busy, lucrative time of year for Petrakis Bakery, and – praise be to God during his holy week – Maria does very well out of it; though, of course, she is far too busy to go to church to thank him in person. Costa called her a hypocrite for it and she almost snapped his head off in response. How was she supposed to bake enough flaounes to feed the whole of Harringay single-handedly if she was sitting in church every night with the little old spinsters? The child didn't think, that was his perennial problem.

Thank God for you. I thought I was going to suffocate in a sea of sesame seeds this afternoon.

Elena drinks chai while Maria rolls up the sleeves of her blue dress and mops the floor beneath their feet with detergent. She must secretly enjoy the pandemonium, Elena thinks. Being surrounded by impatient customers waving pound notes in her face. It must make her feel special. Not that she blames her.

What a way to die, hah? Death by sesame!

You could bake more?

She has a soft spot for Maria. That first day in the bakery, when she looked like she'd seen a ghost, she'd revealed a vulnerable side, and the idea that even the mighty Maria might have a secret soft spot enveloped her in comfort.

Maria finishes cleaning the floor and pulls up a chair opposite Elena. She grabs a handful of pistachios from her apron pocket and cracks them open between her two front teeth, throwing the shells into Elena's empty tea cup and shovelling the nuts into the back of her mouth. Her long grey hair is pulled back into a knot and her lined olive skin glistens with the exertions of her busy day.

She's getting too old for this, she thinks. For all of it. The early-morning baking, firing up the ovens at the crack of dawn come rain or shine. The pressure of ordering in the freshest pastries from the best suppliers to suit the whim and fancy of every customer in north London. Sell Mrs Charalambous a box of stale baklava and word gets out and poof, that's it. That's the end for Petrakis. They'd never forgive you, this lot. They'd brand you a cheat from here to Manor House. Such a huge responsibility. *Retire then*, Costa would suggest.

Sell it, you'd get a good price for it.

Sell it? Sell it? she'd yell back. *As if!*

Child didn't think at all.

Elena asks if she's going to church for the Christos Anesti and Maria looks up at her. Poor, pale, birdlike

Elena. A girl crushed by life and forced, in a sense, into the body of a woman. Her short brown hair hanging lifelessly around her ears and her dark eyes burdened with eternal sadness. Such sadness. It was easy to forget, sometimes, that she was there at all. She is fond of her daughter-in-law, she really is, but there is always something the matter with her.

Church? You bloody joking me? I'm far too busy to sit around praying all night. This problem, that problem. Always with the unsolvable problems. Maria lowers her voice and clears her throat in an attempt to insert some kindness into it. *Look, my darling ...* There was a time in her life she could have easily succumbed to the blackness, she tells her. Very easily. But she chose, instead, to come back to the light and live, if only for her son. It wasn't easy and there are days when it is still tough to be alive, but the alternative to life is a death of the soul. Imagine, to lose the very essence of who you are while your body carries on living without you?

Elena doesn't need to imagine it because her mother-in-law has perfectly described the past long, laborious year. A year of darkness punctuated by baby cries and the constant slamming of doors, of her heart in her ears. She pokes her finger into her cup of empty pistachio shells and whirls them around and around.

Hade, come. Let's change the subject, Maria insists. She's upsetting her now and she didn't mean to. Why don't they leave the nut shells alone and talk about their lovely little Nina instead?

Chapter 4

MARIA PETRAKIS IS in a bad mood. Her husband, Michali, has invited his boss at the base round for dinner so now she has to cook for five at short notice, instead of four. On a Sunday, too. Her supposed day of rest. Day of rest? She should be so lucky!

Michali's excuse is that he feels sorry for Mr Styliano. He lost his wife a few years ago and has nobody to talk to.

Why should I care, hah? She mutters under her breath. *Death comes to us all and what a blessed relief that will be.*

She bangs metal pots and pans together on purpose, leaving cupboard doors open and making more noise than is holy. She's not usually this grumpy or eager to stand up to her domineering husband, but it's even hotter today in Kyrenia than it was yesterday and the kids have been getting on her last nerve with their constant squabbling. Her head throbs with the onset of a migraine as the kids dance around her long skirts like malignant little elves.

Enough! She grabs them both by their hair and hurls them out of the back door so she can skin the rabbits and prepare the tava in relative peace. Kids, who'd have them? She opens the fridge door and takes out a brown paper parcel wrapped in string. She carries it over to the small wooden counter and opens it carefully to reveal the pair of lifeless rabbits Michali bought from the butcher. She expertly lifts off their skin with the sharp edges of her knife, trying not to think of the animals on her parents' little farm. Tava is her signature dish and she hopes Mr Styliano appreciates the extra effort she is going to on his behalf on a Sunday. *Ptu!* She pretends to spit onto the floor. She can't remember the last time she had a day to herself. Even half a day would suffice. She hacks the animals into pieces and arranges them neatly around potatoes in a large metal pan. She scatters chopped onion and fresh tomatoes over the meat and sprinkles cinnamon and oregano over the top. She looks around for the olive oil and swears under her breath when she can't find it. Why couldn't Michali invite the man over on a Monday or a Tuesday when she had plenty to do anyway?

The dish finally soaked in oil, she wipes her bloodied hands on her apron and carries the pan outside to the domed clay oven in the backyard. Costa and Katerina are kicking their ball against the chicken coop, flustering the hens and making her head pound.

Mamma, Katerina hit me!

Costa, if you two don't shut up I'm going to come over there and slap you both until your backsides are on fire, do you hear me? Now get lost, the pair of you!

The kids pick up their ball, hop over the back wall and walk off down the road in their tatty shoes. Maria pushes the stew into the mouth of the oven with the shovel and thinks she'll have to take them shopping for new things tomorrow. It won't do to have them looking like the children of beggars. She and Michali are not rich by any stretch of the imagination, but they can afford to buy their children shoes, God be thanked. There are plenty of people who can't. Like Mrs Kemal across the road whose husband is Turkish and can't get a job in town. Her boys wear trousers that are too short and vests that have holes in them. Serves her right for marrying a Turk, some of them snigger behind her back, but Maria feels sorry for her. She knows what it is like to marry someone who ultimately ruins your life.

Maria sits on the back step beneath the almond tree and dabs at the beads of sweat forming on her tanned forehead with the edge of her dirty apron. Her thick eyebrows soak up the worst of it and shield her brown eyes from the Cypriot sun. A heat haze distorts the neighbouring pink and white houses which surround their yard and the sound of the cicadas is almost in tune with their flickering. The intensity of the summer heat takes her by surprise every year. She looks at the oven, once white and now black with soot, and wonders if it's hotter outside than it is in its furnace. She takes a long, deep breath, grateful, at least, for the shade of the almond tree.

She loses her patience with the kids far too easily

but, she consoles herself, who doesn't? Raising children under the constant glare of the sun, with little money and hardly any input from Michali, who spends every spare moment at the kafeneon drinking kafe and scoffing Greek delight with his cronies. It's enough to test anyone's resolve. Still, she ought to practise a little temperance. Especially with her darling Katerina, who is, after all, only eight years old. True, she can be a grass snake at times, but her blue-eyed cherub brings her so much joy.

Maria remembers when the baby was first born and her mother had come round to visit. She'd peered into the bassinet, pulled back the thin cotton sheet and gasped at the child's beauty. *Those eyes, Maria!* she'd exclaimed. *They will stay blue, too. Mark my words.*

She'd been right, her mother. They did stay blue. The bluest eyes she had ever seen. Bluer, even, than the Mediterranean Sea on a clear summer's day. Her mother had declared that the baby looked just like her beloved sister who'd died in infancy, and had to be named after her. Her name was Katerina, which just happened to be Maria's favourite name. Katerina. The perfect name for the most beautiful girl she had ever seen.

~

Mr Styliano clears his throat and raises his glass.

To the cook! Michali, you are lucky to have her.

He winks surreptitiously at Maria and she reddens at the audacity of the man. Truth be told, she's knocked back a few ouzos while Michali wasn't looking and, despite her earlier misgivings, is rather enjoying this impromptu evening with his handsome boss. A woman can never receive enough compliments in her book. Heaven knows, she isn't going to get any from her own husband.

They sit around the kitchen table, which Michali has dragged into the yard, and watch as the sun dips beneath the roofs of the houses opposite. The oppressive evening heat sticks to Maria's skin, making her arms tingle and loose strands of grey hair curl around her ears. The table is draped in Maria's best white and blue tablecloth in honour of their guest. *The colours of Greece*, Mr Styliano chuckles, pointing to the cloth. *True patriots, hah?*

If only the kids would stop licking their plates like hungry wild animals, she'd be in danger of actually having a good time. She grabs Costa by the ear and hisses into it.

Costa, in God's name! What are you doing? We have a guest!

He kicks the table leg in embarrassment and Michali slaps him hard across the face and sends him to his room with his cheek throbbing.

The silence is quickly filled by talk of politics and Maria rolls her eyes. She pushes back her chair and gathers the plates, relieved, for once, not to be included in the stilted conversation of men.

Michali, let me ask you this, how old is your son?

He's eleven.

Mr Styliano considers this for a moment. He pretends to count, nodding imaginary numbers with his head.

Eleven? Then he is exactly the right age for war.

Mr Styliano pours himself another ouzo and offers the bottle to Michali.

The British have gone and Grivas is hiding in Greece and so now what? You think a Greek president and a Turkish vice president can live together happily? Like husband and wife? You think President Makarios can maintain his grip on an island seething with nationalist headcases shouting for a union with Greece, or do you think there will be a war? Think about it.

He taps his fingers on the table and Michali grows silent, fiddles with his glass. He knows that Mr Styliano is right. He's worked at the air base long enough to have seen and heard things and he recognises an untenable situation when he sees one. There'd been a truce of late, a ceasefire, and Cyprus declared an independent nation, but how long would a fragile peace last?

That night, as Maria is washing dishes in the kitchen, her husband approaches her and puts his hands on her shoulders. He broaches a conversation they've evaded many times before.

I think we should leave.

Maria stops what she's doing but she doesn't turn around to face him.

No.

Maria, if there's a war, our son will be in the front line. Do you understand what that means?

Of course I understand, Michali, I'm not an idiot, but there won't be a war and especially not now. It's in no one's interests to fight.

What would you know? There are more people interested in creating war than keeping peace around here, take it from me.

He tells her about a friend of a friend. A Turkish man stabbed over a loaf of bread. A Greek man struck with a bottle in revenge.

You think they were fighting over bread?

Maria doesn't care about the bread. About war. About any of it. Who cares if the neighbours are Turkish?

I'll take my chances. Go away and leave me alone.

And with that Michali grabs the plate from her slippery wet hands and drops it to the floor.

Chapter 5

London – 1974

A COLD SUNDAY in October. Elena is excited to tell Valentina that she's getting married. Costa proposed this afternoon while they were eating ice creams on a park bench and she accepted. She runs all the way back to her sister's house from the bus stop and paces breathlessly around the front room, waiting for her to walk through the door so she can share her good news.

What is it?

She's barely had enough time to hang her coat up when Elena shoves her left hand in her face. A proposal, a ring! A shiny gold one with a sapphire in the centre. It had belonged to his mother, but he said they could choose a new one together if she wanted. There was a place in London where hundreds of ring shops were lined up in rows like the cakes in Maria's bakery and she could pick out something different. It didn't need to be a sapphire, he'd said. A diamond, perhaps. Something sparkly.

Isn't it exciting?

Valentina unwraps the scarf from her neck and wrinkles her pink nose in disgust.

The baker's son?

Elena follows her sister up the stairs to her bedroom in the small red-brick house Valentina shares with her husband, Taki, in Edmonton, north London.

I said, you hardly know him.

I do so!

She's seen him three times. How much more time does she need?

They'd gone out for fish and chips that first night after Maria had thrown his box of cakes in the bin and marched him down the stairs to meet her. *Costa, Elena. Elena, Costa. OK?* Her cheeks burning in embarrassment at the clumsiness of the introduction and Maria ushering them eagerly out of the bakery so she could close the door and fix herself some supper. She'd eaten half her salty haddock at a café called Paul's on the high street and picked at the other bit while she'd moaned about her mother and blown her nose into the napkin he'd lent her. He'd been solicitous, kind. *She'll ring. You'll see.*

He'd taken her to the cinema in Wood Green a few weeks later. The red, torn seats had stunk of stale popcorn and she couldn't understand the film, but it didn't matter because her mother had called that morning and she was all right and it was a good day. Costa's eyes had widened with genuine happiness and she'd kissed him on the mouth as a reward for his empathy. She'd taken him by surprise, she could tell, and she'd blushed along with him afterwards. *I'm delighted for you.* He was more pleased, she'd thought, about the kiss.

Her mother was in a refugee camp. After they'd lost their house she'd been sent south to wait for a new one along with the women and children and the old men from their town. Elena had imagined her mother sitting on the floor of a hastily erected shelter in a parched field with Mrs Pavlou and had shuddered at the indignity of it. Lenou, forced to kneel in the dust like an animal. *They're throwing the Turks out,* she'd told her. *And sticking us in their homes. An eye for an eye. At least that's something.* And Elena had been relieved then, because despite the two thousand miles and tenuous phone connection standing between them, she'd sounded much like herself.

She'd seen him today as well. They had gone on a date to the park to feed the ducks and he'd bought her a half-melted vanilla ice cream in a cone with a flake in the centre of it. When she'd finished it, he'd dabbed at the corners of her mouth with a tissue he'd rescued from his pocket and he'd asked her to stay in London and marry him. He was nervous, she could tell, and his hands had trembled slightly when he'd pulled Maria's ring out of his pocket in its little velvet box.

Stay?

He'd done on it bended knee.

Valentina snorts.

It's not like you've anywhere else to go.

Elena thinks that she's jealous because, for once, nobody is talking about her.

Besides, he's ugly.

She claims to have seen him, years before. When she'd

gone into Petrakis to buy cheese pastries and he'd served her because Maria wasn't well. Elena didn't believe her. Maria was always there. And besides, Costa wasn't ugly. Not really. He was short for a man and his nose was big and crooked and Maria liked to poke fun at his belly and say it was made of dough, but she liked that he was soft round the edges. Like her dear old Uncle Pedro. Uncle Pedro who would pick her up with one hand and turn her upside down and pretend to sweep the floor with her hair while she swung back and forth and shrieked with delight. *Let me go! Let me go!* When Costa put his arm around her and she nestled into his chest, she felt like that little girl again. Uncle Pedro's favourite niece, smothered by his love.

He's nice.

You can't fuck nice.

And he has lovely eyes.

Dark, like a Turk's?

Dark like yours!

Valentina walks over to her dresser and picks up her hairbrush. She combs her long black hair and flicks it from side to side, admiring her profile in the mirror.

I'm just saying I wouldn't touch him with a bargepole.

Although she doesn't know him and hasn't a clue what she is talking about, Valentina pretends to stick the brush down her throat and laughs at her own unkind innuendo.

Elena sticks her bottom lip out. She's crushed by Valentina's reaction. All those months, she thinks. All those months of covering for her, sitting in the dusty schoolyard waiting for her to be dropped off by her lover so they could walk home together and later, counting down the long, lonely hours until she could reunite with her, and this is it? This is what her loyalty is worth? *Nice to see you've forgotten about the baby.*

She had intended to hurt her. To administer a dose of her own bitter medicine, but the force of her words shakes her. It takes them both by surprise. The laughing stops and the room grows silent. A cemetery on a cold winter's morning. A lost child's grave shrouded in fog. Valentina approaches the bed where she's sitting and Elena recoils in fear at the menacing rage in her dark eyes.

What did you just say?

I'm so sorry.

But it's too late for that. Far too late and Valentina raises her right hand above her head and smashes the brush into Elena's mouth. She yelps with the pain of it and hides behind her hands. She deserves it, for bringing her up like that. What did she suppose would happen?

Valentina walks out of the room and slams the bedroom door behind her, leaving Elena to nurse her bruised and bloodied lip. It's far too late to be sorry and you can't take something like that back.

Chapter 6

Cyprus – 1969

LENOU SITS ON the front step of the small home she shares with her two daughters in Ammochostos, Cyprus, her watch in one hand and her colourful fan in the other, waiting for Valentina to return. She finished work in town hours ago and wasn't on the last bus. Lenou is both furious and worried sick.

Her elder daughter, at sixteen, is becoming far too hot to handle in all senses of the word and is going to get herself into trouble. If only she could be more like Elena. A woman didn't need spirit or looks to get on in life. She herself had been married to a wonderful man for many years, until the Lord decided to call him home. The very best, and God knows, with her widely spaced teeth and large crooked nose, she was far from being magnificent beauty. A woman needed good sense and religious morals, not long hair to fling about, enticing every lecher from here to Paphos. Valentina might possess neither sense nor morals, but she certainly has an abundance of hair. God help her in a town like this, where everybody knows everybody else and people like hair and gossip.

Lenou's had enough. She stands up and pulls her stiff black dress down past her knees and beckons Elena over to the step.

Elena, come here. Do you know where your sister is?

How should I know?

Enough of the lip. I want you to go and knock on the neighbours' doors and ask if anyone's seen her. Go, quick!

Elena rolls her eyes, slips her bare feet into her sandals and shuffles out into the hot dusty evening. She knows exactly where her sister is and certainly doesn't want to announce it to the neighbours.

It's still early enough for people to be sitting on their front steps watching the sun set, shelling peas for dinner or fanning themselves with newspapers. She can hear the sound of radios. Mrs Pavlou is gawping out of her window, pretending to air her laundry and trying to get a better view of their porch. She's heard our conversation, Elena thinks as she waves politely and mutters under her breath. *The nosy cow.*

She walks up the driveway and crosses the road, careful to avoid old Mr Lambri as he wobbles past on his moped as she heads over to the empty playground of their high school, smacking and scratching at the mosquitoes feasting on her pale arms. She tucks herself into a cool alcove behind the sweet-scented jasmine bush and waits for Valentina.

Beautiful Valentina.

It's the same story every night. Valentina is seeing the boss at the factory where she works as a seamstress and the pair of them go off at closing time to do things in the back seat of his car. *What things?* Elena asked her the other day. *Never you mind what things.* When they're finished doing the things they aren't supposed to be doing and she isn't supposed to know about, he drops her off next to the schoolyard near their house and speeds home to make up an excuse to his wife, his tyres screeching in the dust. Elena thinks he must have a great long list of them in his notebook. Lies. *Tonight, my dear, the sun fell from the sky.* Valentina had told her that his wife was growing suspicious of his excuses and that he was going to confess the truth and marry Valentina. Build her a big house on a hill. Elena believed this unlikely tale about as much as she believed that Saint Nicholas clambered down chimneys with a sack of presents on Christmas Eve.

The moon climbs out from behind the white school building and the sky turns from orange to navy. Sunsets are quick; the sun has barely had a chance to bow out before the lights go out and the moonlight takes over. Night brings relief from the sun, but it's still hot and Elena's palms are sticky and damp with sweat and nerves. She wipes them on her legs and she wishes she was at home reading her schoolbook instead of sitting in the dust amongst the mosquitoes and the cicadas, waiting for her sister. She feels silly for her unwavering loyalty to Valentina. There is never any recognition for it, but the alternative is siding with Lenou and that would be so much worse.

A car pulls up opposite and dips its headlights in shame. A shiny black car. A symbol of status in a town where some can't afford to heat their houses in winter. Valentina leans into the driver's seat for just a brief moment and then gets out and slams the door behind her. She searches for her sister in the gloom and waves. A smug, self-satisfied grin plays across her face. Elena has to admit that she has the loveliest hair and the blackest eyes she has ever seen. She walks towards her, a teenage goddess in a pair of denim shorts.

We had sex.

Sex. She knows that to do it with someone who isn't your husband is a terrible sin and that you'd end up in Hell with the murderers and prostitutes. Or worse, the space in between where unbaptised people went. While she shudders at the thought of it, a part of her still feels envious.

They cross the road and head towards home. Lenou is standing beneath the vine, her arms folded ominously across her bosoms and her pale lined face contorted with rage.

Where in God's name have you been? And don't tell me the bloody bus broke down again because I saw the rust bucket trundling past more than three hours ago.

They are showered in the spittle flying uncontrollably from the unfortunately placed gaps in her front teeth.

Mamma, calm down. I was helping my friend after work. She is having problems with her fiancé. I was merely offering advice.

Lenou's eyes narrow. She's a cat on a hunt.

Fiancé? And what would you know about such matters when you are barely sixteen?

An uncomfortable silence. Valentina flicks her hair from side to side and Elena picks at a loose thread hanging from the bottom of her shorts. Will the material unravel, she wonders, if she carries on pulling at the string? Will her shorts fall off her legs and leave her standing naked in the street?

Which friend?

Emilia.

Really?

Lenou grabs Valentina by the hair and twists her daughter's face towards her so they are almost eye to eye.

Aooou, Mamma!

Enough trickery! If you are bringing shame on this family and blackening the memory of your father I will disown you, do you understand me? Now I'm going to go inside and ask God to forgive you for your sins. I suggest you do the same!

Her spittle is everywhere now. In Valentina's hair and eyebrows and on the base of Elena's neck. A sea of their mother's rancid spit, smelling of anger and lemons.

Kyria Lenou, you have found your daughter I see?

It's Mrs Pavlou opposite. Their fat, nosy, neighbour. She's still clinging on to her bed sheets and hanging out of the window. *She's home safe?* Her words are spiteful, loaded. Lenou is in no mood to feign politeness and tells her to fuck off. Mrs Pavlou gasps. She crosses herself three times and mutters a Kyrie eleison. No wonder the daughter is turning out the way she is with her mother with a mouth like a sewer.

They sit on the little bench beneath the long curly

vine hanging from the beams above their porch. They kick their sandals against the stones beneath their feet and wait for Lenou's manic supplications on Valentina's behalf to suppress her ever-growing fury. The street is finally growing silent. People are closing their doors and retiring to their radios or their beds after a long hot day.

Her sister is pensive.

You OK?

She pulls a cigarette and a lighter out of her packet and cups her hands around it. *You want one?* Elena's eyes widen in alarm and Valentina stifles a snort. *Course not.* He told her something tonight, she tells Elena. In the car just now. Something tragic. *His brother killed a little girl in Kyrenia nine years ago. Isn't that just terrible?* She taps her cigarette twice with her long fingernail and the grey ash falls next to Elena's feet. He ran her over. And he didn't stop but he knew it was bad because of the way she hit the car. He could hear her bones crack on his windscreen. People were screaming.

Elena trembles despite the heat of the night. She can see the girl lying in the road, her arms crossed in front of her. There is blood pouring out of her nose. Someone is wailing. Her mother perhaps. She knows she shouldn't look but it's too late. She's been held up for a better view and forced to see her in her coffin and you can't undo something like that. It stays with you. *Take her home,* someone is saying. *This is no place for a child.*

He read about it in the paper afterwards apparently. The brother. That the little girl had died. Valentina lowers her voice and tells her that the mother cursed him.

Do you believe in curses?

She turns to face Elena and her black eyes sparkle excitedly in the moonlight.

I think so.

Her face is shaped like a white sugary heart.

Well this one came true, she whispers to Elena. He couldn't take it any more. He drank a bottle of ouzo five months later and then drowned himself in the sea.

Chapter 7

London – 1983

MARIA TAKES THE key she is only supposed to use in an emergency out of her handbag and lets herself into Costa and Elena's house. She knows the key is for emergencies only because when Costa first handed her the envelope with the spare, there had been a piece of paper folded inside with 'Emergencies Only' scribbled across the top of it. She doesn't remember what these emergencies were now, because she'd thrown the note in the bin in a sulk. Something about fires and gas leaks and hypothetical cats. She wonders what kind of ungrateful donkey writes his mother a letter banning her from his house. Very ungrateful. Especially seeing as she'd given him ten thousand pounds in cash to help him buy the damn thing in the first place.

He'd always been obsessed with the rules, Costa. Even as a child. Always setting alarm clocks and scrubbing his hands clean and straightening his school uniform five times before he left the house. Katerina wasn't like that. Quite the opposite. *A little bitch*, Michali had once called her. *Just like her mother.*

Maria remembers the day she was sent home from

school for scowling at the teacher; she was lucky she hadn't been caned. They had been on their own that day. Just her and Katerina in the house and she'd taken her out for ice cream in town after lunch as a treat. Michali had been livid when Katerina had blabbed to him. *Treat?* he'd spat into her face that night. *Treat?* He said she'd rewarded her for bad behaviour and threatened to put her over his knee and spank some discipline into her himself. He never did, though. He never once hit Katerina. That kind of treatment, the special kind of treatment, was reserved only for her.

Maria smooths the loose strands of silvery hair that have escaped from her neat bun back behind her ears, hangs her bag on her son's banister and breezes into their kitchen. Costa and Elena are sitting at opposite ends of the table, quietly eating faji. The large bowl of steaming rice and lentils sits between them and elicits a loud growl from her empty stomach. She hasn't eaten all day and with a quick *kalispera* and a nod of the head she reaches up and grabs a plate from the cupboard. *Faji, how lovely!*

What do you think you're doing? Costa's fork is suspended in mid-air.

What does it look like I'm doing? This is lovely, Elena mou, bravo.

He tells her that she can't barge into their home unannounced and disturb their privacy whenever she feels like it. *We're not in Kyrenia any more,* he moans. *You can't walk into the neighbour's house with a bucket full of beans for a gossip about so-and-so's wife.* Didn't she read the note?

Of course she's read the note, she replies, and this is most definitely an emergency.

Really, what number was it on the list, hah?

Eleven. Can I sit down?

There were only ten. Ten exceptions and she couldn't adhere to any of them, it seemed. Oh yes, Maria exclaims. The bloody cat and did he know that he was an ungrateful donkey when she'd given him ten thousand pounds in cash? Cash! Elena smiles into her lap, despite herself. She loves Maria and enjoys these semi-serious exchanges. God forbid she'd ever spoken to her own mother like that, she thinks. She'd have hit her across the mouth and broken half her teeth.

So?

So, let me finish and I'll tell you.

Maria shovels forkfuls of rice and lentils into her mouth and mops up the leftover juices with a hunk of koulouri bread. She takes a long sip of her son's lager and belches. Elena looks up at her from under her hair and thinks that, even sitting down, she's quite a tall woman. Certainly taller than Costa and taller, even, than Valentina. Imposing, her mother called her when they'd first been introduced. And a smile like she always knew better than you. 'The mighty Maria Petrakis' she'd heard said many times and it was certainly an accolade that fitted.

It's Maki.

Costa rolls his eyes and groans. *Here we go again.* The infernal Maki Mekkou. Desperate for some help in the bakery, Maria had hired the son of a second cousin to stand behind the counter and serve the customers so she could concentrate on the thing she loved most, making shamali and baking her breads. Nothing much could go wrong, she'd reasoned. She'd still be there, shouting instructions from the back room, dictating the order of things. Maki would be an extra pair of hands, much-needed in her old age. Only it hadn't worked out like that. Yes, the man had hands, but that was about it. He had no common sense whatsoever and standing a good six feet and six inches from the ground, he could hardly hear the customers. Especially the little stooped ones like Mrs Xenophonti, who was nearer to the floor than to the counter. To make matters worse, he didn't know his baklava from his bourekia or his shamali from his shamishi. It was a disaster.

So sack him?

Ha! If only life were that simple. She'd tried to sack him four times. Four! The problem was that she was beholden to this cousin. She couldn't remember how or why or how this second cousin was even related to her, but at some unspecified point in the past the cousin had apparently done her a favour. Now, over twenty years later, she was stuck with the idiotic son and an ever-growing mountain of mistakes.

There was something else wrong with him, as well as his shaky hands and lack of sense. He couldn't stop lying. Not about little things, like why he was late and why he had to leave early, the usual things that people lied about, but about huge things. He'd fabricate stories about heroic battles and space rockets to the moon, gesticulating wildly, his eyes wide with frenzied excitement. Maria thought she'd misheard him at first, but no, he'd definitely said space rocket to the moon.

Costa tells her not to be so unkind. He's heard rumours that he was captured by the Turks in the civil war and sent to a camp for prisoners. He's seen things, horrible things, Costa says, and it's melted his brain. He suffers from traumatic memories. *Ptu!* Maria has heard rumours, too. That he fell off his swing as a baby when his mother was too busy gossiping and landed head first in the neighbour's chicken coop.

Oh, Mamma! Costa soothes and commiserates until finally, like a damp campfire, Maria's ire fizzles out into a wisp of smoke.

You two are very quiet tonight. What's happened?

Elena and Costa cast furtive looks at one another and Costa reaches across to grab his wife's hand.

Elena's pregnant again.

Maria Petrakis claps her hands together.

Pregnant? Why didn't you say? And here I was going on about chicken coops!

Just lovely, she tells them. She leans back in her chair and pulls a toothpick out of her dress pocket. She'd thought Elena had filled out like a cheese puff. It's your swollen face, she tells her. It always gives you away when you're expecting. She was the same. She hopes it all goes well and please to God that she doesn't start seeing the ghosts again.

Elena hasn't spoken to Costa in three days. She's humiliated by his secret confidences to his mother and
imagines them both laughing behind her back as they
drink chai in the flat above the bakery. And now?
Now, she realises that Maria knows the truth. That her
daughter-in-law got sick in the head after having a baby
and wanted to disappear into her skin. Maria will be
lighting candles and praying for her soul and who could
blame her? Certainly not Mrs Koutsouli, or her other
customers or even Pater Thanassi at the church, who
would probably think she was crazy, or cursed, or both.

After all, crazy and cursed were just two sides of
the same coin. Her mother always said that there was
no such thing as a sick head, just an absence of God
and an opportunity for doubt. She'd blame her, her
mother. For bringing it upon herself. *We smash these
things into our heads, Elena, and there is always someone to
blame.*

There's something else bothering her, aside from the
indignity of Maria knowing her secret. She's not
convinced she's entirely herself. At least, not the self
she used to be when they'd first become married. For
a time she'd felt like a flower unfurling in the sunshine,
but since the new baby started growing inside her, the
flower's petals have wilted and she's seeing the grey
again. Not all the time, not like before, but enough to
nag at her. She prays as hard as she can and as often
as possible and sometimes even on bended knee, but
day by day, she can feel the new life sucking her own
out of her. She's frightened that at any moment the

lights will dim and ghosts will start whispering in her ear. The ghost. Her ghost. The ghost she's most afraid of. The curse of Katerina.

Costa tries to reason with her. For God's sake, she was depressed for over a year and he needed someone to talk to or he would have lost the plot himself.

It's only Mamma.

I wasn't depressed. Who says I was depressed?

Costa has to admit that as the years go by, his love for his wife grows but his understanding of her diminishes.

Chapter 8

London – 1974

ELENA TRIES HER best to make things right with Valentina but her anger, it seems, is like a raging fire in a desiccated forest. Not easily extinguished by either man or plane. She follows her around her house like a shadow, making toast and brewing endless cups of cinnamon tea in the hope of being noticed and absolved. Nothing seems to work. When she walks into a room, Valentina walks out of it, her lovely nose in the air and her hair cascading behind her like a black banner blowing in the breeze. It's been weeks, Elena thinks.

You've made your point.

Have I?

It was the same when they were kids. Valentina's moods, up and down like a carousel horse at a funfair. She would grab at Elena's arms after a quarrel and dig her long fingernails into her flesh as punishment for perceived misdemeanours, making her wince in pain and beg for forgiveness. *Stop it!* Scratches and bites Elena could tolerate, but she'll never forget the time her sister screwed up the school project she'd spent weeks perfecting. She'd screamed in agony then. The thick clear snot had run down her face and she'd almost choked from the sadness of watching her article on Alexander the Great burning in the half-lit foukou. *Not so great now!* Her mother had slapped them both that day. Valentina for being a spiteful little bitch and Elena for howling like a pig being butchered.

She's kept their argument a secret from Taki. That is something to be thankful for at least. Crude, obnoxious Taki, who fumbles at his wife's dressing-gown cords and grabs her bottom while she tends to his breakfast plate. Elena, crammed in beside them at the tiny kitchen table with the wobbly leg, wishing, always wishing, that she was someplace else.

I bet you're looking forward to marrying what's-his-face and moving out so we can all fuck each other in peace, hah?

She no longer objects to his vulgarity. It punctures the silence and it's a distraction from the animosity. She finds it strange, though, that despite ostentatious shows of closeness, Valentina has decided not to confess. Still, one enemy is better than two. She imagines Valentina bringing the dead baby up to Taki to look at and she cringes in horror at the thought of it. *Here, look at it, Taki!*

Time is dragging. It's the start of November. Elena changes her approach and stops brewing cinnamon tea. She hides out in the long grass like a twitching rabbit waiting for danger to pass. She makes polite conversation about the change of weather like an English person would. The bite of the wind as it tears around her ears when she walks back from the bus stop. The dirty stop-out more like, Taki sniggers. *You been to lover boy's?* All of this from a safe distance. A sofa or a windowsill or the doorway of Valentina's bedroom. She doesn't dare dip her toe into infested waters.

I'm going to move into his mother's flat after we're married, so you get your spare room back. Taki will be pleased, I bet?

A silence. A crack in the ice, the sound of spring. Valentina standing in the mirror, painting a red smile on her pale face with sticky lipstick. The edges of the bow practised to painful perfection.

As soon as the words flew out of my mouth I swear to you, I wanted to reach out and grab them and stuff them back in.

A long deep sigh. Valentina's black eyes fill with tears and she dabs at the corners with her fingers. Will she forgive her?

I forgive you, Elena. Don't you see what this is about? It's myself I can't forgive.

Chapter 9

London – 1983

MARIA IS SERVING Mrs Vasili when Elena walks into the bakery. Her arrival stirs the atmosphere like a pebble falling into a still pond and Maria has to stop counting out the change and start again. She knows, Elena thinks. She knows I'm upset. She wonders if there is anything her husband won't blurt out to his mother and she is embarrassed all over again.

The door slams shut behind her. The sound of the little bell-on-a-string elicits the curiosity of Mrs Vasili. *Yia sas.* Mrs Vasili turns around to stare at her and Maria seizes the opportunity to raise her eyebrows behind the woman's back. Everyone is scared of Mrs Vasili and even Maki has scurried off to the baking room to cower behind the ovens. Mrs Vasili with the faint moustache, as Maria refers to her. She's apparently related to Nana Mouskouri, *although if you believe that you'll believe anything.*

Maria has finally got round to adorning the bakery with oil paintings. It's been just over twenty years since she bought the place from Mrs Chrysostomou. There's a blood-red sun now, setting behind a row of pink and white houses at the back of the shop, and a cat peeking playfully out from behind a basket of lemons above the cash till. Next to the cat is a picture of a young couple dining in an old-fashioned taverna. The man is leaning eagerly across the table and reaching for the girl's hand but she is looking at something behind him and doesn't return the gesture. The waiter carrying the wine perhaps, or a shadow. It's impossible to tell. The scene reminds Elena of a still from a tragedy. She's not happy, she thinks. The girl. Whatever it is she's looking at.

There's one above the door too. A painting of Her Majesty the Queen. Elena smiles at the incongruity of it. Maria and her English Queen. *Come up.* Elena holds the door open for Mrs Vasili and then follows Maria through the back entrance to the flat upstairs. She walks slowly and breathes heavily, the growing child inside her belly doubling the workload of her heart.

Will he be all right on his own?

Maki? Probably not but I have three different types of insurance.

Maria heads into the kitchen to make a pot of tea and gestures for Elena to sit down on the sofa and take the weight off her swollen feet.

I like your Queen.

Maria chuckles.

You like her?

She tells Elena that she bought her at the market on Portobello Road. She loves the Queen as much as she loves her family and she counts her blessings every morning. First, she praises God and then the Queen for allowing her to live in London, England. If it wasn't for the Queen, she doesn't know what she would have done or who she would have become. So you see, she confides. She is very grateful to her.

Elena doesn't understand but it's enough to be here, near her, basking in the glow of her confidence and the faint smell of orange blossom water. She sighs deeply. She misses the flat, she tells her. The cakes.

Maria pours tea into their cups and sits down in the battered old armchair opposite Elena. She kicks her shoes off.

Well take your pick. No shortage of cakes here.

She winks at her.

I used to feed leftovers to Costa, but now you've both gone I just sit on my own and stuff my face.

She grabs at her imaginary bellies.

I'm getting fat. I should throw more away but I can't bear the waste.

Sell more to the shops maybe?

Maria shakes her head from side to side.

Hah! Does she think Maria is going to arm the competition? George next door would sell his own mother to the Turks to learn the name of her suppliers. No thank you, she replies. She'd rather throw them in the bins for the foxes.

They sip tea in silence. Each knows why the other is there but nobody wants to be the one to initiate the conversation and spoil the mood. Finally, Maria speaks. She tells her that Costa feels bad about breaking her confidence. He was sad, she says, and lonely and needed someone to talk to. It was a long year for everyone and she mustn't think too badly of him.

Elena bursts into tears.

No, no, my girl.

Maria moves her chair closer and pats her on the back.

Hush, hush. Enough of the blackness. Let's talk of happier things. How are you feeling, how is the pregnancy?

Elena blows her nose. She doesn't want to talk about the pregnancy. In fact, another baby is the last thing she wants to think about and she wishes she'd been more careful. *She should have closed her legs,* her mother had cried. Broken plates and a slap in the face for Valentina. How could they not have guessed?

The idea of new life, more responsibility to add to the responsibility she's already burdened with and the return of her melancholia make her feel sick. She wonders how people cope with life when she is so beset with worry. She sees the mothers in the park, the English ones, laughing and joking with their yellow-haired children without a care in the world to plague them, when all she can think about is pushing her pram home as fast as possible before Nina is killed by a falling tree. It's tough, she thinks, when there is very little joy and so much sorrow in the world.

She wonders if not having her own mother around to help makes things better or worse. The occasional overseas phone call, a gift at Christmas and a card on Nina's birthday is the extent of her grandmotherly involvement. Her health, she'd say, prevents her from travelling, otherwise she would, of course she would come. Besides, she is married now with a family of her own and doesn't need her input and the heartbreaking thing was that she'd expected something different from their mother, Valentina once said. Something better.

Does Elena really want her to come to England? Lenou barking orders and taking charge, organising her house and filling it with prayers. Instructing her on how to be a good parent the way she'd lectured her on being a dutiful daughter? Perhaps she does. Perhaps the problem is that she's spent so long being told what to do that now, suddenly, she can't live without direction.

And then, of course, there's her.

Who? Costa asked the other day when he heard her muttering under her breath, opening and closing drawers and looking for the censer. *Who are you talking about?*

Her, she replied. *Who do you think?*

Elena asks Maria if she believes in curses. The horrible kind. The kind that cause bad things to happen. The kind that make you drink a bottle of ouzo and drown yourself in the Mediterranean Sea. Maria is quiet for a moment. She knows that Elena's question is an important one, to her at least, and she wants to answer it properly, to soothe the child's soul and stop her tears from dripping all over her carpets.

I do, darling, but curses don't afflict just anyone. You have to act in a way that attracts them, she explains. An eye for an eye. Your child in exchange for mine. *Does that make sense?*

It makes perfect sense. And that's why Elena's afraid.

Chapter 10

Cyprus – 1969

IT'S THE HIGHLIGHT of Ammochostos, the talk of the town. It's the Mavroyianni & Son factory's annual summer party and Valentina is delirious with excitement. She runs around from room to room in their small white single-storey house, flapping her arms about and shrieking with glee. She reminds Elena of Mrs Pavlou's crazy cockerel. The big black one with the bald spot on its back. Standing on its coop with its neck outstretched, marking the interminable hours. Elena wishes they had a staircase so Valentina could run up and down that and wear herself out properly. Maybe then there'd be some peace.

Lenou is worn out, too, though not from any physical exertion. She's worn out from the worry. She wonders why her daughter is so eager to go to this party and who, exactly, is going to be there. The workers will be there, Valentina replies. Their husbands, I guess, and the former owner, old Mavroyianni.

And?

The new owner, his son, Vangeli.

Who?

Vangeli.

The name sticks in Valentina's throat like a fish bone and she struggles to swallow her words. Elena, eavesdropping from the safety of the kitchen, smiles into her mahalebi. *Isn't the son supposed to be dead?* That's the older son, Valentina explains, honoured to be privy to such terrible things. *He killed himself nine years ago.* She speaks in hushed, excited tones. *Poor old Mavroyianni, losing a son like that.*

Lenou snorts at her attempt at wisdom. Her daughter knows as much about suicide as she does about fictional fiancés. She couldn't give a damn about old Mavroyianni or his dead son. Good riddance. She's heard what he did and he got what he deserved. All she knows is that since her daughter started working at that goddamned factory six months ago, her life has been nothing but trouble. First, Valentina is catching a later bus home every night, then she's being dropped off in the dark by mysterious strangers. Brothers, apparently, of imaginary friends. Cousins of cousins, people and names she's never heard of before. The other day she even caught her curling her eyelashes. *Now why*, she hissed at Elena, *would she be doing that?*

I don't know, Mamma, Elena replied. *Perhaps they were in her way?*

It was all such a joke to them and Lenou's had enough. She's not a stupid woman. She knows that Valentina is up to something and she prays that God deliver her from evil. If it's too late for all that, and she suspects it might be given the local gossip, she hopes

Valentina is at least married at the end of it. Whatever it might be. Lenou believes that marriage is like soap, cleansing all the filth and sin and gagging malicious mouths. Do what you like, just make sure you're married at the end of it. She wonders what her late husband Savva, God rest his soul, would have made of all this. She crosses herself out of respect when she mutters his name. He certainly wouldn't have approved of her beating the girls. He never laid a finger on either of them when he was alive, but then Valentina was only a child when he passed. Things are different now, now that he's gone and left her with two teenagers and one of them a slut.

It had been a love match with Savva. She hadn't been introduced to him on a proxenia. She'd met him on her own, down by the harbour. She'd stopped to watch the fishermen one afternoon on her way home from buying groceries for her father's lunch. It was always cool by the water, and she'd sat on the edge by the rocks to enjoy the breeze and watch the men dangling their lines into the sea, hoping for a catch. One of them had looked up at her and waved. He was the tallest of the group by at least a foot and she still remembers the way her heart fluttered in its bony cage when he'd extended his muscly brown arms towards her and asked her to fish with them. *Come, come!* His friends had teased and clapped. She'd refused, of course. No self-respecting girl would have stood flirting with a group of men, at least, not in public.

He'd asked around the town and found out who she

was, and to her great surprise he'd showed up at her door a few weeks later to ask for her hand in marriage. It had impressed and flattered her, this grandiose gesture of love. Her father had been apoplectic with rage. Who was this strange man she'd brought to the house? Where had he come from? Love? He'd wanted to broker a marriage. You knew what you were getting with a proxenia. Who the family were and whether there were any skeletons rattling around in closets, or worse, unpaid debts that he'd be saddled with. The man standing on their doorstep could have been absolutely anyone.

She'd put her foot down. She remembers this clearly because it was the first time in her life she'd ever crossed the proverbial line. The first, she might add, and the last. She had taken a risk and it had paid off and that was the end of that. *And your mother?* Savva had asked her, as they sat together beneath the lemon trees at the back of her father's house, planning their nuptials. He'd stroked her short brown curly hair and traced circles on the tops of her sunburnt arms. *Will she like me, do you think?* Lenou had cried then. Cried on his big, strong chest. Cried for an eternity, it had seemed like. Finally, she spoke. *My mother is dead.*

Dear Savva. It's sometimes as if he existed in a parallel reality. Now here she is, much greyer and angrier, arguing with her eldest daughter about a party she knows she's too young to attend. Valentina, screaming and crying and stamping her feet like a frightened chicken about to have its head ripped off by a housewife's fingers, disturbing the neighbours. She gives in for want of an easy life. *Enough!* She can go, on the condition that Elena chaperone her. Valentina wrinkles her nose and opens her mouth as wide as it will stretch. Elena is far too uptight to go to a party. Elena? At a party? Can Lenou imagine it, because she certainly can't! Quiet, simpering Elena will embarrass her and want to leave early to read her schoolbooks.

Let's hope so.

~

They head out to the old bus shelter two streets away in their best clothes. It's more of a stop than a shelter because there is no roof to shelter beneath. There are just a few seats and a stick in the side of the road and if you stood there long enough in the midday sun your skin would fall off. They pass Mrs Pavlou's teenage sons along the way: Andoni, Dimitri and Andreas. They're playing football in the yellow dust in their bare feet and the younger two stop to stare and snigger at them as they teeter past in their impractical shoes, pretending to be older than they are. *Hello, pretty ladies!* Dimitri whistles provocatively and Andoni clips him round the ear. Elena imagines them running home to report back to Mrs Pavlou and cringes at the indignity of it, of the four of them mocking over their fish supper.

The familiar evening smells of wood and pine resin are tonight infused with the stench of distant farms. *The pigs must be out.* Valentina snorts. They wobble past

St Peter's Church and turn the corner so they're out of view. Valentina grabs Elena's arm to steady herself and takes her shorts off. She folds them neatly in half and places them under a rock. Then she pulls her white top down over her hips and to the tops of her thighs. *There, now I don't look like you.* She bounces along the road excitedly, like Andoni Pavlou's football, flinging her hair from side to side.

The bus lurches down the hill towards them like an overfed cow and they climb up the steps to ride the eight stops into the town. Elena can see that the driver has altered the angle of his rear-view mirror so he can leer at them from beneath black bushy eyebrows and she tugs at her borrowed skirt and blushes. It's late to be out, especially for girls, and unmarried ones at that. People are strict, judgemental. *I'm glad they're not my daughters.*

They're the only two people on the bus this evening except for an elderly woman who is asleep on the back seat. Her head is wrapped tightly in a white shawl, almost bandage-like in appearance, and there are several teeth missing from her mouth. Her feet are bare and caked in dust and dirt and Elena wonders if she's homeless and riding the bus for refuge.

She feels giddy from staring. She turns back round to whisper to Valentina, who is applying powder to her cheeks in her little pocket mirror and tells her to shut up. *Who cares about the old crone?* Riding in cars and buses always made Elena feel sick. As a child she would inevitably vomit into her lap whenever they took a trip anywhere. Her mother would tut impatiently and dab at her with the hem of her skirts, but her Pappa was always patient with her and he'd stop the car and let her sit on the bonnet and give her a piece of fruit to eat until she felt well enough to continue. Her mother had sold the Morris Minor right after he'd died and the pain of it, of seeing it driving off without him inside, had almost knocked her sideways.

The bus screeches to a halt outside Mavroyianni & Son; they jump out and the driver pulls away indignantly. They stand together on the side of the road, looking up at the factory as the stifling heat of the summer evening closes in around them like a damp, clammy fist. The shop and restaurant owners have closed their shutters for the day, but the relative quiet of the street is disturbed by the sound of muted music. *Let's go in!* The place looks deserted but Valentina knows where she's going and she takes Elena by the hand and leads her round the side and into an open courtyard behind the factory. Elena takes a deep breath as loud music explodes in her ears. Valentina whistles faintly. *Isn't this amazing?*

The courtyard is packed with older people full of drink and jubilation. A young man plays the bouzouki expertly, one leg propped up on a chair, his hot face strained in concentration as spectators cheer and applaud. She can tell Valentina is nervous by the way she is breathing and squeezing her hand. For all her talk, Elena thinks, she's out of her depth. Just like she is. She wants to introduce her to him, she says. The owner. Him. The name they dare not speak of. She pulls her through the crowd impatiently and Elena follows, mesmerised by the scene before her. The music subsides for a second and then starts again, louder and faster. People form a line. They hold on to each other's shoulders and kick their legs in the air, narrowly missing her back.

The odour of cigar smoke mingles with the smell of meat on spits and smarts Elena's eyes. She's never experienced anything quite like it. The atmosphere is charged with excitement and expectation. People stink of sweat and liquor and she can imagine her mother tutting disapprovingly at the drunken bacchanalia and screaming at them to come home before they, too, are converted or worse, ruined.

That's him. She can barely hear her sister but she spots a couple in their thirties standing beneath a string of orange lanterns tied to palm trees to the left of the makeshift dancefloor. The man's shirt is open to his chest and he knocks back a glass of drink before reaching over and grabbing someone else's. There's laughing, it's good-natured banter. A woman hangs on to his arm. She is almost an extension of him. She's dressed in white and she holds a cigarette in one hand and her large swollen belly in the other. The man whispers something into her ear and she leans her head back and laughs the way someone important might laugh. A long throaty laugh. *Is that the wife?* Her light brown hair is piled on top of her head in an elegant bun and her diamonds sparkle in the glow of the light, warning off competitors to the throne. The couple terrify her. The hairs on the back of her arms stand on end and she begins to shiver. She wants to warn Valentina to stay away from these people while there's still time. Please, she thinks. Please leave them alone. A sense, suddenly, that something very bad is about to happen, if it hasn't happened already.

Valentina? She finds her crying in the ladies' toilets. They stink of dustbins, urine and cigarette smoke. Her lipstick is smeared across her cheeks. Women stop and stare at them. Who let the children in? They're mocking. She tries to drag her sister up to her feet but she's limp and won't stand up. Elena crouches down next to her, muttering her apologies into her ear. She's sorry she had to find out like that, she really is, but at least it's done now. No more waiting in the shadows of the schoolyard for Valentina to pull her skirt down and come back home. A narrow escape. They walk back home beneath the light of the stars, neither of them saying a word.

~

She's woken at the crack of dawn by the crowing of Mrs Pavlou's crazy cockerel and pads into the kitchen in her see-through nightdress to pour herself a glass of milk. It's a Saturday. A day for chores and Lenou is already up, rolling out pasta dough on the plastic table-cloth covering the kitchen table, stopping every once in a while to move her short grey hair out of her face and sprinkle flour on her rolling pin. Beads of sweat have already gathered on her forehead, the base of her neck.

You enjoy the party last night?

Not especially. What are you making?

Ravioles. You want to help?

Elena pulls up a chair next to her mother and begins to cut circles in the thin dough with the rim of her empty glass. If she was locked in prison for the rest of her life, she thinks, and could only eat one thing every day, it would be homemade ravioles boiled in chicken stock with lemon juice squeezed over the top.

Valentina was crying all night.

A statement rather than a question, but she stays silent, working quickly and arranging her little dough circles into rows.

Are you going to tell me what happened or do we have to play this silly guessing game all week?

Elena spoons grated halloumi and dried mint into the middle of each circle and buys herself time by making shapes and patterns. Two blobs for an eye, one for a nose. She folds the dough over so it forms a crescent and presses at the edges with a fork.

The person she liked has gone off her.

This person, it's a boy her own age?

Of course.

And it's over?

It's dead and buried, she tells her. Like the dog Mr Lambri ran over on his moped. It's a small, raviolo-shaped lie and therefore easily forgiven, she supposes.

Lenou doesn't believe a word of it but she's tired and beyond caring. It is finished, going by last night's howling. That much she believes to be true. She casts her eyes to Heaven and sends her silent thanks to God. He might not grant every wish. But this prayer, he has answered.

Chapter 11

ELENA ZIPS UP her brown leather suitcase and slides it furtively under her bed. It has the tags from her outbound journey three months ago wound around the handle. Three months ago. Three lives ago. She has no idea how she travelled to London with two bags and has ended up with one. Still, what she's lost in material possessions, she's gained in other ways. She's found peace.

She can't remember the last time she felt happy. Certainly not since Pappa. Her sister, a beautiful caged bird desperate for her freedom and her mother, too afraid to open the door after his death in case the world came tumbling down around their ears. Sworn enemies, constantly poised for war.

Life became harder as Valentina got older. Her blossoming beauty, the talk of the town and men starting to notice. Have you seen her long black hair? they'd confide to one another. The way it falls straight down her back like silk? Her skin, so pale, and completely untouched by the sun, not like the working women out in the fields. And those big, black eyes and red, kissable lips. *Just imagine what she can do with those, hah? A real honey!* A lewd laugh and a long lustful whistle.

It wasn't the boys in her class that were the problem either. Valentina didn't care for spotty teenagers with squeaky voices and secret crushes. It was the older men that were causing their mother grief. The ones who should have known better, who followed her home from the shops and blocked her path with outstretched arms so she'd have to brush past them as they grabbed at her waist. *Hey? Come back!* Elena remembers the time her mother caught a man chasing her almost to the front door and threatened to cut it off with the scissors. *Cut what off?* Elena had asked her afterwards, and there had been a slap in the mouth for her trouble.

Still, at least she was married now. Words she'd heard her mother say a hundred times and to anyone who would listen. *My daughter is married!* As if marriage was the panacea. Perhaps it was. Elena wanted very much to believe that marriage had salved her sister's sadness, but something didn't feel right. Valentina and Taki might hug and kiss each other in front of her face, but she's seen the shadows which flicker in Valentina's eyes when her husband walks into a room. She's seen her cheeks redden with rage and the blood drain from her skin and almost drip down onto their dirty carpets.

She wonders if all of this has something to do with Elizavet. Taki's mother had always thought Valentina no better than a putana who walked the streets for money and could never understand why her precious son would choose to marry a woman with a child in her belly and an irreparable hole in her reputation. Valentina had told her all this when she'd first arrived. *It's been hard on me,* she'd cried. *You have no idea how hard.*

When Taki had first introduced Valentina to his mother, she'd gone on the offensive. *Grivas would be proud of her counter-attack,* Taki's father had bragged. He could use someone like her in EOKA. She had mocked them at first. *Call her a bride? What a joke, what will people say?* Then she'd begged Taki on bended knee. How could he do this to her after all the years she'd wiped his arse? How? She'd faked a few heart attacks after that. Three in total, increasing in severity and the last one so convincing it had led to a stay in hospital and a lecture on lifestyle from the consultant. Eventually, having lost a son, gained a daughter she didn't like and added a bottle of blood pressure tablets to her bathroom medicine cupboard, she'd had to concede that her husband had been right. Taki was always going to choose a beautiful woman over his mother. This realisation had snapped her in two and she'd never forgiven Valentina. Not now that a damaged relationship with her son had been added to her growing list of crimes.

Elena wonders if it's this resentment she can see hiding behind Valentina's eyes. His mother's meddling. She thinks she might ask, but since the mistake with the baby she's been avoiding conversation with her the way someone might sidestep a landmine. Everything, it seems, has the potential to upset her and it's better to stay out of the way.

In the evenings, when Taki returns home from the

building site, kicking off his big muddy boots and shouting for Valentina, *what's for dinner, baby?*, she takes her leave of them and retreats upstairs to her room. Sometimes she writes to her mother and other times she counts the flowers on the peeling paper covering the soot-stained walls. The room they've put her in looks as if it was decorated years ago, for a guest who never arrived – or perhaps who never left.

Sometimes, she can't escape them. *Eat souvlakia with us, there's plenty.* Then she's forced to creep downstairs and sit on the sofa in their dingy front room with the brown carpets and dirty ashtrays and watch Taki picking over his meat. When he's finished with the kebabs he pushes back his plate and picks on her. *Have you done it yet, or are you still a virgin? I can show you what to do if you like?*

She lifts up the edges of the duvet and peers under the bed. Her suitcase. A reminder that she's moving on. A bubble of excitement rises within her and escapes from her mouth. Moving on to build a life of her own. Something she never imagined when she flew over to escape the politics of her island. No longer having to tiptoe in Valentina and Taki's shadows like an uninvited ghost.

A knock at the door. *He's gone out to play poker. Come and drink wine with me.* Valentina moves empty crisp packets off the dirty sofa and hands her a glass of wine stained with her lipstick. If Taki is out drinking it's only fair they get drunk as well. They have a licence.

They talk about Lenou. She's coming over soon,

Elena tells her. For the wedding. *How nice for you.* Valentina sits by the window and lights a cigarette. It's for her benefit, she tells her. The window. She's sick of her coughing. She pushes it open and the sound of cars hurtling down the road drowns her out. *I said, how nice for you, darling Elena.*

They haven't spoken in years, Valentina and their mother. Elena remembers the last time. Two sisters standing in the dark, saying their goodbyes. The emptiness engulfing her after Valentina had gone. Like falling down a bottomless hole without a ladder to climb back out again. It was the same emptiness she'd felt after Pappa died.

Something's happened since that night. She's changed. *Don't worry, I won't spoil your wedding to the baker's son.* The baker's son with his big fat tum. Another attempt at ridicule, but the very thought of Costa waiting for her in the flat above the bakery with his box of shamali fills her with warmth.

Are you OK, Valentina? Why wouldn't she be? she retorts, throwing her cigarette butt out of the window. Such a stupid question. Stupid little Elena, always with the stupid questions.

~

Maria offers to make up a bed for Lenou in her flat above the bakery. *Please, I insist.* It's the least she can do for her new simbethera. Besides, she knows the woman doesn't speak to her eldest daughter and to refuse would have put her in a compromising situation. Maria thinks that you don't work in a shop in the middle of a small community without being privy to the gossip. *Can you keep a secret, Kyria Maria?* They wink. *Oh yes*, she always replies. *Only too well.*

She's heard it all over the years. Things that make her laugh, things that make her cry. Stories that make her hair stand on end. She's quite an accomplished listener these days and she can tell how salacious the information will be by the posture of the informant. If they lean in and grab the counter, their knuckles white with excitement, and whisper wildly in her ear, she knows it's something worth listening to. Something exclusive. Mrs Hatzi's husband dressing up in his wife's frilly knickers while she is out cutting hair all day. You heard it here first, they'd say, eyeing up the fresh kolokotes.

The ones who come in with their heads held high and crow their news from the rooftops like roosters have nothing worth saying, in her experience. Mrs Vasili's husband stuck his tongue inside their cleaner's mouth. She's already heard. Everybody on Green Lanes knows.

In any case, Maria's not interested in tittle-tattle about affairs. Who is sleeping with who is of no concern to her and you can't impress her with the promise of sex. People can do what they like in the privacy of their bedrooms. It's the darker tales she's drawn to. You don't hear them very often, but when you do, they stay with you. Mark you, even. Tales like hers. Now there was a story.

I'm just glad my Elena got out when she did. They huddle around Lenou in Maria's front room, eating soft melo-makarona biscuits soaked in brandy and orange juice. Elena's mother is frail and gaunt, like a shadow of a former formidable self. Her black dress hangs from her body and her skin is brown and wrinkled from years of living in a hot climate. Loose skin wobbles around her neck and flaps beneath her arms. *Tell us.*

After the first bout of fighting there were weeks of peace and she admits that she almost sent for her Elena. She's glad she didn't. They invaded in August. It was awful, she tells them. So awful. People glued to their radios, waiting for the Turkish army to march into their towns and throw them out of their homes. Who will be next? *At least there was notice,* Maria offers. *What notice? We had days. Two at most and what can you pack in two days?*

They said don't take more than you can carry. Lenou packed five boxes and put them in the boot of Uncle Zacharia's car. *Everything else, I left to them.* She thought they were returning. They all did. A few days and it would be over, they said. You'll see. People thought they'd get their homes back after the yellow dust had settled. They were leaving possessions behind. *I even left a hairbrush, covered in hair. Left it for them to find!* This small fact had bothered her more than anything else, she said. Exposing intimate, private things to strangers.

They travelled south in Zacharia's car, like thieves leaving the scene of a crime in broad daylight. They'd built makeshift shelters in fields and they'd sat on the hard, sun-baked floor and prayed. People were mostly kind. Mrs Pavlou was there, she tells Elena. *A broken woman by then of course, and not how you remember her.* And Mr and Mrs Pappas. The nosy witch from the church who used to gossip about Valentina. Then, finally, houses. Hastily erected, but houses nonetheless. Some dignity restored. *You could eat at a table in a house at least.* Others were given property abandoned by the Turks. Lenou got one of those. *You should see it, Elena, such a dump not fit even for a rat and they talk to me about gratitude.*

Maria tuts and nods her head. What a horrible thing to hear. She tells them about Mrs Pantelis, whose eighteen-year-old son, Nico, is officially missing in action. Poor Mrs Pantelis, driven half mad with the grief of it. She comes into the shop looking for him, Maria tells them. Have you seen my son, have you seen my son? She moans and wails and pulls at the cross around her neck and Maria has to call her husband to come and scrape her up from the floor and take her home.

Elena's seen her, haven't you? Elena's not listening. She grabs at Costa's arms, *please take me back.* Anything is better than listening to this, even the cold, empty spare room in Valentina's house. Stories of horror, of war and of loss, hit her like waves and make her lungs ache. *Please.* She can't breathe. Her own mother's suffering blurs with that of Mrs Pantelis like a never-ending tapestry of pain, suffocating her.

In the car on the way home she rolls downs the window and stares as the bright lights of Green Lanes rush by. The cold November air hits her in the face and revives her like a slap. People going about their evenings, darting in and out of the all-night shops, provide renewed context and relief. Life, continued. *Are you OK?* Costa, concerned for her, drives quickly and squeezes her hand between the changing of gears. The car shakes and heaves with effort.

Was it your mother?

It was all of it, she tells him. *But it's OK. I feel better now.*

Chapter 12

London – 1983

WHEN THEY WERE first married, he'd take her to The Parade every Saturday. The sprawling three-storey shopping centre, the crowning glory of Wood Green, used to dazzle and delight Elena. She loved to watch the people wandering around excitedly with small children and spoils in tow, their colourful clothing reflected in the shiny cream floors beneath them. Like sweets in a big glass jar.

Then there were the sounds. Trainers squeaking on floors and voices echoing around in a language she didn't understand and lifts pinging from floor to floor. So many things she'd never seen before. Food she'd never tried, shops she'd never heard of, music she'd never listened to before. *That's David Bowie*, he'd explain. She felt like a child in a magical fairground surrounded by twinkling lights and big hair. *How exotic!* she'd think. *Exotic?* Costa would laugh. *There's nothing exotic about us English*, and she'd be forced to hide a smile then, at the thought of Costa, with his big Greek nose and dark olive skin, passing for an Englishman.

When she'd finished looking at the shop windows,

he'd take her to Just Joe's in the basement and they'd order chips drizzled with ketchup with bread and butter on the side for lunch. She'd drink tea the English way, without the cinnamon, and she'd wrinkle her nose and say it was no different to drinking hot water. He'd call her my little Greek girl and say she sounded like his mother. *You have to adapt a little, see?* To fit in with the English, he'd explain. To blend in, and he'd dab ketchup on the end of her nose while she ate hard greasy chips but tasted only her freedom.

She'd think about her poor mother in her ramshackle Turkish house and her sister in her dingy front room smoking cigarettes with Taki, and she felt like the luckiest girl in the world to be right there, right then, enjoying her English life. So many happy memories. But that was a long time ago. Eight years past and a whole lifetime of difference and she doesn't feel like that any more.

She shouldn't have come back. The sights, sounds and smells which once enthralled her senses have now turned against her and make her head spin and her stomach ache from the nerves. She drifts from shop to shop, directionless and without purpose, the vastness of the place making her eyes swim with confusion, a silent migraine eating at her eyeballs. It's the conversation with Maria that's made her feel like this. She knows it is. All the talk of curses and attracting vengeful spirits. Katerina. Nina. What's in a name? she wonders. It's only a collection of letters and random ones at that. Letters making sounds. There's no real meaning behind them.

A name can't hurt anyone, not really. She buys a coffee and sits at the back of Just Joe's wondering if her future is written at the bottom of the cup, while all around her people are laughing into their plates.

One of their neighbours back home could read coffee cups. Her name was Mrs Mavrides and she lived three doors down from Mrs Pavlou in a house with black shutters and a big black door. The colour of death, her mother would whisper. Such bad luck, to paint your door black, like inviting the damn thing in.

People would sometimes queue outside it to drink kafe with her so she'd tell them their fortune afterwards. She had a real gift for it and she'd take their cups from their shaking hands and turn them upside down and twist them round and round in their saucers, her finger pressed against her lips as she waited for a sign from the other side. *Well, what can you see?* Neighbours would crane their necks for a glimpse of their fate, hanging on to her every word. *A long life, Mrs Polycarpou. It will be a nice long life, God be praised.* Mrs Mavrides had read Mrs Pavlou's cup once and she'd gasped at the horror of the patterns in the dregs. *I've never seen anything like it, Mrs Pavlou,* Mrs Mavrides had exclaimed. *I'm sorry for you, I really am.* Mrs Pavlou had run out of there crying and screaming that day and Lenou had called them both witches when she'd heard the commotion. *Go to church!* she'd yelled across the driveway. *Go and pray and leave the damn spirits alone!*

~

St Mary Magdalena's Greek Orthodox Church is a short ride away from The Parade shopping centre on the 121 bus, and Elena hopes there will be no one there to disturb her meditations on a Saturday.

The heavy wooden doors to the entrance are closed but not locked, and when she pushes against them they creak open, an extended finger, beckoning her inside. She crosses herself three times for the Son, the Father and the Holy Ghost and throws a twenty-pence piece from her pocket into the red velvet-lined dish for her candle. She is careful to choose a spindly one, worthy of her small donation. A long, thick lambatha with a bigger wick and a longer burning time would have been cheating for that price and there was nothing worse than stealing from the church and trying to deceive God while he wasn't looking.

The smell of candle wax and stale bread has a soporific effect and she walks over to the sand table and closes her eyes. She tries to pray but can't seem to focus and she thinks, instead, of Nina. Her little Nina with her sweet little cheeks and her bouncy curls and hands that smell faintly of biscuits. When Elena extended her arms towards her she would shake her head from side to side and run to her father. She loves him best of all, she thinks. Just like she loved her own Pappa. It's to be expected, really. She has spent so little time with the child.

She tries again. *Almighty God.* The sand table is full and Elena can barely find a spot to wedge her candle in. It must be a busy time for prayer and contemplation, she thinks. A Saturday afternoon.

Wait, I'll make some room! Pater Thanassi, the oldest and longest-serving priest at St Mary Magdalena's, comes bustling out of a side door in his huge black robe and catches her unawares. *Yia sas.* He nods a hello, his grey beard moving up and down on top of a smile, and unearths a handful of candles from the sand and dumps them into a bucket of water so Elena has space for hers. He gestures to the empty space at the table, pleased to have come up with an earthly solution to such a spiritual problem. *Put yours here.*

Elena is startled by his appearance and uncomfortable with the idea that twenty or so worshippers have just had their prayers extinguished before God has got round to hearing them. She stands in silence, the candle still in her hand, unsure of what to do next. Pater Thanassi waves smoke from his face and narrows his big brown eyes. Maybe she's here for something else, the girl. And not to light candles at all. *You want confession?*

Her mother used to take them to confession when they were younger. It wasn't enough to fast and cleanse the body of animal fats and take the Holy Communion, she'd say, you had to cleanse the soul as well. Admit, and be forgiven. Elena wasn't sure what it was she was supposed to be admitting to, but she rambled on to Pater Sotiri all the same. She pinched her friend's arm in the playground and lied about why she was late for class. She swore at her mother under her breath and she'd even used the word bitch. Later, when she was older, she'd talk about Andoni Pavlou. She liked him in the way that a wife might like her husband, although she knew it was a terrible thing. She never once mentioned Valentina's sins, though. Some confidences were not meant to be broken.

No, thank you. Pater Thanassi takes the dripping candle from Elena's hand for fear it might set fire to the pews and props it in the sand. He beckons for her to sit down and she shifts sideways so the Pater can squeeze in next to her. The pews have recently been polished and she finds herself sliding further than she means to. She looks up at the gilded icon of the Mary Magdalene, suspended from the ceiling.

Who was she? Pater Thanassi follows the end of her finger. The Mary Magdalene, who else? The eponymous saint of the church. She was a woman of ill repute to begin with, he tells her, leading the wrong sort of life. He stumbles over his sentences, stopping short of using the word prostitute in the young woman's presence. *But then she was saved, you see.* Christ exorcised the devils from her and from that day forth she was restored.

Elena asks if she was happy after Christ had lifted her burdens and restored her. *Of course, who wouldn't be?* Of course, indeed. A fresh start. Mary Magdalene. Elena suddenly knows what she has to do to turn back the hands of the clock and make everything all right again. Her mother and the golden icon of the Mary Magdalene. The same letters and the same name and the answer to all of her problems.

It's late by the time she gets back home and Costa is waiting anxiously by the door. *Where have you been?* His voice betrays panic, a parent scolding a child who has darted across the road and she's shamed by his concern. After her talk with Pater Thanassi she had meant to go home, she really had, but when the bus pulled up at her stop she'd decided to stay on for a bit longer. She'd moved to a seat upstairs by the window and rode the bus down Green Lanes, staring out at the houses and colourful rows of shops from her new vantage point for what seemed like hours.

She'd ended up in Enfield Lock, where the bus terminated, and she'd waited there for ten minutes before climbing onto the next one and riding all the way back up to Turnpike Lane again. Some people had noticed and stared. She did this three times and for two hours before she could pluck up the courage to go home.

She tells him she's been to church and he rolls his eyes. *Please don't do that, Costa. It's so disrespectful.* She hangs her coat on the hook by the door, rolls her sleeves up and walks into the kitchen.

Is Nina asleep?

What do you think?

It was late, he moaned. Past her bedtime. His voice has a sting to it. She feels guilty about this, of course she does, but the child is part of the reason she doesn't want to be here. The responsibility of looking after a two-year-old drains the life out of her and she wishes she could explain this to him in a way that doesn't sound cruel. *She was asking after you again.* It's not that she doesn't want to be with her; she does, in a way. She just isn't very good at it.

She tries to cheer him up. She's going to make patates and avga for dinner. He frowns as she washes her hands and grabs an onion, two potatoes and a courgette from the pantry and begins peeling them frantically over the sink. He pours himself a drink and stands behind her, rubbing his forehead and watching the vegetable peel grow into a giant mound of skin.

We need to talk.

I'll add pastirma, I think.

Elena?

Spice it up a bit.

Leave the bloody sausage for a minute and listen to me.

She can listen and cook at the same time, she tells him. She could do more than one thing at a time. In any case what is so urgent that she has to leave the dinner and have a face-to-face conversation? And she thinks of the girl, in that moment. Staring from the painting in Maria's bakery shop and looking so terribly sad. He says he's concerned about her. About her behaviour. The way she leaves the house and doesn't come home for hours. Once or twice he can understand, but when he's not at work she's never here. Think of Nina. That's all I ever think about, she replies, slamming the knife down onto the counter. She's the problem.

He swills his whisky around in his glass and talks about Johnny. He's highly qualified, he tells her. A very eminent doctor. There are pills, he says, that clear the mind and lift the spirit. Would she consider taking them? Elena drops the onions into the frying pan and the olive oil hisses and spits and it's a relief to her that she can no longer hear him. *Elena?* She adds the chopped vegetables and lowers the heat, the angry sounds gradually dying down. She says she's sorry she left him on his own but she's actually feeling much better after her talk with Pater Thanassi from the church.

Costa sighs. He's not convinced by the hocus pocus. He doesn't believe in anything he can't see in front of him but he's glad she's feeling better, brighter. He finishes his whisky. Will she take the pills for a while and see if they make a difference?

Yes, Costa. She scrapes the sausage pieces into the pan with her knife. *I'll do whatever you want me to do.*

Chapter 13

Cyprus – 1960

THE HOUR AFTER Michali leaves for Nicosia but before the children wake up is Maria's favourite time of day. A time of peace and an opportunity to contemplate the morning's chores before the Cypriot sun has fully risen. Collecting the eggs from the chicken coop, making the kids' breakfasts and taking them into town to buy new shoes. She makes herself a cup of sweet kafe in the jisveh and opens the back door to sit on the step beneath the almond tree. The heat is already making itself felt and she grabs at her hair and forces it back into a knot behind her ears. She's missed the dawn and the sky has already taken on the hues which promise the start of a new day. Blue and yellow. The colours of a bruise. She is no stranger to bruises. She once counted seven on one arm. A pinch or a punch for every day of the week.

When Michali is at work the house groans with relief. Even the chickens are happier, clucking away at the back of the yard like a group of contented old grandmothers. Her parents used to keep animals. Chickens and more besides. Pigs, goats, rabbits. Maria loved the rabbits best of all and would often sneak off to play with them when she was supposed to be watching Thora. She liked the way they wriggled beneath her fingers like warm, pulsating balls of fur, and she'd spend hours tickling their soft pink ears.

She'll never forget the afternoon she came home from school to discover that her mother had slaughtered her favourite, Achilles, and was preparing it for their dinner. His lifeless grey body stretched out callously on the kitchen table while her mother whistled a merry tune and the pots boiled angrily on the fire. *What's the matter?* Her voice full of disbelief at her sensitivity. She didn't visit the rabbits any more after that. She stuck to the animals nobody wanted to eat. The tough old goats and the thin, leathery cows.

The only trace of her husband this morning is the pieces of broken plate scattered across the kitchen floor. A reminder of last night's argument about leaving the island. A familiar refrain. Michali's monologues about war and his conviction that he knew something others didn't. She was lucky, this time. She'd escaped unscathed. No black eyes for her to hide today, the plate had taken the blow for her instead. *Does he hit you, Mamma?* Costa had once asked her, and she'd winced in shame. *Of course not, son. I fell over in the backyard.* Sometimes she caught her arm in the door or was attacked by the neighbour's dog. Once, when he'd almost snapped her shoulder off and put her in the hospital, she'd had to invent a collision with Mr Kypriani's bicycle to pacify the hysterical children.

She tuts to herself as she scoops up the shards with the brush and empties the debris into the bin. She thinks about Mr Styliano. Maria enjoyed being in the presence of a handsome man who complimented her cooking and paid her attention. Maria remembers him winking furtively at her over the table and blushes at the memory of his warm brown eyes and white smile. She wonders if Mr Styliano was nice to his late wife. He didn't strike her as a man who would beat a woman. But then, what did she know? Nothing, evidently. Look at the choices she'd made. She was thirty when she'd married Michali. Old enough to see a brute for what he was, or at least run a mile the first time his fists had hammered into her face. Instead she'd tried to get pregnant in the hope of subduing the ever-flowing rage within him. It had taken five years and three miscarriages to hold a son in her arms and his anger still burned hotter than the sun.

Her doomed relationship. As doomed as the girl's in the painting hanging above the refrigerator. She'd hung her next to the sunset over Rizokarpaso and the picture of the cat playing with the lemons. She'd even painted the kitchen walls bright yellow to cheer her up, but nothing seemed to work. Perhaps the girl was also married to an animal. *Don't worry darling*, she'd say to her under her breath. *We'll get away one day. You and I.* Or maybe he should be the one to leave. She fantasises about plunging him into the well in their backyard head first and leaving him there to rot in the heat while maggots feast on his eyes.

Her parents hadn't liked him but she'd been too in love to care. Too far gone with the fantasy of it. The day before the wedding her father had sat her down and poured them each a glass of zivania. It wasn't too late, he'd said, as she sipped the potent spirit and wondered how he could drink the stuff all day, every day. It wasn't too late to change her mind. It was a long life with the wrong man. *You can do better.* Maria had laughed then. At the suggestion that she could do better. She was too old and plain to meet anyone else and everybody knew it and there had only ever been one proxenia. With her long brown spindly arms and legs and already-grey hair, she was hardly the town's catch. *If I don't marry him this is it for me, Pappa.* A life on her parents' farm, missing her sister Thora who had married years before and moved to Paphos to start a family. Besides, when she thought about her fiancé her stomach flipped and her cheeks reddened with excitement. Isn't that how you knew? Isn't that how you knew that somebody was right for you? All that flipping and churning and your heart drumming in your ears like the harbinger of joy.

What's for breakfast? Costa walks into the kitchen in his too-tight clothes and rubs at the sleep in his eyes. He is getting fat. She's had to let out all his trousers and his T-shirts no longer fit. *Let him eat fruit for a couple of weeks,* Michali had shouted. *To deflate his gut.*

Can we have pites and syrup? Maria chuckles, despite herself. She could never deny Costa food and while the cat is away … Just this once, she tells him. To celebrate going into town to buy new shoes. Costa's eyes widen in alarm. There are rules in Michali's house and nobody goes anywhere without his permission. Even he knows that. *It's OK*, she lies. *He knows*. The poor child. Eleven years old and already saddled with the burdens of an adult. Of course Michali doesn't know she is taking the children into town. She barely speaks to him unprompted these days for fear of acquiring a bruise. That being said, she will need to find a way to keep Costa quiet so that he doesn't go blabbing to him later. Perhaps she will cook his favourite meal. She sighs. No wonder he's getting fat.

Chapter 14

London – 1974

MARIA OPENS THE door of the large silver oven she calls the Champion and peers inside. They're done. She grabs a pair of metal tongs and carefully places the fresh koulouri breads on a tray. The heat blasts into her face and makes the skin around her collarbone tighten and tingle. She once caught the side of her arm on the rack when she was half asleep and the pain of it had driven her half mad. *Ooof!* The perils of running a bakery. She's more cautious now, much more cautious.

Mid-morning is late to be baking in the back, especially when the shop is busy, but Mrs Papavasilakis pretty much cleared her shelves of the sesame breads this morning and it wouldn't do to have the place looking sparse. People would think she had fallen on hard times. She suspects, and not for the first time, that Mrs Papavasilakis is buying her breads to stock her own shop. *Of course not, Mrs Petrakis,* she'd retorted when Maria had confronted her. *We just love your bread, Mr Papavasilakis and I.* A doubtful tale, she'd said later to Costa. How much bread can the pair of them eat? She decided to send him up the road to Papavasilakis Deli and Fresh Groceries to spy on them and nothing, apparently, was amiss. *What do you mean?* she'd replied. *Were they selling my bread or not?* They were selling koulouri, he'd told her, but in their own branded bags and a person needed proof, you couldn't just go around accusing two upstanding members of the community of fraud. Besides, one koulouri looked pretty much like another koulouri. *You bloody joking me?* Maria thought they were trying to poach her clientele. *Nonsense. They're a deli and this is a bakery. You wouldn't go in there for freshly baked bread and you wouldn't come here for salami. Right? Plenty of room for everyone on Green Lanes.* She'd called him an idiot then. What did he know? So she was getting up at five in the morning to bake koulouri bread so that Mr and Mrs Papavasilakis could repackage it and sell it for a tidy profit? No thank you. What was next, Mr and Mrs Papavasilakis dancing on her back in stilettos whilst prodding her with the profits from her breads?

Maria restocks her shelves with the fresh loaves and carefully lowers one into a brown paper bag to take upstairs to Lenou. Nobody can resist her warm koulouri bread. It might cheer the woman up a bit. God knows she needs it. Maria is eternally grateful that her and Costa packed up and left the island when they did, although war was not her motive. Michali had seen it coming, of course. Every night at dinner there would be a different account of the same story. A Greek Cypriot policeman attacked a Turkish bus driver and left him for dead. The Turkish community was up in arms. Grivas is laughing at us from his hidey-hole in Athens, he'd say. *Warmongering fool.* She'd dug her heels in and still refused to leave. Mrs Kemal and her family weren't leaving, she'd say. If things were so terrible, why was Mrs Kemal sitting on her doorstep shelling peas, hah? *Answer me that?* He'd laugh. *How should I know, woman?* But he wasn't going to base their future on the comings and goings of Mrs Kemal and her colander of vegetables.

Maria thinks there might be more to Lenou's black mood than her recent ordeal and wonders if she's feeling guilty about her elder daughter. The one she threw out of the house and didn't speak to any more. She's heard all about their troubles. News travels fast in a small community and scandal practically flies. She has to admit, it's not how she would have handled things, leaving her teenage daughter to fend for herself like a lamb among rabid dogs, but each to their own. They had an odd family dynamic, the three of them, Lenou, Valentina and Elena. The overbearing mother and the hysterical daughter and shy, retiring Elena, always striving to please.

She can't imagine what it was like, all of them living together under the same roof. And then there is her son, Costa, stuck in the middle of it all like a healthy man in an infirmary. Good luck to him. She likes Elena, but he is certainly going to need luck and she isn't planning on helping any further. The bed is now his to lie in.

~

Lenou thinks that someone must be talking about her as her ears are burning in embarrassment. The mighty

Maria Petrakis, no doubt. Hovering around downstairs among her breads and portokalopites, casting judgement on others. Who's to say she wouldn't have done the same thing in her situation. *Hah?* she asks Elena. *Answer me that?* The very thought of her situation still makes her stomach cramp in pain and her acids bubble and froth like water from a hot geyser. She grabs at the gold cross dangling around her sagging bosoms. Making small talk over breakfast and laughing behind her back with her array of dishevelled customers.

It was a terrible time, she cries to Elena when she arrives at the flat the next morning. Such a terrible time. Elena remembers it well. *You?* Lenou scoffs. *You were just a child! What could you possibly remember?* The stares, she continues, the gossiping, the disapproving looks from the neighbours. Mrs Pavlou rubbing her hands with glee, revelling in their misery.

She tells Elena about the day the wife came round looking for Valentina. *His wife?*

His wife I tell you! A tall pale woman with a long thin neck and a big expensive coat. *She looked like a malevolent swan.* She was shouting at Lenou to let her in. *Where is she?* The indignity of it and she was glad, then, that she'd sent her daughter away. She even had a babe in her arms, as if things couldn't get any more humiliating. She seemed to know things, she tells Elena. Private things. Valentina must have blabbed it all to him. Elena had no idea. *Yes, that and plenty more besides!* Like the day she'd gone into town to buy groceries and Mrs Alexandro had spat in her tomatoes. Whichever way you spun it, she was at fault and everyone had something to say. She'd brought her up badly, she'd been too strict a mother, and she'd treated her unfairly in the end.

A gentle rapping at the door. Maria's brought up fresh koulouri bread. *Eat it while it's still warm,* she implores, *and there's real butter in the fridge.* The room falls silent and Maria looks from one woman to the other. She knows, Lenou thinks. Everybody knows. She marvels at the legacy of gossip and the power of the malicious tongue, wreaking havoc from two thousand miles away and four years past. Elena claps her hands together. They can eat the bread later, she's going to take her mother out for lunch and a change of scenery. They can talk about the wedding. Somewhere in the vicinity where they don't need to speak English. Maria laughs. Two mouths and not an English word between them. She suggests Koko's. He makes the best halloumi sandwiches on Green Lanes.

Tell him Maria Petrakis sent you. He might even offer me a discount next time.

How typical of the mighty Maria, Lenou thinks. Always looking out for herself.

~

The elderly violinist is called Frixo. Proudly sourced from Maria Petrakis' extensive network of Greek Cypriot émigrés living in and around Green Lanes, for the sole purpose of serenading Elena on the morning of her wedding. He was actually Mrs Koutsouli's recommendation and, given that he sounded like a cat being drowned in the sink, she wonders why Mrs Koutsouli had bothered. Sour grapes, most probably.

Mrs Koutsouli was not a malicious woman, not like some, and she was still her favourite customer. She wasn't in the same league as, say, the evil Mrs Papavasilakis, but Maria thought that perhaps Mrs Koutsouli was a little jealous of her fortune. After all, she was about to marry her son off to a nice Greek girl and have a nice Greek wedding, while her son had run off with an *Englesa*. It wasn't an accident, Maria would tell her, when Mrs Koutsouli came into the bakery to moan. Elena didn't just happen to fall off a tree like a shiny red apple and roll towards her feet. What's more, while her Christoforo was out at the clubs and the bars looking for loose women, her Costa was upstairs eating *shamali* and waiting for his mother to find him a wife. It's Christopher now, Mrs Koutsouli would reply. His Greek name was a source of embarrassment, apparently. *Exactly my point, Mrs Koutsouli. Exactly my point.*

They are crammed into Maria's front room, Maria, Elena, Lenou and Frixo the violinist, performing the traditions which precede the wedding ceremony. Circling the bride's waist with a red scarf and blessing her with holy incense. *Lots of spiritual insurance*, Maria whispers. *So that nothing will go wrong.* Lenou shoots her a look. *It's a prayer, Simbethera. Insurance is what you buy for your house.*

Of course. Maria takes the censer from her and circles it three times over Elena's head. She wishes the woman would at least try to crack a smile, today of all days.

She kisses Elena on both cheeks. Small, pale Elena, in her long white gown and her head poking out of the top of it. She looks like an adorned candlestick, Maria thinks. Like a little lacy lambatha candle. She strokes her short dark hair and rearranges her pearl tiara on top of her head. Her large brown eyes are heavily shadowed with makeup, lending new, hidden, depths. She looks like a woman this morning, Maria thinks. Older than her nineteen years.

Very pretty, my darling girl. Lenou makes a noise which sounds like a snort. *Pretty, yes. But my Valentina, now she was a beauty. With her long black hair and her big black eyes. As black as midnight.* Maria pinches Elena's cheeks. *It's better to be pretty.*

Beauty, she tells her, is a curse. Maria Petrakis was neither pretty nor beautiful. She was an old woman of sixty now, of course, and couldn't care less what she looked like, but even as a younger woman she was plain. *Passable*, they referred to her as back home. *She'll do*, they'd say. Her mother used to call her a boxamati, a breadstick, because she was tall and bony and her skin was tanned and rough. Prematurely cracked by the sun. A sesame boxamati, neither enticing nor offensive. Nobody could really object to it but people weren't exactly queuing up to admire it.

Her hair was long and dark but by the age of twelve it was streaked with grey, so she'd scrape it back and wear it out of sight in a knot. Her trademark bun. Her ears protruded from the side of her head but she quite liked them that way. They provided extra support for her bun and their angle was such that she could hear for miles. She looked better for her years, she thought. At last her hair and her skin befitted her status. She'd oozed into the edges of herself. Besides, she had known passion, even with a face that was merely passable. A passion like no other because it came from somewhere real. She was glad about that. That it hadn't come from Michali. The last laugh.

He'd started to hit her after their wedding. They'd just moved into their new house and she remembers the day clearly because she'd been helping him to move crates out of the car he had borrowed from his friend. She'd grown tired of the heavy lifting after a while, and she'd wandered outside into the yard for a breath of fresh air. She'd been excited to see that there was a well in the garden. Most houses had a well in their vicinity, but this was an old-fashioned one, with a rope and a bucket instead of a motorised pulley. She imagined herself throwing the bucket in and pulling the fresh water out of the earth for Michali and her. Not for her parents or for their animals, or for her sister Thora, but for her own husband to drink. How responsible that sounded! How grown up! She'd leaned over to look inside it, marvelling at its narrow black depths, when Michali had stormed outside.

His strides were long and purposeful and his face was contorted in rage. She'd barely recognised him. She'd thought at first he must have hurt himself, dropped one of the crates on his feet, and she'd started to go over to him, her arms outstretched in kindness. *What's wrong?*

He'd hit her then and her hand flew to her throbbing cheek in shock. She gasped at the shame of it rather than the pain and she'd run to their bedroom and locked the door behind her. She'd sobbed quietly and for hours, her tears soaking the pillows and sheets. She'd sobbed until the sun had set behind the neighbours' houses and the moon had made a sad face in the sky. What had she done? she wondered. What had she done to upset him?

He'd returned hours later. He'd been at the kafeneon drinking liquor with his friends and he stank of alcohol and cigar smoke. He'd rapped gently on the bedroom door and asked to be forgiven. He didn't know what had come over him, he'd said. He'd seen the box with the broken white teapot, the teapot that his mother had given them as a wedding gift, hidden in the back seat of the car and he'd seen red, convinced she'd dropped it on purpose to spite him and his family. *Why*, she'd asked, *would I do that?*

Her instinct that evening had been to run. Pack a small bag and go back home and leave everything to him. Their wedding gifts, the money, the house. She didn't care any more, he could take all of it. But then she imagined her Pappa opening the door and seeing her standing there with her flaming cheek and her shabby case and shaking his head in disappointment. *I told you so.* Her mother, weeping from the humiliation of it. A daughter of thirty with a divorce under her belt and no suitors for miles. And she'd stayed. Persuaded herself that it was a one-off and that the stress of the wedding had momentarily clouded his judgement.

Underneath it all he was still her Michali, the man she'd ambled around the neighbourhood with and who had told her he was a hero.

She had wanted to believe this more than anything, but a few months later he'd punched her square in the mouth during an argument over the chicken coop. She'd wanted to put it near the door so she didn't have to walk to the back of the yard to collect the eggs every morning and he'd claimed the noise of the chickens would drive him crazy. *Cluck! Cluck! Cluck!* He'd clapped his hands in her face. She'd brushed him aside and tried to lift the damn thing herself to prove a point and the blow had knocked her backwards. His wedding ring had cut her lip and she'd howled for hours then, and didn't care who heard the commotion. Mrs Kouli had even knocked on the door at one point to see what was going on.

You OK?

I'm OK, thank you.

She'd carried on sobbing and screaming and pulling at her hair and Michali had at least found the decency to leave the house. She wasn't crying for her split lip or her pale blue dress, spoilt with the blood that would never come out, she was crying for the loss of the rest of her life. She was the stupidest woman on Cyprus, or at least, the most naïve. She remembers walking over to the mirror in the bathroom and kissing her teary reflection. Bloody smears distorting her swollen face. I've married a monster, she whispered to herself. Can you help me?

Finally, the racket stops and Maria manages a half-hearted clap. *Bravo!* She drops a few coins into the violinist's hand and shoves him out of the door. As well as charging her to play an out-of-tune violin, he'd stunk to boot. You'd think the man would consider having a shower and squirting a bit of aftershave over his shirt before gracing a bride on her wedding day. Was there no decency any more?

It's OK, darling, you can put your arms down now. Elena is still standing with her arms outstretched, unaware that the blessings have ended and unsure of what to do next. Her face is hot and sweaty and fixed into a grimace. Her makeup is sliding down the side of her face, leaving milky white streaks. *Here, let me patch you up!* A woman can never have enough patch-ups, she tells her. Maria reapplies her blusher and whispers quietly into her ear. *It's OK, it's going to be OK.* She looks around the front room to make sure her mother is out of earshot. *Your sister, she didn't want to come to the flat this morning to listen to the violin?* She can't resist. It's a big day and the sister should have been here. Elena's eyes widen in embarrassment.

Oh no. She's not really into prayers. She'll be brushing her hair and choosing her dress.

Good. Then I'm sure she'll look quite the picture when she finally does finish doing herself up, hah?

Over the years Maria has developed a skin to rival that of a rhinoceros and the extrasensory perception of a cat.

Quite the picture.

~

St Mary Magdalena's dingy old church hall has been transformed. Rows of white paper chains camouflage the dirty peach walls; pink helium-filled balloons hover near the ceiling; white linen and pink organza bows cover the tables and chairs, and even the head table where the four of them now sit perched, Maria, Costa, Elena and Lenou, has been spruced up with silver tinsel. Not bad, Maria thinks. Not bad at all.

She would have loved to have hired The Sotiris Palace for the happy couple, of course she would have. The fashionable suite with its proud arches and pillars painted gold and decked in fairy lights would have truly befitted the wedding of her only son, but it was all on her nickel and way out of her league. Costa's friend Johnny had got married there last year and the room had looked spectacular. When the bouzouki player had started strumming at his strings her heart had leapt and she'd felt, for all the world, like she was dancing on the Acropolis.

Still, Costa wasn't a trainee gynaecologist with a lawyer for a father like Dr Johnny, so St Mary Magdalena's church hall would just have to do. It's not like she could have asked Lenou for a contribution either. She'd arrived at her front door with a broken spirit and an empty purse and it wouldn't have been right to confront her with a bill. I can offer you the dress on my back and a blessing, she'd said to Maria after she'd unpacked her suitcase. Yes, Maria had thought. And a scowl that could sour the milk in my galatobourekia.

A good turnout. Maria surveys the room: almost eighty guests. Good going for a woman who'd travelled to London with only a few bags and her son for company. Fled, a better word than travelled, she supposes. Elena peers shyly over the tinsel and wonders where Maria has managed to find all these people who now queue up in their best clothes to kiss her on both cheeks and raise their glasses and their koubes in her honour. She recognises some of them. Maria's customers from the bakery. Mrs Koutsouli with her wispy grey hair and broken heart. Mrs Vasili, clutching her handbag in one hand and her husband in the other, her large backcombed quiff almost blocking out the lights. And Mrs Loizou, whose baby was born on the floor of Petrakis Bakery ten years ago, while Maria was calling for an ambulance.

That's Johnny. Costa shouts into her ear, his voice loud and proud. A friend from his schooldays, *he's married to an actress. And that man there is my Great Uncle Stassi. He's a hundred and three next month.* It turns out that everyone is referred to as an uncle and Stassi is not really an uncle at all, but another friend of Maria's. A hundred and three. The old man sits hunched over a walking stick and she notices that every inch of him has succumbed to gravity. His cheeks, his eyelids and even his earlobes surrender themselves to the floor. *He's fought in two world wars on the side of the British but now he wants to die.* A small black drawstring purse sits in front of him at the table. *What's that for?* Elena asks. Costa leans into her ear again. *They say he's made a bargain with Death and the coins in his purse are a bribe. Is that your sister?*

Even her name is beautiful, Elena thinks. Valentina. The syllables glint like diamonds. She's sitting in the centre of the room in a dress made from different-coloured sequins. A shiny peacock in a park full of fat grey pigeons. She can feel her mother stiffening next to her. Elena wonders how many more hours she has to sit at the table greeting enthusiastic supporters. She looks down at her gold rings. The engagement ring from Maria that they never got round to replacing and her new wedding band. She's glad to be married. To be Mrs Petrakis, wife of Costa, but she's not a natural for the attention a day like today demands. She doesn't think she's pretty enough. People have travelled from the far reaches of Green Lanes to admire her and here she is, a slip of a girl in a too-long dress and with hair that neither straightens nor curls. A disappointment, she imagines them saying. The wedding was nice but the bride was a disappointment. She wasn't worth braving the traffic for. *You look marvellous, darling,* Costa whispered to her when she stood opposite him at the altar. *Just marvellous.* Kind, caring Costa. You didn't marry for much more than that.

She wonders what Valentina's wedding was like and her breath catches in her throat at the thought of her sister in her magnificent gown with her long thick hair cascading down her back. Just like in the photograph she had pored over for years. *A real beauty!* The guests would have gasped and clapped their hands together as she stepped out of the limousine. *Now that's a bride, a true nyphi.* It would have been worth braving Green Lanes to see her.

She searches for Valentina, to offer a smile, but she's nowhere to be seen. The chair next to Taki is empty and he's playing with a packet of Marlboros. He looks jaded, uninterested. She extricates her fingers from Costa's damp palm and jumps up from her seat, suddenly in a hurry to find her. She picks up the bottom of her dress and heads to the foyer where she encounters Mrs Koutsouli coming out of the toilets. *Darling mou!* Mrs Koutsouli grabs her by the ears and sinks her soft prickly lips into her cheeks. They leave sticky wet marks. Maria is lucky to have her, she says. A good Greek girl. Did Elena hear about her son and what he did to her? Mrs Koutsouli fingers her hair. He's prematurely aged me, look at these whites. Elena nods in sympathy and wonders if Valentina has stepped outside to the car park. She'll be freezing, she thinks, in mid-November with nothing around her shoulders.

Three young schoolboys play football with an empty can of Pepsi at the back of the foyer and distract Elena from Mrs Koutsouli's lament. *She dragged him to Kent afterwards. How am I supposed to get to Kent, hah? Answer me that? Does the 329 go to Kent? Does the 29 go to Kent? She couldn't care less, hah? That's why she's a xeni and not a Greek. Can you imagine a Greek girl doing that to her mother-in-law?* Elena thinks about Andoni, Dimitri and Andreas running up and down the hot dusty streets in their bare feet, chasing after their ball. And, later, Andoni dressed in his military uniform ready for war and his mother crying on her porch. Lambs to the slaughter, Lenou had said. What a tragic waste of life. Although Elena had thought she was glad, at least in part, that Mrs Pavlou was suffering.

She appears in the foyer like a ghost from the past and Elena escapes from Mrs Koutsouli's force field to embrace her. *Congratulations.* Her hair is wet and her eyes are swollen and mascara stains her cheeks.

Is it Mamma?

Of course not. It's raining outside. Why, has she asked after me, our darling Ma-mma?

She drags her words to make a point and Elena shakes her head and regrets it. She wishes she'd said something to appease her soul, but there was no coming back from the lie. Valentina links her arm through hers and shouts into her ear.

Who are all the crazy old women?

Customers. Mrs Loizou who's sitting with her back to you had a baby in Maria's bakery. She only popped in for a box of pastries and she ended up going into labour.

Valentina wrinkles her nose.

How disgusting. Remind me never to buy bread from there again.

Elena giggles and Valentina wipes the smile from her face.

Never mind the old crones. I need to tell you something. Something truly terrible.

Her breath smells of cigarettes and alcohol and her eyes bulge from her head. Elena's heart begins to pound. *What is it?* But it's Maria Petrakis who finishes off the sentence.

Elena! The money dance, come, quickly! The band is already

*playing your song and Costa is waiting on the dancefloor like
a stuffed vine leaf.*

Maria marches over to her and tugs at her hand,
frustrated with the speed at which she's moving. She
leads her back through the foyer and whispers conspir-
atorially. *The best bit of all, we can make some of our money
back, hah?* When they get to the doors leading into the
hall Elena turns around. The three little boys that were
playing football and her beautiful Valentina have all
disappeared into the night.

~

Lenou refuses to go to sleep. To close her eyes and have
the same scenes play out on the backs of her eyelids like
a terrible distorted film is more than she can bear tonight.
Better to sit on Maria's sofa and stare at the walls than
to lie on it and indulge in uninvited memories.

It's the same images that she sees over and over. The
look of embarrassment on the doctor's face as he
delivers the unwelcome news. Finally, somebody to tell
her the truth! Mrs Alexandro spitting in her tomatoes
as she shops for groceries, her sympathies unclear
despite the slight. Worst of all, that woman showing
up at her front door, unannounced, to compound her
humiliation in person in an expensive feathery coat.

A morning in late October. She'd been sitting outside
on the wooden bench beneath the drooping grapevine.
It used to grow right the way over their front porch
and afford them all a welcome shade in the summer.

The heat was finally abating and the light breeze carried with it the smell of the sea and the promise of the autumn. Relief from the sweltering sun, for a few months at least. She'd been drinking a kafe and thinking about her, of course, always her, and Mrs Pavlou with her evil eye. Wishing them harm from behind closed shutters and cursing what was left of her family. Why would she do such a thing to us? Elena would ask. Why would she wish us bad luck? Why, indeed. Who knew what went on in the minds of others? Perhaps the motive was jealousy or perhaps there was no motive at all. Maybe Mrs Pavlou had enlisted help in her endeavours from her crazy neighbour, Mrs Mavrides, the witch with the coffee cup compulsion, and the pair of them had conjured up a spell just for fun.

The woman had caught her eye earlier on. She'd seen her marching purposefully up and down the road as if lost and she'd wondered who she was and what she was doing. It was a weekday. The kids were at school and people were diligently going about their business so who could she be looking for? Then she'd started to walk down the driveway which separated her front porch from Mrs Pavlou's, her white high heels wobbling unsteadily in the gravel, and Lenou had felt afraid. She'd slipped her feet into her sandals and walked back into the house, standing with her back to the door and hoping that the woman would pass by her like a storm. A knock. *I'm looking for Valentina.* Lenou's chest had trembled with the panic and her fingers had fumbled nervously with her cross. *Open the door!* The woman's voice had grown louder and more insistent. Any façade of friendliness had vaporised into the breeze she'd been enjoying moments before. She'd opened the door to try and pacify her lest the noise awoke Lazarus from his grave, but the woman had been too quick for her and had stuck her shoe into the gap and forced her way inside. *Where is she?*

She'd recognised her then. Kyria Mavroyianni. The cuckolded wife. Her side of the family were wealthy and she'd seen her face in a brochure once, advertising shiny apartments. A tall, formidable woman in her early thirties with heavily outlined eyes and hair sprayed onto her scalp. She was wearing a curious white coat made from feathers and had an infant tied to her chest. *Well?* She'd paced from room to room, pushing at the bedroom doors and calling for her daughter. *Well?* Buzzing around like an angry bee trapped in a see-through jar. *She's gone*, Lenou had replied. *Gone to England*. And the woman had thrown her head back and laughed in her face. Of course she had, how silly of her to have asked when it was all here in her letter. Isn't that what stupid little girls did? Write little letters? She waved a brown envelope in Lenou's face. The letter that a young man had pushed through their letterbox. Another one of Valentina's lovers, she supposed. *Perhaps he is the father of the bastard?*

Lenou was rendered speechless for the first time since her own mother's burial. She had no idea what the woman was talking about. Letter? *Tell her from me, he doesn't want it and he doesn't want her!* She was screaming in Lenou's face and the baby in the sling was mewling like a startled kitten plucked upside down from its basket. *I certainly will.* It was easier than arguing and she'd have said absolutely anything to make her disappear. She'd stood by the front door for ages afterwards, thinking how she'd failed as a mother. She'd failed as a mother and her daughter was a whore, although which had happened first was a question for God.

Suddenly galvanised, she'd dragged the rusting metal foukou they used for cooking the meat out from beneath the bench and dumped it onto the driveway with a satisfying clang. She'd set the coals alight and fanned the flames until they'd glowed bright red and she'd thrown the letter the woman had shoved in her face into the fire. She'd watched as it had curled and burned and she'd almost expected to see goblins leaping out from behind it to clap and dance around her feet. What a spectacle! No goblins, but Mrs Pavlou, who'd appeared on her porch in her dressing gown with a shawl wrapped around her head and a bucket of soapy water in her hands. *Everything OK, Kyria Lenou?*

She'd decided, then, to burn every image of her eldest daughter that she owned and she'd gone back inside and swept the mantelpiece clear of her school pictures. She'd cracked the glass frames by smashing them into the table and she'd ripped the photographs out one by one and thrown them into the foukou. *Kyria Lenou, I think you will regret this, hah?* Go and fuck yourself, she'd said, and for once she'd meant for it to be heard. *Go and fuck yourself, Mrs Pavlou.* She watched as Valentina's smiling face turned into cinder and she felt like she'd achieved catharsis. Good, she'd thought. Now I never have to think of her again.

An impossible feat. How could she stop thinking of her when her love was woven into the fabric of her bones? Photos or no photos, she'd always be there. Then, of course, there were the pictures that she'd missed. When the radio stations had announced the invasion she had found them in an album that she'd grabbed on her way out of the door. Valentina as a baby. Innocent and unsullied, her little teeth protruding from her lips and her chubby face flushed with happiness. Lenou's eyes had been blurry with tears as they'd driven down to Thekelia, but she wasn't crying for her possessions. Uncle Zacharia had patted her on the knee. I know, I know, he'd said to soothe her. *They'll be gone soon, and we will get our lives back, you'll see.* He'd told her stories of people who had refused to leave their property and had been thrown out or killed by the Turks and buried in their own backyards. Terrible tales of torture and worse. Better to leave and come back when the war has ended, he'd said. When the British and the Americans have seen enough bloodshed and forced the Turkish army to retreat.

Shall we pray? They'd chanted the psalms together as he drove them south and she'd stared out of the window at the parched yellow fields and the olive groves and the sea shimmering in the distance and she had cried for Cyprus then, as well.

Such pain, she thought. It was a wonder she was still breathing at all. Seeing her today, at the wedding, for the first time in five years, had reopened old wounds that had never truly healed. It should have been her, Maria thinks. She should have been the bride, her elder daughter. So much conflict. She tried to do God's bidding, she really did, but she was first and foremost a mother and she couldn't disown her in her heart. What would she say to Him, on Judgement Day? she wondered. I'm sorry, God, but please make allowances for me because I love my daughter still? God didn't strike bargains. He struck people, not bargains. *Tell me, Mamma, what should I do?*

The lights flick on in Maria's front room and Lenou looks up to see her host standing in front of her in her white cotton nightgown, her long grey hair hanging loose behind her back.

Simbethera, what are you doing up, your flight isn't until the morning, no?

I couldn't sleep, Kyria Maria.

Lenou reddens at the sight of Maria in her thin night-clothes with her unbound hair tumbling behind her and apologises for disturbing her sleep. *You're not disturbing me. Shall I make us a nice pot of tea with fresh cinnamon?*

She looks different with her hair loose, Lenou thinks. Softer, almost. A benign ghost. She'd prefer a cup of cold milk, she replies. *If it's not too much trouble.* With a little nutmeg if she has any to hand and maybe a few aspirins. It's no trouble, Maria sings, suddenly happy to oblige the woman in her final hours in London. The relief of it, of her imminent disappearance, sending her almost skipping to the fridge like a young maid.

She hands her the glass of milk and lowers herself into the armchair opposite.

You allright, Simbethera?

Not really, Kyria Maria. Not really.

The war?

In part.

Lenou doesn't feel like holding up her family's misery for further scrutiny. Least of all to the mighty Maria. This war, she tells her, has destroyed her. *You should see the house they've stuck me in, Kyria Maria. It belonged to them and you can tell. Not a cross in sight and the roof is made of corrugated tin. God willing, it's only temporary.*

Maria nods.

Corrugated tin? Ptu! God willing.

Lenou's missed the point of her tongue and it's just as well at this early hour.

You know, Kyria Maria, you are lucky that you'd already left Cyprus. I lost everything we'd worked for, my Savva and I. Everything except five boxes of hastily packed belongings and my memories of my daughters as children.

Maria sighs then. A long, deep sigh. There it was again. That word, lucky. Why did people always presume she was lucky? You are lucky, they'd told her. Lucky that she could still sleep. That she could get over it. That she had her son to live for still.

Lucky? No Simbethera, I wasn't lucky. You see, I lost everything before the war ever started.

Chapter 15

Cyprus – 1960

THE SUN IS at its highest point in the sky and it's scorching hot in Kyrenia. Maria regrets leaving her fan at home. She dabs at her brow with a dirty handkerchief she has rescued from the bottom of her bag and arranges herself beneath the rusty tin roof of the bus stop for shelter. Costa and Katerina, newly bathed and coiffured, are pinching each other's arms.

Mamma, look he's bruised my arm!

Enough!

Maria wonders whether she's going through some sort of change. Her head is always throbbing, she's interminably hot and moody and can barely tolerate her own children. Menopause, isn't that what they call it? The start of a woman's decline.

Mamma, what am I going to have for my special dinner tonight?

Maria's heart sinks. More shopping, more cooking. Housework, housework. Always bloody housework. Some days she wishes she could pack a bag and leave and never come back.

Anything you want.

Anything? How about stifado?

No.

Afelia?

No.

You said anything! That's not fair. I'll tell Pappa we've gone into town, then.

Maria shoots Costa a look that would silence a man a mile away.

I'm making patates and avga and let that be the end of it.

Potatoes and eggs? Rubbish. No thanks.

Maria raises her hand to slap Costa across the mouth, but catches sight of the bus blundering over the hill and thinks better of it. He'd disturb the other passengers with his wailing and snivelling and draw more attention to them all. *Hade, get on. Before I change my mind about this whole damned trip.*

The bus into town is old and rusty and the black plastic seats are so hot that Maria has to sit on her bag for fear of excoriating the back of her legs. They're only going a few stops down the road but she relishes this short time to herself. She bats a fruit fly from her face and gazes out of the open window at the dusty yellow plains, dotted here and there with prickly trees and bushes, and the white single-storey houses in the distance. On the other side, the sea. A contrasting, ever-present wonder, blending seamlessly into the horizon and providing some relief from the stifling air.

She likes to imagine what people are up to in the privacy of their homes. Baking bread, skinning rabbits, tending to the animals. Sweeping the sand from the floors. The sand, a constant and pernicious enemy. Everywhere at once and never to be got rid of. She wonders what Mr Styliano is doing right at this moment. Perhaps he's drinking his morning kafe with his workers and complimenting her food to Michali. *I had a lovely time last night, Michali. Your wife is extremely accomplished.* Michali nodding in politeness, but marking her cards and desperate to come home and hit her. At the thought of this, and of Michali in general, her body crumples in sorrow. How in God's name is she going to stay married to this man for the next thirty years?

Katerina turns around in her seat then and smiles at her. *Are you OK, Mamma?* Her beautiful Katerina, with the shiny braids and dancing blue eyes. She wonders where she came from, this magnificent girl. What she has done to deserve her. That's how she is going to stay married to Michali, by remembering that it isn't about what she wants any more. It's about the children now, she thinks. Only them. Her little fantasies about Mr Styliano and the life she could be living can go to Hell along with her other dreams. *Of course I'm all right.*

We're here! Costa leaps off the bus and Maria steels herself for a morning of shoe shopping under a baking hot sun with two unruly children. *This way, head to Gregori's.* The town is bustling with people and bicycles and cars and Maria stops to look at the window displays along the way. Louli's fabric shop catches her attention. Long rolls of brightly coloured material stand proudly inside the entrance and Maria thinks of a market somewhere exotic and far away. Somewhere where the spices grow. She wishes she could have travelled. Seen something of the world before she married Michali and consigned herself to a life of domestic drudgery. Swapped one mundane existence for another. Animals for an animal.

She steps inside the shop, unable to resist its allure, and fingers the edge of the dusty rolls. Who buys these fabrics? she wonders. She doesn't know anyone who wears these colours, these crimson reds and fuchsia pinks. The colours of a princess. Or a queen. She certainly doesn't know anyone who wears silk. She can just imagine the look on Michali's face if she were to wear a red silk dress to church on a Sunday. She'd be in for a beating then. Especially if she told him she was wearing it for Mr Styliano and not for him at all.

No children today?

Louli waves at her from behind the till and Maria looks up and waves back.

Kalimera. Sorry, I was miles away. Thinking about the beautiful clothes I could make with your materials if only I had the pleasure of free time.

Buy! Buy!

Louli flaps her arms around her head.

God knows I could use the money. I was just saying, the kids, they're not with you?

Maria looks over her shoulder and realises that Costa and Katerina are no longer behind her.

They were with me a minute ago. Insolent brats must have gone on ahead. I have to go!

She makes her way over to Gregori's shoe shop

expecting to find the children already in there causing mischief, but there's no sign of either of them and the shop is closed for an early siesta. For goodness' sake! Why now, of all days, in this damned infernal heat?

She jogs over to Christo's cake shop where Costa loves to stop and stare at the sticky golden pastries, but they're not there either. Maria can feel the panic rising within her and her heart is beating in her ears. She is hot and confused and shoppers are swimming around her like colourful boats out at sea.

Costa! Katerina! She's shouting but she doesn't care. Let people stare, she thinks. Let them stop and stare open-mouthed at the mad woman running down the street with her skirts hitched up around her knees. *Costa! Katerina!* She shouts louder now, running faster and screaming their names at the top of her voice until her mouth goes dry and she can no longer speak. She turns left at the end of the street and sprints down the main road towards the old cinema. A hundred feet in front of her, a small crowd has gathered. Maria thinks they are waiting for the cinema to open, but as she runs towards the group she can see that people have their hands over their mouths. Something has happened. A young man turns around and points at her. *It's the mother, out the way, let her pass!* Maria drops her bag to the ground and finds that she's suddenly wading through a river of thick red tar.

She pushes her way through the crowd, her breath coming in short, shallow bursts as the river grows wider and threatens to engulf her and finally sees Costa sitting on the kerb. Confusion clouds her eyes and relief washes over her. She seeks momentary footing on slippery stones. *Why are you sitting in the road?* Costa is crying and when he raises his hands in the air, his palms are covered in the same tar. *My God! Are you hurt?*

Maria grabs him under the arms to bear his weight and starts pulling him towards her. Behind him, a lifeless body lies in the dirt. Maria absorbs the scene in slices as she pulls at her son. A bloodstained knee, a pink skirt, a purple hand. She attempts to look at the face on the body but finds that her eyes won't focus. Someone, a man, hugs her tightly from behind and starts dragging her away. She's drowning in it now, the tar. The pair of arms squeeze her tighter and tighter until her ribs feel like they might break. Maria claws at his hands. *Get off me! Get off me!*

The screams are coming from someone else's mouth. This is someone else's tragedy. The last thing Maria Petrakis sees before she passes out in the stranger's arms is a small girl talking to a young woman with short dark hair. The girl is dressed in Katerina's clothes but she doesn't recognise the woman. Come, the girl is saying to her. Come with me and let me show you to the well.

Chapter 16

Cyprus – 1969

THERE IS SOMETHING wrong with Valentina. Something very wrong. She's gone off her eggs in the morning, pushing the metal egg cup back across the kitchen table and leaving for work on an empty stomach. She loves eggs, Lenou complains. *She's had runny eggs and toasted bread for breakfast since she was three!* Then she stops eating chicken. Roast chicken, chicken tava, boiled chicken with macaroni. Lenou is beside herself with rage then. If she thought she was going into Ammochostos town every day to buy her a goddamned pig like she was some sort of empress she had another think coming. Then it's tea and kafe and Lenou almost flings the teapot at her head in frustration. *What do you mean the tea tastes of metal? Fetch your own bloody drinks then!* Finally, and most perturbing of all, Valentina stops smoking.

This is enough to send Lenou over the proverbial edge and she calls crisis talks with Elena. *What the hell's wrong with her, hah?* The two of them, sitting at the kitchen table on a Saturday afternoon in late September, wondering what is going on. Elena brings a sheet of

carefully transcribed notes to the meeting and Lenou
has brewed a fresh pot of chai.

A comparison of symptoms. A meeting of minds.
Elena clears her throat. *So, I've written down heartache.*
She's particularly proud of this point because she thinks
it makes her appear wiser than her fourteen years to
her mother. *Heartache?* Lenou mocks. *Pah! Don't give me
that rubbish! She's a sixteen-year-old with a crush on a boy at
the factory, not a ninety-year-old woman who's lost the love of
her life.* Elena continues with her list undeterred. Polio,
diphtheria and typhus. Lenou accuses her of reading
out the diseases on her school immunisation card then,
when in actuality Elena's copied them from the medical
encyclopaedia she accidentally stole from the school
library when her friend Giovanna was sick. *Give me
something real to work with, hah?*

Giovanna Johnston. Her little English friend. Her
father was a British artist who'd moved to Cyprus for
the good weather and cheap rent and her mother was
a Greek Cypriot from Ammochostos. She had straw-
berry blonde hair and blue eyes and freckles and looked
unlike anyone Elena had ever met. The kids in their
class used to say she looked like a fairy or a magical
princess from an American film. When she spoke
Greek they all gasped. The incongruity of it, of the little
girl who didn't appear to be one of them but who actually was, never wearing thin. She knew how to speak
English too, and this seemed to fascinate the class even
more. The Little Englesa, they used to call her, and they
all had a soft spot for her, even the teachers. The Little

Englesa of Ammochostos. She died a few months after they'd turned ten. It was too much, someone had once said. Too much for a child to bear.

C for cancer and L for leukaemia although leukaemia was also listed under C in her encyclopaedia. She'd turned the edges of the pages over so she could find the entries again if she needed to and she'd know what to look for in herself. *Mamma, will I get cancer, too?* Maybe her nose would start to bleed when she played skipping rope and that would mean she had caught it too. Was it contagious? she wondered. Could it be spread by a kiss? She'd kissed her once, towards the end and Lenou had almost hit her across the mouth when she'd confessed, because to say something out loud, something bad, was to invoke it in her book. *You understand? Do you?* You called upon a fate which was never meant for you by shouting these things out. Elena didn't understand, not really, but the idea of it had terrified her. To imagine things, truly terrible things, and then to have them come true because of those thoughts and not in spite of, was more than she could bear.

Maybe Valentina has cancer? She says the word out loud now, but she crosses herself afterwards like Lenou has taught her and that seems to appease her mother. *It's not cancer.* She's not even cross at the thought of it and Elena wonders why. Sometimes she has made her kiss an icon after crossing herself just to make doubly sure that she hasn't opened one of her mother's unwelcome doors. *Next?* But there isn't anything else on Elena's list except for cholera, and she decides to leave that one for the next meeting.

She forgot about Giovanna soon after she died, but she didn't do it on purpose. She just realised that she could stop the thoughts and the pain they inflicted by locking them away in her mind. Pappa and Giovanna, sleeping soundly together in a box in her head while she carried on with life. It was easier that way. Like falling asleep and waking up when the film had ended and everybody had gone home. Only they had to go somewhere, Valentina had once said. Bad things didn't just disappear. *Elena?* Lenou is tapping impatiently on her piece of paper. *Leave the stupid notes alone and go and talk to her.*

Valentina doesn't want to talk to Elena or anybody else and she's even locked her bedroom door, something she hasn't done since Pappa died. *Are you sick?* Valentina's voice, barely audible over the sound of her favourite singer, Giorgos Dalaras, crooning in the background. *No.* A song about unrequited love. Weren't they all? *Open the door!*

Elena's own bedroom is across the hall from her sister's and she decides to hide out in there and wait for her to come out. She'll have to use the toilet at some point, she reasons. Elena's white bedroom walls are also plastered with posters of Dalaras, but only in homage to Valentina. Valentina loves him and says he is a god, so Elena loves him too. And silver icons, of course. Lenou won't let either of them paper their walls with popular culture without leaving space for the religious relics. Her encyclopaedia lies open on her messy, unmade bed and she takes a deep breath and flicks to P for pregnancy. She remembers their pregnant neighbour, Kyria Jordano, telling their mother about her fascination with lemons when they were queuing up to light their candles in church last year. The only things, she'd claimed, that could neutralise the taste of metal in her mouth. Elena hadn't a clue what Kyria Jordano was talking about. All she knew was that the woman had a belly the size of a watermelon and was allowed to sit during the liturgia when everyone else had to stand. *It's not fair,* she'd whine. *Shut it, Elena,* her mother would reply. *The woman is carrying a child.*

Carrying a child. She looks down now at the entry for pregnancy and decides she's being ridiculous. It has been almost three months since her sister stopped talking to him. Since the fateful party. Besides, he is about to have a baby with his wife and everyone knows that a man can't make two babies at the same time. More likely to be polio than pregnancy. She closes the book then, afraid that if she spends too long thinking about the worst-case scenario, she will conjure it into existence.

Chapter 17

London – 1988

HAVE YOU FOUND my son?

The lights go back on. The room is a luminous white. The woman sits behind a desk so big and imposing that Elena thinks it would take weeks to reach her. Maybe it's deliberate, the distance. Maybe she thinks Elena will jump across the desk and somehow harm her too. The woman's blonde hair is pulled back away from her face and she wears black-rimmed glasses. They look like a smudge. A footprint in the snow.

Why am I here?

Since she walked into the police station to write the truth in the mist for all to see, Elena has been in and out of garish white rooms. She misses Costa. Why isn't she allowed to see her family, to join the search for the lost child? She hopes they are out there looking for him at least and not just wasting their time talking to her. The woman intimidates Elena with her unspoken authority. Her questions are probing, intimate and they make her head spin. She puts her hands to her face.

Please! Have you found my son?

Elena?

Someone is saying her name over and over. She digs her nails into the bottom of her seat to stop herself from falling off the edge and she rocks back and forth as if in pain.

Chapter 18

London – 1983

APRIL. THE ENGLISH spring air is filled with the scent of honeydew and the neighbours' freshly cut grass. The sound of a bee, trapped in the curtain which is flapping around in the breeze from the open window, transfixes and relaxes. *She's beautiful, darling!* The new baby is a girl just as she'd hoped. A month of optimism. A month of expectation. *Just look at those little fingers.* Ten perfect fingers curled into two little fists. *She's so small.*

Elena sinks back into the pillows and stares out of her bedroom window like an exhausted queen claiming a hard-fought victory, while Costa ambles round the bed, rocking the baby in his arms. She wonders if the world has always been this bright and colourful or if someone has painted it so today, just for her. A canvas of hope. The blue sky, the top of the apple tree, bright yellow flowers peeking tentatively out from the ground. Yellow, the colour of Maria's bakery. The colour of Maria's cakes.

They've just arrived home from the hospital, and the relief of it, of not having to spend another day trapped on the noisy drab ward with the strip lighting and surly nurses, sends her soul soaring into the stratosphere.

What are we going to call the little miss?

I'd like to name her after my mother.

She doesn't hesitate, she knows what she has to do. Costa's eyebrows shoot up like rockets. The baby, with her tiny delicate mouth and porcelain skin, doesn't look much like a Lenou to him. It's a clumsy name to inflict on a baby, he winks, but I guess it's your decision. Elena almost laughs out loud then, at the thought of anybody being christened Lenou. *That's her nickname, Costaki-mou. My mother's name is Magdalena.* An audible sigh of relief. *Magdalena? All these years, I never knew.* He tells her he likes it.

Katerina and Magdalena. *Our Nina and our Magda.* Elena gives Costa her hand and he kisses it tenderly, his lips brushing her skin. He looks up from her fingers and lowers his tone. Afraid to broach the subject and burst the bubble of bliss, but eager, still, to know. *The tablets, they are working? You feel OK this time?* He steels himself for the reply but Elena has never felt better. Of course, she doesn't have the heart to tell Costa that the lifting of her spirits has nothing to do with the medication his friend prescribed. She knows that Mary Magdalena, newly cleansed from sin by Christ, has banished the curse of Katerina from their home. A new name and hope, at last, for a new beginning.

~

At midday, Maria unties her apron and hangs it on the hook behind the till. It's time. Time to take a break. To pour herself a glass of cold water and take the weight off her feet. The long shifts are a trial and some part of her constantly hurts, be it her knees, her back or her neck. She keeps her aches and pains to herself, though. Costa would only harangue her to retire. No thank you! Retire and do what exactly? Look after his children? Sit upstairs like an old gojiakari in her rocking chair waiting for Death and his scythe to come for her? She's not quite ready for that yet. Not quite ready.

Besides, Petrakis Bakery is more than just a business to her. It's her home, her life, and in many ways, her salvation. It had started with the baking back home. Just after Katerina. It had been a way to make Costa fat and happy again in those early months after he'd returned from Thora's, grey and emaciated. But it had become more than that. So much more. The kneading of the dough at five in the morning when the world was still asleep, digging her knuckles into the soft, malleable zimari, letting the lump take her weight and absorb all her troubles. The rolling out of the pastry into a circle or a square, the effort of it momentarily wiping her mind of thoughts and leaving her free and empty to concentrate on making her shapes. Then, the best part, loading her creations into her ovens, the Champion and the Apprentice, and watching her pale mounds magically transform into giant golden-brown loaves and cakes, like unformed foetuses unfurling in their mother's belly. The smell of warmth, of food, of life, filling the bakery and drifting into the flat upstairs. The birth of things rather than their end. How could Costa expect her to give that up?

Then, of course, there are her customers, many of whom she's seen grow up over the years. Like Anna-Maria Loizou, who was born on this very floor. Named, in part, after Maria Petrakis who had practically helped deliver her. Mrs Loizou had only come in for a box of tiropites. She'd been dreaming of them, she said. Big flaky puff pastries shaped like triangles, with cheese and mint in their centres. Every time she thought about them the baby would kick and press down on her back, so she'd decided to drive to Petrakis in her Jaguar to buy a few and the rest, as they say, is history.

She'd made a bloody mess of her shop that day and Maria had said to her afterwards, *didn't you know?* She'd come in to show the new baby off in her fancy pram with the shiny silver wheels. The husband had plenty of money and she couldn't resist letting everyone know. A little red thing she was, with a shock of black hair, swaddled in pink and white blankets. *Didn't you know you were in labour?* She'd been in pain all day, she'd replied, but she thought she just needed to fart. Maria had laughed then. First baby. You forgive anything when it's the first. She had almost given birth to Costa underneath the almond tree in the backyard. Mrs Kouli's son riding frantically across town on his rusty old bicycle to fetch the midwife while she'd kneeled up against the tree with her underwear around her ankles and hoped she'd arrive in time. It's just a bit of backache she'd said to Michali that morning. *You go to work. It's not due for weeks, yet.* Not that he'd have stayed around to welcome the baby anyway, and it was just as well as she couldn't stand him by then.

Anna-Maria is about to become a pharmacist and her mother is very proud. The first person in their family to go to university, she beamed. And the first chemist in a long line of fish and chip shop owners. There are the sad stories too, of course. Mrs Pantelis and her missing son. They never did find his body and the woman has been driven half mad with the pain of it. No bones to mourn or bury. Imagine that? she has said to Costa and Elena. Imagine the pain of having nothing left at all? Maria ended up on the floor with her last Saturday. Mrs Pantelis crying into her hands and Maria whispering soothing words into her ear. *Have you seen my son, have you seen my son?* Perhaps the phone lines were still down, Maria said to reassure her. She patted her hand and moved her hair out of her swollen wet face. It's a lie they've carried on for years, the pair of them. Maria complicit in the charade and Mrs Pantelis oblivious. *Can I call your husband for you?* Maria running behind the till to call Mr Pantelis and wondering how long it would take him to drive through the weekend traffic in his gold Mercedes 190 to come and collect her. Poor Mrs Pantelis with her black patent shoes and her matching handbag. It broke Maria's heart to think of her still taking the time to match her shoes to her accessories despite her overwhelming anguish.

And then there is Mrs Vasili. Who will serve Mrs

Vasili if she retires? Not Maki, that much is for certain. Mrs Vasili with the faint moustache and the hair that grows upwards instead of downwards because she thinks it brings her closer to God. She came in yesterday for a box of semolina halva cake and it had been an absolute fiasco from start to finish.

She'd been in a hurry because she'd parked on a double yellow line. *Hade! Hade!* she'd screamed at Maki, her arms flapping and her chins wobbling and the man's hands had started to tremble although it didn't take much. *Four pieces of halva!* He'd begun to place the soft cakes into the little white box with a pair of tongs, meticulously lining up the almonds on each slice so they all faced the same way and wasting precious minutes in the process as she moaned about the state of the roads. *This whole place is covered in yellow lines! Damn Haringey council! What are you bloody doing?* Didn't she say she was in a hurry and here he was playing a game of backgammon with the cakes? Poor Maki's forehead had broken out into a sweat by that point and even Maria had felt half sorry for him. *Hurry!* Mrs Vasili had fixed him with her cold black eyes, her white quiff standing on the top of her head in an almost predatory manner and Maki had lost his nerve and dropped the box upside down into the tray of baklava. Maria had gasped then, because the sticky yellow halva cakes had broken into a thousand pieces and ruined the baklavas as well. There was so much syrup everywhere that they'd become inextricably linked and therefore completely unsaleable.

Maki had bent over to clean the floor and Maria had

gently taken Mrs Vasili aside to apologise and to explain about the war. *You see, Mrs Vasili, the man lives in a world entirely of his own making and Costa tells me it's because he was taken prisoner in '74 although personally I still believe it was something to do with falling into the chicken coop.* And Mrs Vasili had pretended to spit on the floor at the thought of clumsy Maki fighting in the war for Cyprus. *Him? If he was a soldier in the war then I am related to Nana Mouskouri!* she'd scoffed before flouncing out empty-handed, and Maria had finally understood after all these years that Mrs Vasili had been being sarcastic when she referred to Nana Mouskouri, and she wasn't her cousin at all.

At the mere thought of Mrs Vasili and her badger's quiff, Maki's eyes widen in fear and Maria promises to rush straight back down to serve her should she happen to come looking for free halva by way of compensation. She chuckles to herself as she climbs the stairs up to her flat and closes the door behind her. Peace at last. She kicks off her shoes and heads into the kitchen to pour herself a glass of water before dragging her armchair across to the window and clipping the net curtain back so she can watch the world go by. Her second favourite pursuit, staring out of windows. Green Lanes. Miles and miles of densely populated road, stretching all the way from Newington Green to Winchmore Hill, where the posh Englesoi lived. She'd seen it change a fair bit over the years. More shops had popped up, more Greek Cypriot bakalies and even a few Turkish ones too. Funny, she thinks. How they can live together here quite happily, but were killing each other back home not so long ago. The Green Lanes effect, George next door called it. Peace, love and pastirma.

More cars, more buses. The number 29 stopping right outside her window when traffic was at a standstill so she could peer inside and stare at the weary passengers sitting hunched over their newspapers. It's busy today, she thinks. A warm Friday afternoon in spring and the shoppers are out buying bags of charcoal for their weekend barbecues and watermelons for afterwards. It's a wonder those watermelons taste of watermelon at all, she'd said to George. What with all the bloody pollution.

George of George Groceries. He'd taken to cutting his best watermelons in half and displaying them on little tables outside his shop and then standing next to them in a string vest and gesticulating at passers-by. *Lovely watermelons!* She'd taken offence at this ridiculous marketing campaign after a few weeks because of the black smoke from the cars and she'd told him in no uncertain terms that customers would be dying of lead poisoning and it would all be on him. He'd told her to piss off, but he'd obviously taken her comments to heart because he'd started to put little bits of clingfilm over everything after that. To appease the mighty Maria Petrakis, he'd joked. It had been amiable banter between them, despite the bitter words.

She had fallen out with both Themis of Themis Continental to her left and George to her right when she'd first bought the bakery from Mr and Mrs Chrysostomou. She had decided to take the original sign down and replace it with a white and blue one with Petrakis Bakery on the front and they'd objected to the colours. *What's wrong with the colours, hah?* she'd replied. *Are these not good Greek colours?* The problem was that both Themis Continental and George Groceries had white and blue designs on their shopfronts and they had accused her of trying to steal their custom by putting up a larger and newer sign. *Pah, rubbish! Maybe you should give yours a clean, wipe the bird droppings off?*

In any case, she'd chosen white and blue because she'd told Mr Styliano that she would, and she wanted to fulfil her promise. She owed him that much. *Your tablecloth is like the Greek flag,* he'd said to her when they'd first met, and it had become a thing between them. *See, Mr Styliano,* she'd say if she could speak to him again. *I am a true patriot after all.* Not that she would be seeing him again. That was another one of her promises to him. *Never contact me again, Mrs Petrakis.* She'd ignored the pain that his words had evoked and she'd agreed to his demand and not a day went by when he didn't cross her mind.

There's another reason why Maria's come upstairs. She recently went round to Costa and Elena's house to meet the new baby and things didn't seem right. The atmosphere was charged, like the sky before a storm, and it has been playing on her mind ever since.

They'd left her standing on the doorstep for what felt like hours, for a start. She'd had to ring the bell three times like she was a cheap salesperson come to show them her catalogue – or worse, a xeni, not the family matriarch. When Costa had eventually opened the door, his dishevelled appearance had knocked the wind out of her body. *What took you so long?* she'd said. She'd thought she was going to have to pay for her own funeral. He hadn't shaved for weeks, it looked like, and there were dark shadows under his eyes. His pyjamas were gaping at the navel, his hairy stomach was sticking out and the buttons looked as though they were about to fly off and take someone's eye with them.

She'd thought things couldn't get any worse until she saw Elena. Floating down the stairs in a pink glittery nightdress that looked like it belonged in Nina's wardrobe, with Costa's dressing gown draped over her shoulders. She was hugging the child to her chest like it was a lifebuoy and almost suffocating her with the force of it. *Here, give her to me!* She'd reached her arms out to take the sleeping child before Elena smothered her to death and she'd practically flinched in shock at the suggestion of it. No, no, she'd cried. She only wanted her mother and screamed if anyone else tried to hold her. It was all very peculiar. Nina she would barely touch and this one she was holding on to for dear life. The workings of Elena's brain, once again an undecipherable mystery.

They'd ushered her into the living room while the pair of them had crept off into that shiny white kitchen of theirs to whisper over the jisveh, no doubt, about how inconvenient her visit was. Maria had looked around the small untidy room with the brown carpets and green velvet curtains and the battered wall units covered with spider plants and felt like she was in a horticultural time capsule. The kitchen belonging to one decade and the rest of the house older than hers. Why didn't they paint the walls, at least? Buy a few new cushions and add a bit of life?

They'd deigned to come back into the room, after what seemed like an eternity, with a cup of kafe for her, Elena still clutching the child and Costa muttering apologies and making excuses. Always with his excuses. *Where's Nina?* she'd asked. *With the childminder.* But neither of them could remember her name. This had alarmed Maria further and Costa had snapped at her. *We have a ten-day-old baby,* he'd replied, irritably. *What do you expect?* Pity he was too old for a slap across the mouth, she'd thought, but she kept her feelings to herself. How dare they insinuate that she had no idea what it was like to raise a child when she'd dragged up two on her own on a scorching hot island in a house with practically nothing to hand. The electricity coming on for three days at a time and then going off again. Washing dirty nappies in a clay pot in the backyard with a sprinkle of detergent she'd borrowed from Mrs Kemal and a bucket of water from the well. Her mother before her, boiling water on hot stones and washing dishes with ash she'd collected from the oven in their garden because she didn't even have that. Soap, too much of a luxury. It was 1983, for God's sake! These kids didn't know they were born.

She'd bitten her tongue and said nothing. She'd sat back on the sofa and drank her too-bitter coffee and studied a photograph of Lenou perched peremptorily between the plant pots. Pride of place. She was looking rather garish, older than her supposed years and Maria wondered what had become of her since the wedding. *Your mother, she's OK in her new home in Dhekelia?* Elena had followed her finger and feigned a brief smile, while the baby was forced deeper into her dressing gown and Costa tried not to fall asleep with his eyes open.

She'd got up to leave without having held the baby at all. Costa had walked her to the door and she'd asked him then, what is the matter with Elena? Nothing, he'd tutted. She's just tired. They were both very tired. She had thought about them as she rode all the way back to Harringay on the bus because she'd been angry and then concerned. She'd stared out of the window at the people rushing past and wondered if she had caught the blackness again. The one she'd suffered from after having Nina.

She thinks about Elena now as she finishes her glass of water and contemplates going back downstairs. Life was tough and some people were just not cut out to make the journey. Her Katerina, God rest her, had been one of them. Elena, she suspects, is another and Mrs Pantelis was slowly heading that way too. Not her, though. When it had truly mattered she had dug deep into the well inside her and found something buried there and she'd changed her designated path like a

stream circumnavigating a rock. She had escaped from
Michali and his brutality and she had saved her own
life in doing so. It had cost her, though. Her soul, at the
very least, and probably Mr Styliano's as well.

Chapter 19

Cyprus – 1944

WHEN THEY ARRIVE back home from the young man's house, Maria's mother opens the back door to let the heat escape, ties her tatty white apron around her slender waist and begins preparing a lunch of bread, black olives and tomatoes. It's been a long morning and there's a lot to consider. She carries the plates outside and the three of them sit around the small wooden table in their backyard in Kyrenia. The sound of the cicadas and the smell of the farm animals mingles with the jasmine and keeps them company as they eat.

Maria's father, Manoli, is thoughtful. He sips zivania and eats sesame koulouri bread dipped in the juices of the tomato. He rubs his long black beard and scratches at his cheeks. He did not like the suitor, Michali. Something wasn't right about him. He looked fine enough, he'll grant him that, and his manner was polite, but Manoli had caught him out in several small lies about his job at the base and if he can lie about the little things, Manoli thinks, what else is he hiding beneath that long girlish hair of his? It showed a deceptive character at best and it left a bad taste in Manoli's mouth. A very bad taste indeed. He washes it away with more zivania and carries on stroking his beard.

Maria's mother, Andrianna, feels much the same way as her husband. Michali was a strange young man and his mother had made her feel ill at ease as she hovered around them with walnut preserve like an eager waiter in an empty restaurant, but it was the first proxenia their daughter had been invited to and beggars could not be choosers. Not in Kyrenia. Nicosia maybe, but not in Kyrenia. Besides, what else would Maria do, if not marry and have children of her own? Andrianna carefully spits the stones from the olives into her hand and arranges them neatly around the edge of her plate. She once cracked a molar biting into an olive and the pain of it was always there, nagging away at her like the memory of the meeting with Michali. She would be relegated to a life of farm work and caring for her elderly parents if she didn't accept Michali's proposal. Not a good outcome for a nice girl. The man exuded a disconcerting air, granted, but that didn't necessarily equate to a bad match, and even a bad match didn't spell disaster. Women got on with things. That was life. Nothing was ever perfect.

Besides, Maria was no great beauty. Not like Andrianna had been in her day. Her high cheekbones and large hazel-green eyes had been the talk of Kyrenia when she was eighteen, but Maria had inherited her father's features. His pinched olive-skinned face and long, bony arms. And that hair. Grey as a wolf she was, and barely thirty.

She sighs as Maria bounces around in her chair with excitement, her silver bun dancing on top of her head like a rag doll. She chews on her sesame bread and thinks that the arranged date couldn't have gone any better. Michali was tall and slender and handsome, with long brown hair which brushed his shoulders and large brown eyes. When they had walked out into the neighbourhood together after their sweet, he had put his arm around her waist and squeezed it. He'd told her about his job at RAF Nicosia and Maria had been so impressed. There was nothing as enticing as a man who worked for the army, and especially during a time of war. She had thought him a hero and wondered if he wore a uniform and fought brave battles against Adolf Hitler in planes that flew upside down. She could imagine herself marrying this mysterious man who called her father Kyrie and her mother Kyria and running her fingers through his hair as he made love to her at night. Finally, someone to love her.

You liked him, the young man?

Maria looks up at her father and blushes as her private thoughts collide with the present. *Yes, Pappa. I really did!* She tells him that they had a long conversation after their coffee and she'd thought him solicitous and intelligent. He'd even held the door open for her afterwards. A frown creases Manoli's forehead and he sighs in disappointment. There were no signs of either of those qualities to his mind, certainly not from where he was sitting. He pours himself another caustic drink and drums his fingers on the table. It's not what he wanted for the girl, not at all, but his wife was right. At thirty, her childbearing years were practically behind her and fairly soon nobody would be knocking on their door to offer proxenia. She would be left behind to rot in the heat like the carcass of a cow.

You are sure? He didn't strike you as a little odd?

Odd? Why no, Pappa!

Andrianna and Manoli exchange clandestine looks over their daughter's grey head before his wife gets up and gathers the empty plates noisily. Then it's done.

Maria crosses herself three times and squeals with delight like one of their pigs. In one morning, all her dreams have come true. Thank God, she thinks, as she clasps her hands together and looks to the sky. Thank God for answering my prayers and sending me Michali.

Chapter 20

London – 1975

MARRIED LIFE SUITS Elena well. Being Elena Petrakis, wife of Costa, is far preferable to being plain old Elena, daughter, sister and mediator. In gaining her gold rings she's added a spring to her step and a smile to her face. Marriage earns you respect, her mother used to say in the days after she'd kicked Valentina out. *Pray to God your sister finds that out.*

Those days seem a distant past now, like the stars her Pappa used to point out to her at night, twinkling away a million lifetimes ago. She wonders if there is a Turkish family living in their old house yet and if the new occupant of her room is taking down her pictures of Dalaras and thinking about her, their owner. What did she look like, this mysterious girl who had inherited her life? Did she have black hair and black eyes and an unusual, exotic-sounding name? Dilek, Ayse, Hamida?

Did she really want to be there, living in her shadow in their abandoned street with its boarded-up buildings surrounded by all the ghosts? More ghosts than at the bottom of one of Mrs Mavrides' coffee cups. She remembers Mrs Pavlou running out of her house in terror that day, her face as white as a bed sheet and her short black hair standing on end like a terrified cat's. What could she have seen in those dregs to make her scream like that? she'd wondered. The unimaginable, Lenou had replied. A mother's worst nightmare.

The smells from the bakery waft up into their bedroom. Orange and mastic, this morning. And cinnamon, of course. Always the cinnamon. The start of a new day. She envies Maria her baking. She's lucky, she thinks, that she has something she loves doing, something she excels at. Maria had her bakery with its tantalising smells, Valentina had her beautiful, almond-shaped face and even her old friend Andoni Pavlou had his ball to perform tricks with. She wishes she had something to mark her out from everybody else, make her feel special. *What am I good at, Mamma?* she'd once asked her, but there had been no discernible reply.

She can hear Maria shouting at Costa as she washes her face and brushes her hair in the mirror. Costa insisting that his mother find new suppliers to increase their profits and Maria arguing that money is money but her reputation is priceless. *You think George thinks like that, hah?* Costa replies. *You think he imports water-melons from the most expensive company he can find? What about Themis, you think he buys olives from the rip-off merchants too?* Maria raises her voice in response. *Pah! What do I care what those two are up to, they're the biggest crooks on Green Lanes!*

Green Lanes, Harringay, with its Greek Cypriot outlets interspersed with a few Turkish marketler and the odd Chinese or Indian restaurant. A colourful array of grocery shops, restaurants and bakalies selling traditional produce to members of its small, vibrant community. Each shop with its own unique selling point to recommend it to its frequenters. George Groceries and his giant green watermelons, Themis Continental and his pungent, garlicky salami, Koko's Cafe and his cheap halloumi tucked inside slabs of sesame bread, Tasso Kebabs and his renowned chicken skewers that taste of the summer, and her very own favourite, Paniko's Paneri. A bakali twice the size of all the others with a flimsy multi-coloured canopy dangling outside and rows of old-fashioned wicker baskets lining the aisles. Baskets brimming with black and green olives, white cheeses, pink loukoumia, golden pasteli and bright red tomatoes rubbed in olive oil to make them extra shiny. Elena is reminded of Ali Baba and his cave as she peruses the shelves. A veritable treasure trove of sparkly things surrounded by scoops and scales.

The owner, Paniko, a man in his late fifties with a bald head and a protruding stomach, struts around proudly, greeting shoppers with a nod and a welcome. He used to work on the ships, he tells her when the tills are quiet. Many moons ago. He's seen every country there is to see and several of them twice. She listens in awe as he fiddles with his bushy black moustache and regales her with his adventures. He once fought off a lion in Tanzania and he has seen sunsets to rival great paintings. He's even been to India, she tells Costa excitedly, and seen the Taj Mahal! Elena can't imagine going that far when to her, the top end of Green Lanes is a challenge. Take the bus, Costa suggests. Go into town and see the things that tourists like, but the thought of it turns her legs to jelly. To be lost in London in a sea of xenoi is a nightmare that haunts her. Or *you could call your sister*, Maria chimes in knowingly. *Go and do something with her?*

Elena hasn't spoken to Valentina since the wedding, when the pair of them stood in the foyer of the hall and Valentina hissed in her ear. She had wanted to tell her something then, something truly terrible, she'd whispered, before Maria had spirited her away. Elena had thought about her during the money dance and then afterwards, when she'd lost her virginity on the squeaky bed in the room adjacent to Maria's. *What is it?* The secret, perhaps, to the sorrow that torments her sister and casts shadows across her face.

A cold, dark evening in February. It's started to rain and the wet pavements of Green Lanes shimmer in the yellow light reflected from the street lamps. Shoppers stop to put up their umbrellas before scurrying back to their cars or bus stops and Elena buttons up her large cream coat and runs into Varosi Butchers. Tony spies her standing in the doorway while hacking at a joint of meat and he beckons her over to the counter. *Come, come, I'm about to close!* His big bloodied hands more intimidating than inviting. The smell of dead animals hanging in the windows tugs at her stomach and she thinks of her grandmother back home plucking

chickens out of their coops and breaking their necks
with her hands. She'd cried in horror at the sight of it
once, and her Pappa had sat her on his knee and
explained that creatures were meant to be eaten. *See?*
It's OK. He'd kissed her cheek and smoothed her hair
while her mother tutted that he was making her soft,
and her job harder. *This is life, Savva.* Poor Pappa. Always
trying to take the cruelty of things to appease her delicate soul.

She walks tentatively across the slippery blood-
spattered floor of the shop and thinks that she will miss
shopping for Maria when they move out of her flat. *Buy*
something Mamma likes for dinner, Costa said earlier. *To*
soften the blow. I'll tell her tonight. She picks out a leg of
lamb large enough to feed the three of them and wonders
why all the things that make her happy have to end
abruptly. *This one?* Tony wraps the meat in brown paper
and fumbles with the long, thin string until she eventually offers to tie the package herself. *Here, let me.* Pappa,
Maria and her cosy flat above the bakery, and her friend
Giovanna with the bloodied nose. All of them taken away
from her before she was ready to let them go.

~

A postman? Are you bloody joking me? Maria bangs her fist
into her plate and sends the leftover kleftiko flying
across the table like a missile. *And what about this place?*
Who's going to help me in the bakery when you're off pretending
to deliver mail, hah? Costa says he'll help her look for

someone before they move out and Maria throws her fork at him. *Eiyy, watch my eye!* She thought he needed the toilet when he raised his hand and told them all he had an announcement to make but this, this she can't believe. *Judas!*

Elena twists her napkin around her chapped, dry hands and stares uncomfortably at her half-eaten meal while Costa and his mother argue. The memory of blood-soaked feathers lying on the floor of the butcher's shop ties her insides into knots. *Well, tough.* Maria shrieks. *The answer is no! This is a family business and last time I checked you're still family!*

Costa tries to reason with her with his hands in front of his face to avert blows from passing cutlery. *Please, Mamma!* She tells him to get lost and storms out of the kitchen in a rage as black as the winter sky. Elena's face crumples and her eyes fill with tears. *It's OK, darling, she'll come round, you'll see.*

How can she tell him? she wonders. How can she admit that she'd rather live here, in the flat that smells more like home than her own home ever did, with a woman she loves like a mother? That the past few months have been the happiest of her life because people have been kind to her? *And we can try for a baby, too, if you like.* She's crying properly now, at the very thought of it, and Costa puts his arms around her and tells her she's too sensitive. Here he was worrying that his wife would hate his mother and instead she loves her too much. Imagine that! Such a happy situation to be in, he thinks to himself. What a fortunate man.

Chapter 21

London – 1988

THE WOMAN WITH the blonde hair and the black glasses hands Elena a tissue.

Have you found my child?

Elena wipes her face and stares out of the window.

Do you need a translator?

The voice is gentle but it is impatient to continue.

No.

There was a time when the English language surrounded her like a dark and impenetrable ocean. She, a drunk swimmer, with lead tied around her feet.

Can you tell me about the letters, Elena?

Which letters?

The sky outside is red and she can't tell whether it's early morning or late evening. It's hot and dusty in the room, a scorching Cypriot summer and she can feel her palms sticking to her seat. The snow beneath her has melted to reveal dust. Dust everywhere.

A funeral. She knows it's a child's funeral because of the size of the coffin and the way people hold on to each other for support. Relatives are on their knees. The sound of wailing fills the air and Elena can taste

the earth in her mouth. She wonders if it's Mrs Johnston
screaming like that. It must be – who else?

I'm hot.

I'll open a window.

Elena pulls at the collar of her mourning dress. The
sky breaks open. It's a crimson colour. The colour of
blood on the pavement after a game of skipping rope.
A nose bleed. A bruise. The start of an illness without
an end. Trauma travels into her knees and makes them
knock together. A trickle of urine escapes from within
her and runs down the inside of her legs. A kindly voice
speaks to her mother.

This is no place for a child. Take her home. It's too much.

This is life.

She's distressed, Kyria Lenou. Take her home.

She needs to see, to know how things can be.

She wants to crawl into the kind woman's mouth
and slide down into her body for comfort. More than
anything, she wants to go home.

What do you see?

The woman's voice tugs at her and she's momentarily
back in the present, but the memories knock into her
like the Mediterranean Sea and she's back again,
beneath the crimson sky.

I see a white coffin.

A face. A name from another life. Her father's star.
It comes at her from the past like a bullet through the
brain. The pain of it ripping through her body and
tearing it in two. It's too late. Someone is telling her
that it's too late. Her mother is holding her up and she's

already seen the unimaginable. A mother's worst nightmare sealed into a coffee cup. The loss of a child.

Who died, Elena?

The Little Englesa of Ammochostos.

She died of leukaemia and they buried her in the
dust while her mother fell to her knees and tore at her
chest and screamed until she had no more breath left
in her body. The kindly woman was right. It was no
place for a child.

Chapter 22

Cyprus – 1969

WHEN VALENTINA STARTS being sick, Lenou raises her hands to the heavens and makes an appointment with Dr Verras. Going off her eggs in the morning is one thing, she tells Elena as she buttons up her long black dress. Throwing up food is quite another matter. *I'm not made of money and the very least, this thing might be contagious.* Elena sits on her mother's cream crocheted bedspread and looks on as she pins her short, curly grey hair up with a clip and arranges a black scarf around her head. She takes a few steps back from the mirror. There. It wouldn't do to look shabby for Dr Verras. The most judgemental man in Ammochostos, Elena thinks. Dishing out medicines with a side order of criticism. He's allowed to look down on us, her mother had retorted after she'd whined about her last visit. He was a doctor and therefore much closer to God than they were.

She studies the photographs of her Pappa that hang from the bedroom walls. Pappa in his khaki green Cypriot Volunteer Force uniform and matching hat. Her parents on their wedding day. Baby Valentina in her lacy christening gown sitting on Pappa's knee. She wonders what poor Pappa would have made of Valentina's mystery illness. She doesn't look very sick to Elena as she skips along the gravel driveway behind their mother like a schoolgirl sucking on sweets. Lenou walking three paces ahead in her best dress, her nose in the air and her gold cross swinging from left to right like the pendulum of a ticking clock.

They head to the bus stop and disappear from view. Elena sits on the wooden bench beneath the vine and draws her knees to her chest. Their absence brings relief, if only for a while. It is a Saturday afternoon in late September. The cooler air which now flutters through her hair smells of lemons and she thinks of Kyria Jordano waddling around the church with her giant belly sticking out, red-faced and vying for a pew. P for pregnancy. Mrs Pavlou is out sweeping her porch again, the wooden handle of her broomstick darting backwards and forwards like the tongue of an insidious snake. Elena wonders if she can sense that her victory is near. Just a few more hours of sweeping left, she thinks. Not long now, Mrs Pavlou. *All OK, Elena? Yes, thank you, everything is fine.* Her son, Andoni, barges past her at that moment and nearly knocks her off the step. *Eiyyy, be careful!* She jabs at his sides with the tip of her broom and shouts at him to slow down. He ignores her, and shuffles across the gravel towards Elena in his denim shorts and white T-shirt and carrying a football under his arm. He's going to the schoolyard to kick his ball around for a bit. Does she want to come?

Andoni Pavlou is fourteen and in her class at school. He's the eldest and the nicest of the Pavlou brothers. Andreas is a spiteful little brat who would smile in your face and happily spit in your hair and big fat Dimitri has a mouth larger than the entrance of a cave. Radio Pavlou, they called him at home. If you wanted something broadcasting you'd tell it to Dimitri.

Andoni is different. He is thoughtful and considered and when he raises his hand in class, it is because he has something interesting to say. He is also the most handsome. Elena breathes in his musky scent and thinks that he's changed in the weeks since she's seen him. He's taller than she remembers him and his shoulders are broader. When he speaks, his voice is low and deep, no longer the voice of a boy. She doesn't remember it sounding like that before and her heart misses a beat with the thrill of it.

They make their way to the top of the driveway and cross the road to the dusty playground of the Gymnasio Ammochostou. The playground of their local high school is surrounded, in part, by its large grey buildings and hidden from the adjacent road by a row of small gnarled olive trees. He likes the deserted yard, he says, and often comes here to be by himself. *Me too.* Although she doesn't admit that she's spent the past six months here, sitting in the alcove beneath the fragrant jasmine bush waiting for Valentina. One night she was late. Elena had already watched the sun set beneath the school's water tank and the moon rise up to take its place. The sky had turned mauve and then black and there was still no sign of her sister. She had scratched at the mosquito bites on her arms until they'd bled and practised telling her mother that her sister was dead. Strangled by a stranger in the back of a black car. She'd turned up eventually, of course. She always did. Wearing the superior look Elena had seen on her face as she skipped off to the doctor's this afternoon.

The sound of Andoni's ball hitting the ground echoes around the quiet playground like pistol shots.

I love this time of year best.

Me too. I hate the heat and I get devoured by the bugs in the summer.

It's because her skin is sweet, he replies, flicking his light brown hair out of his eyes and winking at her. His eyes, the colour of sand. That's what they say when you attract mosquitoes. Only special people do. He kicks the ball in her direction and Elena misses and has to run after it. *Unlucky, pass it back.* He likes her hair short, he tells her, as he balances the ball on one foot and then tosses it up to bounce it on his knee. It's different. It marks her out. Long hair is too obvious. His attempt at maturity impresses her. He thinks she's the second prettiest girl in the class. After Nicoletta Nicodemou.

You're good at that.

Thanks. Practice.

Nicoletta Nicodemou. All the boys like her because her bosoms are big and she looks older than fourteen. Andoni throws the ball towards her and teaches her how to stop it using the side of her foot. *Like this, kita.*

You try. She kicks it back. *Bravo.* He asks about Valentina. *What about her?*

My mother says your sister, you know, with lots of different men. He sticks his right finger into his left fist and wiggles it around.

She also says your sister has a secret and when your mother finds out she's going to be knocked off her pedestal.

Your mother's a bitch.

I know. Is it true?

About the secret? I think so.

Eiyyyy!

He tells her that he'll pray for her soul in church. His mother makes them go every Sunday. *Mine too.* They kick the ball back and forth between them until their shadows begin to stretch across the playground and the lights of the houses in the distance glow brighter.

It's late, let's go. He picks up his ball and they walk home together in the gloom. Andoni declares that if there's a war he might be called up to fight for Cyprus. Imagine that, he says.

Are you scared?

A bit.

But he's excited, mainly. Someone has to stick it to the Turks and he'd get to wear a uniform and hold a Sten gun. They say their goodbyes and Elena watches him disappear inside. Then she sits back on the bench beneath the vine and braces herself for the inevitable.

～

Who is the father? Lenou is a giant volcano. When she erupts, she's going to cover everything in molten lava and strip the skin from their bones. *Who?* She's screaming now and pulling at her hair and Elena imagines the neighbours leaving their suppers half eaten and rushing to their windows in excitement. Mrs Pavlou, crossing herself in mock concern and Andoni praying for their souls like he promised he would. *Who?* She pulls the green plastic tablecloth out from under them, sending cups and plates crashing noisily to the kitchen floor. Elena buzzes around like an unwelcome fly unsure of where to land, the answer to her mother's question on the tip of her tongue, though she doesn't dare betray Valentina. *Is it the boy? The boy from the factory?* There'd be hope, then. A teenage boy can be pressured into marriage or, at least, lectured by a priest. A married man more than twice her sister's age will do as he so pleases. *Well, is it?* Valentina has the good grace to keep quiet. The reality of a baby slowly sinking in and erasing the smirk from her lips. A baby. A child inside a child, Elena thinks. Who would have thought? Certainly not Lenou, who was knocked sideways by Dr Verras' news and had to be treated for the shock.

Sorry.

Sorry? You think this can be fixed with a sorry?

The screaming continues and Lenou opens cupboards and reaches for heavy silver pots to hurl across the kitchen. The pots and pans joining the shattered cups and plates. *Eiyyy, Mamma, you'll wake the dead!* A look from Lenou warns Valentina that she will soon be joining them in the cemetery. Anything for the peace. *Get out, get out both of you!* She grabs Valentina by the hair and throws her out of the room. Her sister, half tangled in her chair, almost taking it with her down the hall. Elena runs to her bedroom and locks the door behind her, grateful, tonight, not to be sharing with trouble. She stands with her back against the door, breathing heavily, and wonders if she'll pass out again.

She's been fainting ever since the night Valentina was late to meet her and she was left to sit alone in the school playground imagining all sorts. Valentina locked in the back of his car, banging on the windows and begging for help and headless torsos floating in the Mediterranean Sea. Her mother screaming in her face and accusing her of murder. The guilt of it worse than her sister's actual demise and the blame eating away at her insides like a corrosive poison. It's my fault, it's all my fault, Mamma. I knew and didn't tell. There was even a small white coffin in these flashes of horror, and the fear and panic it provoked continued long after Valentina crossed the abandoned yard and extended her hand towards her. *Sorry I'm late.*

Later, as she lay in bed replaying the events of the night, she found that she couldn't catch her breath. It was as if she knew that the danger had passed, yet couldn't stop a collision. She began to hyperventilate, breathing in short shallow bursts like a person drowning in putrid waters, and eventually black spots exploded at the sides of her eyes and she fell into a black hole head first. A hole that led to nowhere. A place without dreams. When she came around again, she felt all right. Better, even. The terror of before seemed distant and blurred and somehow unrelated to her. Like the disembodied memories of her Pappa and Giovanna, locked away in their box and unable to hurt her.

She knew she'd fainted because she'd seen her mother pass out once, a few months after Pappa had died. They'd gone into town to buy aubergines for dinner and her mother had collapsed in the queue and fallen into the vegetables. The shopkeeper, Mr Gavril, had come rushing round from behind his counter to help them, and he and Elena had half dragged and half carried Lenou down to the waterfront. They'd sat her down on the pebble-strewn beach by the harbour and splashed the cool sea water in her face to revive her. Elena had been petrified that she would die like her Pappa and leave them entirely on their own. Two orphans rummaging around in the rubbish for scraps of food like Panteloni the cat.

She'd said it was because she hadn't eaten breakfast that morning and she was hungry and dehydrated. It was a blisteringly hot summer's day and she'd had a funny turn, that's all. *Don't worry, child.* She'd patted her hand to dispel her fears and Elena wondered if she was sad about Pappa. They'd met just over there, she'd told Elena, pointing to the pier. He'd been fishing with his friends and he'd noticed her staring coyly at him. Of course she had stared, he was the most handsome man she'd ever seen. She'd laughed then, with her head tipped all the way back and her face pointing to the sky and they'd watched the fishermen working and the colourful little boats bobbing up and down in the blue water for hours together. Elena had tried hard to imagine her mother as a carefree young woman who wore pretty, brightly coloured dresses and attracted the attention of men. It didn't seem possible, somehow, whichever way she visualised it.

She can hear her howling in the kitchen now. The destruction of their earthenware has stopped, but the crying has intensified. Lenou is no longer angry at the father of the baby, but outraged by the neighbours and sorry for herself. What has she done, she shrieks, to deserve all of this? This is Mrs Pavlou's doing. It has to be. Mrs Pavlou and her jealous evil eye, willing their downfall from the other side of the driveway. *We're cursed, cursed I tell you!* Elena decides that she's not going to faint after all. She walks over to her open bedroom window and peers out from behind the wooden shutters. Mrs Pavlou, it seems, has found the last decent bone in her body and retreated indoors to gloat in private.

~

They decide to skip their last class of the afternoon and head a quarter of a mile up the road to Brokobi's Beriptero to buy orange sodas. Andoni pretends to march like a soldier and kicks dirt into Elena's face from the dusty brown street beneath them. His cries to attention and his exaggerated swinging arms amuse the bored neighbourhood kids, who run after him in their shorts and bare feet and get on Elena's nerves. *Eiyyy, Andoni!* She knows he's only trying to cheer her up. It's been weeks, he says, since he's seen her smile. *Would you be smiling if you were me?* Probably not, he replies. He asks her if it's true that her sister is going to have a baby and he sucks air through his teeth when she confirms that she is. Is he impressed, Elena wonders, like the boys in their class who look at her with a new interest, or disgusted like the rest of them? Perhaps a bit of both.

It's not just the Pavlous who are talking about Valentina. They're all gossiping behind their backs. Mrs Mavrides, Mrs Pappas from church, the kids at school, and even big Brokobi now stares at them disdainfully as they stand outside his tin-roofed kiosk and drink their sodas beneath the Coca-Cola-branded shop sign. Andoni kicks a stone into the wall opposite and mutters into her ear: *Don't let him bother you. Big Brokobi has enough problems of his own.* Has she not seen his huge chins and the way he sweats when it's hot? Like Niagara Falls.

Last week it had been old gojiakari Eleftherou who had insulted her. She'd been sitting outside her front door in her long black dress with her walking stick propped between her bony legs and she'd shaken it at Elena as she'd walked past on her way to school. She'd even spat on the ground and muttered a curse. *Maybe she's spitting out her teeth?* Andoni had ventured when she told him what had happened. She doesn't know what she would have done without him and his sense of humour these past weeks. Her mother has barely stopped crying long enough to peel the potatoes and barbecue a chicken for their Sunday lunch, and her sister has all but disappeared. She's sending her to England, she tells him. *My sister. To live with my mother's cousin.*

She'd arrived home yesterday to find two black leather suitcases standing ominously in the front room. *Are you going someplace, Mamma?* She'd kicked off her sandals and poured herself a glass of milk. It was Valentina who was leaving, her mother had announced. Her and the bastard in her belly and a damned good riddance to them both. Elena had stood in the doorway and gasped at the thought of it. Valentina, exiled to a country she'd never heard of, her baby wrapped in dirty sheets stripped from her lover's bed. Whatever happened to mercy, she wonders. The merciful God of her mother's prayers. Where was He? She was going to London to live with a relative and it was all arranged. *Can you hear them laughing at me?* She'd started crying again. *They are saying, look at that stupid woman. She has fallen off her perch and she is crawling around in the mud like a blind beggar.* Elena had dropped her glass then, and it had cut her feet into a million milky pieces.

Lenou had been sympathetic and had even helped her pick up the shards. It was the shame that had caused it to slip from her hands, she'd explained. The other day she'd sliced her own finger open with a carving knife, so she knew the feeling, and it was just as well Valentina was leaving or they'd have no digits left between them.

Valentina comes to see her before Elena has a chance to knock on her door. *Can I come in?* Her long black hair, the source of all their troubles, wound tightly around her head in a knot. They crawl under the bed sheets together like they used to when they were small and Valentina tells her that she's being vanished. *Like I never existed.* Valentina and her illegitimate child erased from memory to silence malicious tongues and appease the next-door neighbours.

Promise me. Her tone is urgent. *Promise me that you won't let her turn you into her.* Elena promises, although she doesn't understand the request. *She's crazy, Elena.* The things she hides behind, she tells her. The spiritual stuff, it's an excuse. Valentina's dark pupils dance in the light from the open window like a pair of tragic ballerinas.

Elena wishes Pappa was still alive. Good, kind Pappa. He would have pulled their doors and shutters closed and told them it didn't matter what anybody else thought, least of all Mrs Pavlou. It's OK, wife. The girl made a mistake. She's still young. Hadn't they all made mistakes at one time or another?

She takes her sister's hand.

You are so beautiful, Valentina. Sometimes I wish I was you. Isn't that funny?

Her sister's voice sounds disembodied, like it's coming from someplace else.

I've always wanted to be more like you.

Chapter 23

London – 1984

HE CALLS HER crazy. It's a turn of phrase more than anything else and he doesn't mean to hurt her, but it hurts her all the same. It reminds her of the night Valentina had crawled into her bed and they'd whispered about their mother in hushed, forbidden tones. Valentina had said the same thing about her, and Elena had jumped to her defence. There was no such thing as crazy. Not in Lenou's eyes. You were either standing in the light or crouching in the shadows and there was nothing at all in between. Elena knew exactly what she meant, even if nobody else did.

Mrs Pavlou had called Lenou crazy once too, a few weeks after she'd thrown Valentina out. Her mother had opened the front door after an episode of strenuous crying and screamed at the top of her voice that Mrs Pavlou was cursing them. First she'd killed her husband and now she'd ruined her daughter and she hoped that she was happy casting her spells like the wicked old witch that she was. She'd yelled so loudly and for so long that eventually the light over the Pavlous, front step had flickered to life and Mrs Pavlou had appeared in the doorway in her nightclothes. *You're crazy, Kyria Lenou. You know that?* she'd shouted. *Absolutely crazy!* Elena had been sitting outside on the little bench, hiding in the dark, and she'd seen and heard it all, but Mrs Pavlou hadn't realised she was there and neither had her mother.

When she was growing up it was always Pappa who would comfort her mother when she was angry. Big, strong Pappa, standing in front of his wife so she couldn't hit them or pull at their hair, and sometimes taking a blow inadvertently. He'd never called her crazy, he was far too respectful of her to say something like that, but she still remembers the look of disappointment in his eyes the night her mother had spoilt their trip to the bazaar.

The St Peter's Day Fete was a near-famous event in their neighbourhood, honouring the saint of their eponymous church. Elena had been so excited to see the brightly coloured stalls selling cheeses and honey and little cubes of toasted coconut, and Valentina had been too, but her mother had started screaming at them for not finishing their chores. Her wrath had gained momentum apropos of nothing, it had seemed, and within the space of a few short minutes it was threatening to engulf the house.

She'd thrown things across the kitchen, breaking a shutter and damaging the wall and she'd finally achieved what she'd set out to do and ruined the outing for them all. Pappa had insisted on taking them anyway, but he'd been sad and the night had felt spoiled. Like gone-off milk. She'd looked around at the other families, parents holding hands and children squealing in delight as their ribbons trailed behind them like kites, and she'd wondered why *her* mother was always so angry.

Her anger grew, ironically, after Pappa's passing. Lenou seemingly realising in those dark, blurred weeks following his death that she'd had nothing to feel angry about beforehand. Her resentment escalated and she aimed it at her daughters. *It's not my fault*, Valentina would shout as their mother chased her around the kitchen with a wooden spoon. *I didn't kill him*. And that's when the idea came to her. That somebody probably did and it was most likely Mrs Pavlou.

You're being crazy, he says, which she supposes is not quite the same as calling her crazy. To be fair to Costa, she had opened the window in Magda's bedroom and screamed at him to come upstairs because the baby wasn't breathing. He'd dropped the lawnmower while it was still turned on and he tells her he's lucky that it didn't tear his leg off in the panic. He'd run up the stairs two by two, his large soft chest heaving with exertion beneath his shirt and he'd almost broken the baby's door down to get to them. The pair of them had stood in Magda's little pink room with the pink carpets and grey elephant shapes on the wall and watched her sleeping and there had been nothing wrong with her at all. That's when he'd said it. *You're being crazy, Elena. There's nothing wrong with her at all.*

The same thing had happened at the start of the week and a few days prior to that. Costa tells her that she's tired. Why doesn't she try to rest in the day when the baby naps and Nina is at her nursery? She takes her to the doctor the next morning anyway, just to be sure. She pushes her all the way there in the pram to avoid getting on the bus and aggravating her anxiety and she sits in Dr Stein's too-white room and watches nervously while she gently lifts her vest and listens to Magda's chest, feeling, all the while, like she's about to be sick.

She's a perfectly healthy eighteen-month-old baby, she assures her. *There's nothing wrong with her at all.* The doctor smiles in a way that disconcerts her and gives her a leaflet on what to look for if a child is really sick. *She's smiling, and babies who are sick don't smile.* She feels silly, afterwards. Like people are laughing behind her back and, indeed, into her face. Mrs Pavlou and Mrs Pappas and maybe even Big Brokobi. *They're all laughing at us,* her mother used to scream at her sister. *Are you happy now?*

She doesn't tell Costa about the doctor's visit and she does well, she thinks, to carry on with the rest of her day despite the strange feeling unfurling inside her. She even collects Nina from nursery with Magda in tow and prepares the children a snack. The semblance of normality. Isn't that what Costa wants at the end of the day? A normal wife and a normal family?

When he arrives home she can no longer pretend that she's all right and she runs up the stairs to crawl beneath her covers like she used to do when life back home was insurmountable. *What's wrong?* She almost laughs at his question. Such a silly question! How can she tell him what's wrong with her when she doesn't even know herself?

~

Maria's irritated when Costa calls her and begs her to come over. It's the third time this month, she barks down the phone. *What the hell's wrong with her now?* She'd been standing behind the bakery counter, her long dark silhouette framed by all the yellow, thinking of all the things she had to do and, instead, daydreaming of tsipopites.

Not the kind you buy in this country, made with fresh cream, but her tsipopites, the ones she used to bake back home after Katerina died. The secret ingredient, she confides to Maki, other than the fresh tsipa of course, is the nut oil she used to add to her filo pastry. It gave the cake that extra special something, a flavour to tantalise the tongue. There was another secret, too. After she'd rolled out her pastry into a square, she would make sure the tsipa was spread right to the very edges of the thing so that when it was coiled around the cake tin like an old lady's braid, the creamy butter filling would seep into every inch of the dessert. When it was assembled she'd shovel it into the clay oven with the ftiari to bake, and the smell of the sheep's milk bubbling away would lift her spirits and restore something to her that had been lost in tragedy.

They were almost legendary, her tsipopites, and they'd even coax the neighbours out from behind their little brown shutters and doors. Mrs Kemal would pretend to run out of peas to shell at the very moment the pita came out of the oven and she'd appear on her doorstep with her colander to borrow more. Mrs Kouli would find herself at a loose end as well, despite the housework she was always grumbling about. She'd stand by the little wall separating her yard from Maria's and practically stick her head into the oven for a slice. *Of course, Kyria Maria, if you are offering some of your tsipo-pita with a kafe, I wouldn't say no.* Maria wasn't a stingy woman and wouldn't begrudge the women a slice of cake, but the pites and the bourekia and the breads she had baked in those early months were to nourish their own souls and nobody else's.

Ah, Costa. She would do anything for him. Anything for her son. She would walk over hot coals for him and stick a knife into her side and watch the world slide out of her body for him. But asking her to take two buses down Green Lanes during rush hour was a step too far. He pleads with her then. *Please, Mamma.* She only has to sit with Nina while he gets the baby ready for her bed. He only has one pair of hands and she doesn't have to wash the dishes and sweep the floors like last time. He talks her round but she slams the telephone down in regret afterwards and Maki smiles and raises his eyebrows and asks if there is trouble in paradise. There is no such thing as paradise, she retorts. And if anyone is ever stupid enough to marry him he'll discover that for himself. She stomps up the stairs to fetch her coat and her handbag, muttering to herself all the while, and she's so exasperated with the world by then that she slams the door closed on her way out into the busy high street.

She's not quite sure she believes this herself, about relationships. Relationships are not meant to be this difficult and wives are not supposed to behave like Elena. Poor Elena. She feels sorry for her, she truly does, but to lie in bed all day when there are two little girls to take care of and a house to run is completely incomprehensible to her. If only she'd had the luxury of a fairy godmother when her kids were little, and she'd said as much to Mrs Koutsouli the last time Costa had called on her for her help. *If only I'd had a fairygod mother to do all my bloody housework.*

Costa, of course, is in complete denial. *She's just tired, that's all* and at the end of the day, there is nothing as convincing as the lies we tell ourselves. She climbs onto the number 29 with considerable effort and looks around for a seat. The boy is like an ostrich, burying his head in the sand and hoping it will all go away. Well, it isn't going to, she can assure him of that.

The bus is packed, like she'd told him it would be at this time in the afternoon, and she can feel her ageing legs wobbling unsteadily beneath her. A woman with a giant double pushchair stands blocking the aisle as her children scream, and people cough and splutter into her hair. She pulls her handkerchief out of her bag and holds it up to her face, tutting to herself about insolent, ungrateful sons. The windows are misty from too much breath and she's starting to feel faint. *Oof!*

Eventually, a man with pink hair and a jacket covered in metal studs gets up and lets her take his place. *Thank you.* A smile. The English a continuous mystery to her. A man with metal protruding from his jacket and big pink triangles sticking out of his head. Last time there had been a passenger holding a giant stereo to his ear. Whatever next?

The bus terminates at Wood Green Station and she stands outside Zara's Patisserie to wait for the 121 or the 329, whichever should arrive first and if at all. The cake shop is new, and Themis and George had teased her about it mercilessly when it had first opened. *A bit of competition, hah, Kyria Maria?* Pah! she'd replied. Competition indeed! It was too far down Green Lanes to pose a threat to her bakery and besides, scrawny Zara was no match for her. A slip of a woman in her early thirties who'd overzealously plucked out both her eyebrows and had recently married for the fourth time. No wonder she could afford to buy her own shop, Maria thinks. She'd be rich, too, if she'd divorced as many times as this woman had, and she wonders where she puts all the leftovers.

And her cakes, she'd said to Themis, looked more like fried eggs than pastries. Round yellow things with orange blobs dumped unceremoniously in the centre. No thank you. Petrakis was a proper Greek bakery, not a pretentious patisserie selling plastic pites. Themis had lowered his voice then and told her he'd heard rumours that the shop was just a front for her other ventures. *What other ventures?* she'd asked curiously. *She's a porn star,* he'd replied. On the side. George thought he'd seen her in a film he'd rented from Cyprus Videos next to Paniko's, although he was only in there looking for Demis Roussos' latest album and not for adult entertainment at all. *Oh, of course not!* Pornographic pastries! Maria had crossed herself three times at the thought of it. She thought she'd seen and heard it all over the years, but evidently not, and the lewd blobs in the patisserie shop window made more sense to her now.

Costa is warming up the baby's bottle in the kitchen when she arrives and the girls are hanging off him like shiny baubles on a wilting Christmas tree. The desperation in his eyes tells Maria everything she needs to know. Elena has been in bed for most of the day. *Is she sick?* She unbuttons her long black coat, slips off her shoes and scoops Nina into her arms. *How should I know, Mamma?* Always the same reply. Well if he didn't know what was wrong with his bloody wife how the hell would anybody else? She sinks into the sofa in the front room with the spider plants crawling out of every crack and orifice while he disappears upstairs to bath the baby. She tells him the clock is ticking. He has thirty minutes and then she's leaving. She doesn't intend to get the bus back home in the dark and it's bad enough she's had to travel all the way down Green Lanes to Palmers Green during rush hour when she offloaded him onto Elena years ago.

Nina sits cross-legged on the brown carpet in front of the television and Maria sighs. Such a beautiful child, with her dark curly hair and milky chocolate eyes. Pray to God she isn't picking up on the madness but of course, they always did. *You OK, my darling?* The little girl turns around and smiles at her then and Maria thinks of her Katerina sitting on the bus that last time. The thoughts coming at her like cars when she least expects them and knocking her into oncoming traffic. If only she had known what lay ahead.

She's suddenly indignant. What she would have given to have been able to raise her own child and here was her daughter-in-law, blessed with two healthy babies, wallowing in self-pity. How different her life might have been if her Katerina had lived to tell her own tale and if Mr Styliano had been her husband instead of the brute she'd married. And people called her lucky.

Chapter 24

Cyprus – 1960

AFTERWARDS, PEOPLE SAID that she was lucky to have passed out at the scene. It was a blessing from God, they said. To spare a mother from the unspeakable pain. People talked about grief as if it was a bus. Maria had fainted and missed it and that was that, it had rattled off down the hill and it was all over. Grief is more like a fist than a bus, Maria thinks. Striking her in the face until she doesn't recognise her bloody reflection in the mirror. Until she is bent over the bathroom sink, torn to shreds, retching and moaning and spitting out her teeth.

Grief is like Michali.

He had been kind to her at first. In the beginning, when Costa had gone to stay with Thora so they could mourn her without restraint and it had been just the two of them, screaming into the dark. They had even held on to one another as they'd cried, wounded animals running from the barrel of a gun. And he'd been every bit as vulnerable as her, then.

But later, the man she'd met at the proxenia disappeared for the second time and the real Michali was back. The Michali she knew. Asking her what had happened over and over, making her repeat the events of that morning, looking for the loopholes and trying his best, it seemed, to catch her out and make her the true perpetrator of their daughter's death. How long had she stood in the fabric shop gossiping with Louli, how quickly had she run down the road and why did she go into town without his permission in the first place? He picks at her scars with his nails and enjoys watching them bleed. These are the same questions she has asked herself a million times, she tells him. If and only. The most painful words that ever existed.

If only it hadn't happened, if only she hadn't taken the kids into town.

There is only one person to blame and he drove away without stopping. She tries to tell him that. There are rumours. Cyprus is a small island. People supposedly saw his car and know who he is. They knock on her door day and night and tell her *Kyria Maria, we know who did this*. He's from Ammochostos and his father owns a factory making clothes. Friends, relatives, even neighbours offer to assemble a mob to eviscerate him and hang his bloody guts from the nearest palm tree. People are outraged on her behalf. An eye for an eye without concrete proof. Is this how God intended us to live? Maria wonders. And what comes next, a child for a child? You kill my child, I'll kill yours? On good days, Maria turns and hides from thoughts like these in the palms of her hands, but during the darker times she allows them free rein and she curses him, whoever he may be. The man and his family and everyone who knows him. Cursed for an eternity, in the name of Katerina.

After the funeral, which she can barely recall, Maria closes her door to well-wishers and revenge seekers and begins to curl inwards like a spiny hedgehog. She sleeps for hours at first, then days, and then weeks. The seasons change and the heat dissipates into a cool mist but Maria is oblivious to this continuation of life, just as life is oblivious to her loss.

Dr Pantazis visits once a week at Michali's insistence. He exchanges small talk with her husband before creeping respectfully up the stairs to her room. He says that she is bearing up well considering her pain and that she's lucky she can, at least, sleep. *God is kind to you, Kyria Maria.* There's that word again, she thinks. My child is dead and people tell me I'm lucky.

Tell me, doctor. How am I lucky?

Because God is kind to you.

She laughs long and hard, then. As if someone has told her a terrible joke.

Chapter 25

London – 1975

I'M TELLING YOU, it's true. *They put the wrong man in there. They would have buried him as well, had the priest not insisted they open up the box at the last minute.*

Mr Panayioti is the master of the tall tale and Maria doesn't believe a word of his concocted nonsense. For a start, she retorts, why would the priest demand they open the lid of the coffin right there and then, and in front of the family?

How should I know? Maybe God had a word in his ear, hah?

He winks at her mischievously and orders four of her biggest kolokotes.

You were there, you saw all this with your own eyes?

She places the little pumpkin pies into a box and thinks that it's most unlike Mr Panayioti to order vegan pastries when he usually ate koubes filled with mince or bourekia made with Anari cheese and sugar for his breakfast. *You fasting?* No, he tells her. He's just taking a break from the animal fats. He lowers his voice in embarrassment. He has gout, of all things. Doctor's orders. He wasn't there although God knows he seems to be going to enough funerals these days and this could easily have been one of them. He read about it in the local Greek Cypriot paper. The story next to those pitiful adverts.

There was a time when Mr Panayioti was sweet on her and Costa used to joke that she should paint her nails and invite him upstairs for a chai. Wash and curl her hair. Make a bit of an effort. Why not? he'd laugh when she shook her head in disbelief. She deserved some happiness. No thank you. Mr Panayioti was twenty years her senior and, truth be told, he reminded her a little of a tortoise, with his small beady eyes and his wrinkly neck protruding from his polo-necked sweaters. His wife died many years ago and he was lonely, she could tell. He'd started driving a mini cab after she'd passed away just so he'd have someone to talk to during the day, and he'd even learned how to cook for himself. She'd been impressed by that. He could cook all sorts now and not just soups and boiled macaronia, but stifado, kleftiko, moussaka, the tricky dishes that required years of practice and an array of complicated spices. Recipes even she had to think about. Bravo, she'd said to him after she'd tried a piece of his bechamel pastichio. Truly delicious.

Which pitiful adverts?

She places the box of kolokotes into a bag and hands him his change. She must know the ones, he says. People looking for love, that sort of thing. Lonely hearts columns. Or married men seeking affairs, as he preferred to call them. Be honest, he asks her, would she ever look for romance in the local newspaper?

Maria chuckles at the thought of finding love again at her age. *Pah!* he replies, tapping his bag of kolokotes with his forefinger. Sixty-one is no age at all. He's nearly eighty and still looking for a girlfriend.

She wishes him luck with it and she thinks that there's another reason why she never bothered to marry again. Nobody would come close to Mr Styliano and the feelings he aroused within her, and there was little point in looking. Even now, after all these years, her old heart lurched at the thought of him. There are ways, he'd said, after she'd told him that Michali hurt her. Ways of making people disappear, and the hairs on her arms had stood up on end as his words had changed her life.

A young woman with long black hair enters the shop and the little bell above the door sounds twice to signal her appearance. There's a sudden silence, and Mr Panayioti turns around to gawp at the stranger who has stolen his limelight and thrown him off his podium. He leans back into the counter and raises his eyebrows approvingly. *Mashallah!* The young woman is wearing a pink T-shirt and long flares and her large brown sunglasses almost cover her face. When she pushes them back over the top of her head Maria recognises her. Elena's sister.

Mr Panayioti almost convulses in his excitement. She can upstage him any day, he mutters under his breath. Here he was thinking that his pies and his afternoon run to Heathrow were going to be the highlight of his day, when he crosses paths with Aphrodite herself.

Maria raises her hand in the air. She's heard enough about gout and goddesses and funeral fiascos.

Will that be all, Mr Panayioti? Only, dead bodies and marital indiscretions aside, I really must talk to this young lady.

~

Downstairs in the bakery, Maria can hear the girls' footsteps and the sound of chairs being scraped across the kitchen floor. She looks up at the ceiling and sighs. What drama has the sister visited on Elena this time? she wonders. She doesn't hear from her for half a year and then she reappears like the harbinger of doom in shiny high-heeled shoes.

When Costa announced his engagement to Elena, the customers flocked to Petrakis in their multitudes to warn her against the new family. *Mah, the sister she got pregnant when she was just a child*, they whispered loudly and in mock concern. The lover was a married man twice her age and the mother threw her out! A harsh punishment, but what else could she do, the poor woman? There was obviously something wrong with them and the younger sister might turn out much like the older one. Like rotten apples falling from a tree.

Maria tuts at the memories. People pretending to be concerned for Costa when in reality their eyes shone with glee. Mrs Vasili practically crowing over the news and even Mrs Koutsouli deriving some malicious enjoyment from the scandal, she could tell. Still, she's never been busier than she was in those weeks, and their self-satisfaction almost paid for the wedding.

Maria had to admit that they were all a bit strange. The family. The religious mother was bordering on crazy, the sister was beautiful but melancholy, and then there was the husband, Taki. Maria often wondered where he fitted into all of this. The timings didn't make any sense if the rumours were to be believed.

Valentina is sent to London in disgrace with her belly protruding and while pregnant with another man's child she marries Taki. Why would Taki want a girl with another man's baby flourishing inside of her, and why would Lenou agree to such a match? Unless her mother was trying to pass the baby off as Taki's? A firm possibility if the man was stupid or couldn't count backwards from nine. And his mother, truly apoplectic with rage she was. *My son is marrying a whore, what did I do wrong?* Maria knew all about Valentina before she'd ever met Elena and, at one point, everybody on Green Lanes had heard of her too. *Tell me, where did I go wrong?* Sticks and stones and tongues break bones.

All these mothers, Maria thinks, as she sprinkles icing sugar over the kourabiethes for her window display. The real centre of the shop. Frothing at the mouth because their children wouldn't do as they were told. Jumping up and down and banging their fists on their foreheads like malevolent little goblins. Faking heart attacks and taking blood pressure tablets and rolling around on the floor. Lenou, Elizavet, Mrs Koutsouli. Did it ever work out for them, she wonders, all this anger and despair? It didn't work out for her when Costa told her they were moving out. She'd sat in her room for days at first, sulking over the betrayal, and the Judas didn't even bother to knock on her door. She'd crept in a few times. Dear Elena. She'd unlocked the door for her and they'd sat on the edge of her bed together and Maria had shown her the photograph of Katerina that she carried around in the pocket of her apron. It was an old school picture and she'd given one to Costa too. It's the anniversary, she told her. Fifteen years this summer. She hoped that Costa would remember.

It had upset her, she could tell. The picture. She was a sweet, sensitive girl who couldn't stand very much reality. She couldn't face the thought of it, she'd said. Of her blue eyes staring forever at the sky. It's OK, child, Maria had replied. *Let's put it away, hah?* And she'd put the photograph back in her apron and she'd told her she didn't mind that they were leaving. Not really. The two of them were going off to start their own family and that was exactly how it should be. Grab the happiness while you can, she'd said, as she patted Elena's knee. Grab it and run and don't look back.

She was pleased with herself, then. For overcoming her selfish desires and letting the children live their own lives, unlike all these other mothers. Besides, when it came down to it, there were far more effective ways of influencing fate than screaming and crying and tearing your hair out. And she should know. She should know full well.

~

She's surprised to see Valentina standing at the top of the stairs. Maria announcing her arrival and shouting at her to put the kettle on. *Your sister's here!* Her excitement ringing around the little shop. She's pale and thin and the dark, revealing circles beneath her eyes contrast with the colour of her snow-white skin. Elena pours hot water into two cups of coffee and slides one across the kitchen counter to her sister. It's been months since she heard from her. *Is everything OK?* Valentina picks up the mug and laughs at the thought of Elena drinking instant coffee. Since when, she teases, did her sister drink coffee like an American?

Can I smoke?

Elena opens the window so she can dangle her long pale arm outside. *How is Taki?* Her long black hair seems to consume her tiny frame and her hips stick out of her trousers. *Taki is Taki.* It's strange, having her here. The smell of her too-strong perfume and cigarettes mingling with the aroma of cakes. Distant galaxies colliding. She asks Elena why they're still living with Costa's mother. *We're moving.* Valentina rolls her big black eyes. There'll be babies soon. Her tone is accusatory. Legitimate ones, she tells her. Ones she gets to keep, wasn't she just the lucky one?

There's a silence as she finishes her cigarette and flings the butt out of the open window. Elena wonders where it might have landed and whose scalp it may have singed. Valentina says she's sorry. It was cruel of her, she admits, but she still thinks about her every single day and the pain of it is practically eating her up. She tugs at her waistband. *Look at me.* She would have been five now, she tells her. *My little girl.*

Valentina pulls up a chair next to Elena at Maria's kitchen table and she grabs at her hands and threads her fingers through hers. She needs to know, she demands. If she delivered the letter, the one she gave her before she left with Uncle Zacharia. Of course, Elena replies. Always the same question. She went with Andoni Pavlou. She still remembers the white and gold railings which surrounded his house. She doesn't mean to interrogate her, Valentina tells her, but it's important to her to know that Elena did what she'd asked. It meant everything. It was life and it was death.

Another cup of coffee and a change of subject. She pulls her hands away from Valentina's. She mentioned Andoni Pavlou. Did Elena know that he was dead? His brother, Dimitri, knew a friend of Taki's and he'd told him the news at a football match. One of those embarrassing ones where fat, out-of-shape men run around on a field full of dog shit.

Elena sips her coffee and stares out of the window at the back of the flats opposite. Were they flats or shops? she wondered. She didn't know. She hadn't heard. A man dumps black rubbish bags into a large metal dustbin in the alleyway and wipes his palms on his apron. A butcher, maybe, with blood on his hands. He went missing in the war, Valentina continues, and they identified his bones last month. He was still wearing his tags, so at least that was something. They didn't tear them off him like they did with some. *It's sad, don't you think?*

They found his body in the undergrowth, blackened by the sun. It's warm out today, Elena thinks. And the meat in those bins will start to stink by lunchtime. The stench of rot and decay. What a shame for his life to have ended like that. Poor Andoni and poor Mrs Pavlou.

Do you remember her?

How could she forget her? Elena thinks of her now, hunched over her broom and supposedly cursing their family. Why would she do that? she'd asked her mother. Why would she wish harm on us, didn't she have enough problems of her own? Didn't they all? She tries to imagine Andoni scoring a goal, but sees only his mother's face as they tell her the news.

Her own hands are suddenly on fire, red flames at first and then long black ones. The colour of Andoni's skin as they carefully untangled him from the brush and dragged him out in pieces.

Elena? I'm sorry, it was a shock. Here, let me help.

She's spilled her coffee everywhere and she didn't even notice.

~

Elena is staring out of the window at the moon. How strange, she thinks, that no matter where we are in the world we are all looking at the same moon. Costa pulls on his pyjama bottoms and climbs into bed. He throws back the duvet and taps the space next to him. He's sorry, he tells her. About Andoni Pavlou.

Really strange.

Mrs Pavlou and Mrs Pappas and her mother, they can all see the same thing as she can right now. Does she want to talk about Andoni? Not especially, she tells Costa, but she's grateful that he cares. She wonders what Mrs Pavlou is doing now and why her mother didn't mention Andoni the last time she'd called. It's because of the resettlements, Valentina had thought, she probably didn't know. What a shame for his life to have ended like that, she'd said, and it had bothered her for a moment.

Just a moment. Confusion, that's what Dr Verras had told her mother she was suffering from after Giovanna died. She's confused. She'd started having dreams about little white coffins being lowered into the ground and she had no idea where they came from. *Take her home, Kyria Lenou.* A kindly voice from the past mingles with her mother's.

She doesn't want to talk about Andoni Pavlou, she tells Costa, but she'd quite like to learn English. She's been feeling rather muddled of late and it is time to make a bit of an effort.

Chapter 26

London – 1988

SHE WONDERS WHY the woman is asking her about Giovanna.

The sunlight is streaming through the windows and Elena can see dust particles suspended in mid-air. At last, time is slowing down and objects in the white room appear to be in focus. There's a shelf full of brightly coloured book spines and a painting of a robin in a frame. Detail. A desk. A window. A bookcase. A woman wearing black-rimmed glasses. Her missing son is fading like a child's memory of a long-ago Christmas. Once upon a time there was a little boy. His eyes were the colour of the sea and he lived in a snow globe made out of glass. She knows that he is gone. More importantly, she knows now that he is not coming back.

The woman tells her that sometimes events are connected in ways that are not at first clear. Could there be a link between Giovanna and her missing child? Elena shakes her head. Giovanna Johnston is dead. She knows she is dead because she saw her laid out in her little white coffin. It was cruel of her mother to make her go. So cruel. Giovanna's funeral had traumatised her so deeply that she could barely remember what she'd seen. She doesn't want to think about her any more, she tells the woman. The Little Englesa.

What would you like to talk about?

She wants to talk about her son. The way his blue eyes shone in the sun and in the school photograph that she carried around in her apron pocket. He was a very beautiful child and when he smiled he lit up the room.

He liked to play football.

He carried a ball around with him everywhere he went. He was good, too. Always practising. The light outside the window is changing again and the steely white sky is turning blue. A deep, dark blue. The surface of Mediterranean Sea. There is yellow dust blowing inside the room through the cracks in the walls. So much sand that she thinks she's going to suffocate or pass out in her bed and wake up with the covers tied around her neck. A hanged man, dangling from a noose. She joined him sometimes, in the empty school-yard behind their house, which smelled of jasmine and olives. He'd kick the ball towards her and show her how to stop it with the side of her foot. Like this, see?

A memory. She's drinking coffee in Maria's kitchen when Valentina tells her that he's dead.

My son is dead.

She hadn't meant to shock her that day. How could she have known, she asks the woman, that Elena had been in love with him and that it would affect her as much as it did?

Who do you think died?

They found him in the undergrowth. Beneath the dust, decomposed and blackened by the sun. She'd told her it was a shame for his life to have ended like that and she hadn't flinched. Thinking about it now, it had cut her to her bone. A butcher's knife hacking at her limbs and putting them in a big metal bin to rot in the summer heat.

Suddenly there's screaming.

It's OK, Elena.

The woman is trying to comfort her, but she's struggling too much and she presses a button to summon help. Who is she calling? Elena wonders. Her Pappa, perhaps.

Elena?

It's no use shouting out her name, she thinks, when the screams are coming from Mrs Pavlou's house. She can hear them a mile off and it's a wonder she didn't wake the whole of Ammochostos that morning. They reverberate now around the small white room, shattering the glass. She'd screamed for her Andoni and her sons feared she would never stop. She tore all her hair out when she learned the news, or so Elena imagines when she closes her eyes at night.

Have you seen my son, have you seen my son? He went off to war with a big black gun?

The door flies open and a man comes in to kneel beside them. He's here to soothe her, to stroke her hair, to call her husband so he can pick her up off the bakery floor. Take her home. The woman with the glasses tells him about somebody's sister. *Gentle. It's still very recent, very raw.*

Poor Mrs Pavlou, pricked with a needle and told to relax. *Nobody's going to hurt you,* the woman says. The man is here to help. His arms are big and strong, but they're comforting and they cradle her like a baby until her legs stop kicking. Someone is telling her to relax and she laughs then because she saw it all in the bottom of Mrs Mavrides' coffee cup and she knew it was coming, that it would hurt. How could it not? She'd gone round there for a bit of a laugh and to pass the time, and instead she'd seen a mother's worst nightmare. The loss of a child, written into her stars.

Chapter 27

Cyprus – 1969

NOVEMBER. THE DAYS are cool and misty and the nights are slowly drawing in. The inevitable descent into Cypriot winter. People in Ammochostos spend more time in their homes, behind closed doors and shutters, listening to their radios or playing backgammon and drinking cinnamon tea to pass the time. Those who have a television watch the news and wonder what's going to happen in the coming months. Years, even. The cold, the damp, the uncertainty. It's not a good time to be alive, Lenou tells Elena. Not a good time at all.

There might be a chill in the air but there is a fire raging inside of Lenou. Someone is intending them harm. Causing the death of her Savva, the demise of her daughter, and her stomach acids to bubble like a boiling pot of avgolemoni soup. She has a pretty good idea who it is, too. The neighbour. Mrs Pavlou. Her with the unruly brood of barefoot boys and the evil, prying eye. Hanging out of her windows with her wet laundry and projecting her malevolent glare in their direction. *Why?* Elena asks. Always why, why? What did it matter what the woman's motives were? Perhaps she was jealous of them or maybe she envied her daughter's beauty? Perhaps it was all for self-gratification, to while away the hours. A crazy puppetmaster pulling strings from behind a stage. Who cared? What mattered was that her eye was bringing Lenou misfortune.

Talismans. That's what she needed. More talismans. Around the house and around their necks too. Little blue amulets shaped like unblinking, vigilant eyes. And prayer. Her own mother had taught her how to pray. To pray on her hands and knees until her legs went numb and her arms felt like they would buckle under her weight. It wasn't enough to quickly cross yourself and hope that God was feeling generous. You had to pray properly, like you meant it. Only then would He listen to her.

Her mother, Xanthe, had been a fearsome woman. So fearsome, in fact, that Lenou considers herself lenient in comparison. The sharp tip of her legendary wooden cane was a prospect so terrifying that Lenou and her three younger brothers would run around the streets of Ammochostos for hours in their bare feet to avoid feeling its sting across their backs, sometimes even making it as far as the sea.

Growing up, there were consequences for every type of transgression, but the gravest sin of all in Xanthe's book was offending the name of God. It seemed that many things offended God, at least according to her mother. Crossing your legs in church, folding your arms, and sitting back down on the pew halfway through the priest's sermon was positively sacrilege. Lenou will never forget the beating her little brother, Pedro, received for coughing during Communion and showering the priest with holy wine. He couldn't sit down for days afterwards, the poor boy, and Lenou had found it hard to comprehend that any child, least of all her dear sweet Pedro, could be deserving of such a punishment.

She'd died of a sudden attack of the heart the summer Lenou turned thirteen. One minute it was beating, they told her, and the next it wasn't. *It was God's will, clear as day.* They were at school when it happened and arrived home to the terrible news and a house full of mourners shrouded in black.

Their grief-stricken father had ushered them into the bedroom to bid her a farewell and Lenou still remembers the shock of seeing her bloated blue face poking out from beneath the white sheet. The incongruity of it, and the way her cold leathery skin had felt beneath Lenou's fingertips when she'd traced the outline of her mother's cheeks. The smell of death and decay already hung in the air and she had understood, then, the point her mother had been trying to make all those years. Seeing her once formidable body laid out lifeless on the bed and awaiting its burial, Lenou had finally comprehended that life was brief and futile and that the only thing worth striving for was the promise of an afterlife. *I'm sorry Mamma,* she had whispered in her ear. *I'm sorry I wasn't better at listening.* She had remained steadfast in her resolve from that moment on and, of course, some days it had been difficult, she was only human. But everything worth having is difficult to achieve.

It's this lesson, the lesson that was seared into her brain that day, that she tries to instil in the girls. How can she call herself a mother otherwise? How can she walk out into the street and raise her hands to the skies and profess her love for her daughters if she doesn't impart the only truth worth imparting to them? What use or point are temporal pleasures if they jeopardise immortality, and what use is any mother if she doesn't nurture her children's souls? They didn't understand, just like she hadn't when she was their age, and neither had Pedro.

He used to visit them when the girls were little. He'd never married – women were far too much hassle, he'd chuckle – but he loved children and Elena best of all. Two kind souls, kindred spirits. How Elena used to laugh when Uncle Pedro scooped her off her feet and tickled her stomach. *Mamma, Mamma, look at me!* Afterwards, there'd be a bar of pasteli for her, but only if she'd finished her dinner. She'd loved him too, her Pedro. She truly had, but he'd stopped coming round after Savva died. It was too painful to watch, he'd said. Too painful to watch her metamorphosis into their own loathsome mother.

~

She's standing on the bench beneath the vine, picking leaves for their dinner. She puts the fresh ones into a pot for her mother to wash and the ones with holes in their centre into a pile on the table for the vegetable compost. It's cool out, and she rubs her arms to keep warm. November, and with the changing of the seasons, the dimming of light and colour. Yellows, blues and dark greens morph into greys, browns and blacks. She's cold now, in the mornings, and she shivers on her way to school. Grateful for the short walk and cup of hot milk that awaits her when she arrives.

Yia! Andoni Pavlou comes over to join her, his hair parted in the centre and his hands in his pockets. She's making dolmades this evening, Lenou, with the leaves from the vine. She'll boil them in hot salty water and wrap them around minced meat and rice. Valentina's favourite meal.

You need help? He jumps up onto the bench next to her and it creaks beneath his weight. They pick leaves together, side by side, and she can feel the hair on his arms tickle her skin as he reaches over to pick the best ones at the back. *Look at the size of this one,* he exclaims proudly. *Save this one for me.* She asks him if he can keep a secret and tells him that Valentina gave her a letter the night she left for England. He asks her what kind, but Elena doesn't know.

They'd been standing at the top of the road, her bags at their feet, waiting for Uncle Zacharia. It was the middle of the night and Elena had pointed out the stars in an attempt to cheer her up. They glowed like diamonds in the pitch-black sky and reminded her of Pappa. *Do you remember,* she'd asked her sister, *when he*

*used to take us to the beach at night when it was cool and tell
us the names of the stars?*

Valentina had tucked her loose hair into her jacket
and hugged herself tightly as she smoked. There had
been barely anything left of her by then, despite the
baby inside. She said that she remembered and she'd
pulled out the envelope and pressed it into Elena's
hands. For him. The father of her baby. A *plea*, she'd
said, shifting her weight from one leg to another to keep
warm. And the truth. She'd made Elena swear on her
life, and on that of the baby's, that she would give it to
him. *Put it in his hands.* She'd made her promise again
and again and Elena had looked up at the stars and
crossed herself. *I promise.*

He'd come to take her away at that moment, Uncle
Zacharia, and her sister had dropped her still-lit cigarette on the ground. He bid them a kalinihta as he lifted
Valentina's bags into the back of his car. *Yia, sister.* She'd
waved out of the window and it had been sad to watch
her drive off with Zacharia. Alone and friendless, with
only Elena to bear witness to what she had been.

Can I see? She takes the small brown envelope out
of the pocket of her jeans and shows it to Andoni.
The baby's father's name is written on the front and
his address is on the back. Andoni holds it up to the
fading November light. In the weeks since Valentina
left, Elena has memorised every inch of it. The way
the letters in his name swirl up and down like musical
notes, written in black and smudged at the edges.
Valentina in such a hurry that she couldn't wait for

the ink to dry. She holds it as if it is hot. As if it might somehow burn her fingertips.

They jump off the bench and sit next to each other, their arms touching and the pot of vine leaves on the table almost full. He asks her why she hasn't delivered it already. It's been ages since Valentina left. Guilt, she tells him. Whatever she chooses to do from this point on will bring consequences. Someone will be hurt. Her mother, especially. *Then it's easy*, he replies, leaning over to squeeze her hand and whisper warm words into her ear. *Let's not tell her.*

Chapter 28

London – 1985

MARIA QUITE ENJOYS attending the funerals of the
distantly related or acquainted. There is something very
life affirming about standing at a graveside on a brisk,
chilly morning, knowing that you are not going into
the carefully prepared hole, but allowed to pick up
where you left off afterwards. To go home and read a
book or drink tea. Perhaps that's why people have
wakes, she thinks. Not to toast the dearly departed but
to celebrate their own, brief, stay of execution.

St Mary Magdalena's Church in Wood Green is practically empty and there are only a handful of mourners
sitting in the front two pews, herself included. Maria
hopes for a better turnout when her time comes. Costa
and Elena and all of her customers and maybe even Mr
Styliano, should he somehow learn of her demise. To
know that he might be there, despite everything that
has passed between them, gives her something to hope
for.

She smooths the skirts of her long black dress and
looks around. George and Themis are here this morning,
and Mr and Mrs Papavasilakis. Local shopkeepers who

knew her well and have come to pay their last respects. And the precious son, Christopher, sitting with his xeni wife. The pair of them, the cause of all Mrs Koutsouli's problems. He did it to spite her, she'd eventually concluded. Why else? Maria would feel sorry for her and let her sit at the table at the back of the bakery and enjoy an eliopita on the house while she worked. Ignorant, insolent sons.

She didn't much blame Mrs Koutsouli. It's not that she didn't like English people, she liked them well enough. They even came into the bakery sometimes and their eyes would light up at the sight of all the cakes and pastries lined up in colourful rows and she would ask them if they were lost. They would laugh at her little joke and she would chuckle too, and tell them the names of the different sweets and explain what was inside each of them. Cream, cinnamon, oranges and nuts!

There were even one or two customers she was especially fond of. Like Mrs Baxter, who had a villa in Halkidiki and said complimentary things about her breads. She would even try to bid her a farewell in Greek on her way out. Her 'yia sou' sounding more like a 'hi Sue'. She was nice, though, and Maria is sure the xeni wife is perfectly pleasant in her own English way, but it's one thing to jest over pastries with someone and another thing entirely to marry them. Differences, Mrs Koutsouli used to say. There are fundamental differences between us and they'll get in the way in the end.

Like what? Costa used to say when they discussed it

over dinner, and he'd call them peasants and say that Mrs Koutsouli deserved to be alienated from her son. He was right, in a way. Not that they were peasants, that was just plain rude, but that Mrs Koutsouli could have handled things better and not driven her son all the way to Kent. It was to protect them, he'd told her when they moved away. From her vicious tongue. She was upsetting Linda and scaring the girls. He'd changed his name to Christopher so he'd blend in with the English and told her that she was not welcome in their new house. And that had been it. The final rusty nail in the coffin of Mrs Koutsouli.

Poor Mrs Koutsouli. Laid out cold in her shiny brown coffin with the rusty nail through the top of it while Maria warms her face in the rays of sun streaming in through the church windows and daydreams about a cup of tea. She looks up at the icon of the Mary Magdalena hanging from the ceiling and thinks it's been ages since she last came to church. She used to make an effort for the name days of the major saints, for Easter and Christmas, but these days she barely manages even that.

Elena seemed to come here enough for all of them. She's lost count of the number of calls she's received in the past year from Costa, asking her to come over and help with the girls because Elena was in bed or in church praying. *Praying for what?* she'd ask when her bad mood had got the better of her and she couldn't get a seat on the 329. *A nanny for the kids?*

She'd felt like that at first. Angry and inconvenienced,

but lately she's been thinking that there's something very wrong. Elena's long afternoons in bed or in church, the way she looks right through the girls, as if they aren't there at all. Maybe she needs to see a doctor, she'd suggested to Costa, and she'd tell him the same thing every time he called her and asked for her help, but nobody seemed to be listening to her except possibly the cracks in their living-room walls.

Did you enjoy the service, Mrs Petrakis? Maria looks up to see Pater Thanassi in his black regalia standing next to her at the side of the pew. *Yes, thank you. It was very comforting.* At the front of the church, mourners form a short queue to cross themselves and kiss the top of Mrs Koutsouli's coffin. Maria realises she's missed most of it and reddens in embarrassment. He'd like to speak with her, he says, before she heads to the cemetery with the cortege, but only if it's not too inconvenient.

Maria's heart sinks to the shiny, cold floor. She was rather looking forward to a quick burial and a nice cup of tea, but Pater Thanassi's grey beard shames her into doing as she's told. The teacher's cane. Of course. She follows him to the back of the church and into a dusty, windowless office with books and ring binders arranged haphazardly on shelves. Pater Thanassi closes the door behind them and bids her to sit down opposite him. *I haven't seen you in church in a while.* An accusation, or perhaps a plea for a donation, so she begins to fumble in her handbag, pulling her purse out and spilling coins into her lap. *No, no, no.* He shakes his hands, his palms in her face, and asks her to put her money away. Maria's curiosity begins to eclipse her disappointment at missing a ride to the cemetery.

He strokes his beard and smiles disconcertingly, reaching around the room for a suitable place to begin, and he tells her it's about Elena. *My Elena?* Yes, a lovely girl, and he's sure he's not breaking any confidences by revealing that recently she's been coming to the church almost every afternoon to pray and that she seems more than a little sad. Could there be something bothering her?

Maria can think of one or two things and plenty more besides, but she's physically lost for words. He's pleased, he hastens to add, that Elena is taking her spiritual journey so seriously and he wishes other members of his congregation were as committed, but she looked like she could use a companion, somebody to pray with, didn't she agree? Her husband, perhaps?

Of course, Costa would just love to come with her, Maria replies. When he isn't pretending to be a postman, she thinks, and her cheeks burn in shame as the priest's righteous gaze penetrates her face, looking for the truth. *Good, then that's settled.* Pater Thanassi gets up from his chair with almost no effort, the relief of concluding the conversation seemingly lightening his load, and Maria realises that everyone has left the service and that Elena's problems are more serious than she'd feared.

Oh, and one more thing. What now, she thinks, rolling her eyes as he turns to rummage around in the drawer of his desk. What could he possibly have to add to that? He has a book for Elena. She's been asking him about the evil eye and this was a particularly good one. He's pleased with himself. *It's very informative.* Would she be kind enough to pass it on?

Maria Petrakis puts the book in her bag without looking at it and trudges out of the church, the weight of it pulling her shoulder towards the ground. She decides to give the funeral a miss and head straight to Costa's for immediate crisis talks. She's sure Mrs Koutsouli would understand, given her own troubles with her daughter-in-law. Besides, it suddenly looks like it might rain and while a sunny funeral is quite uplifting, a wet one is a different proposition entirely.

~

It's Friday lunchtime and Elena's house sounds and smells exactly as it should. The kettle is whistling and the washing machine is whirring and the scent of frying onions wafts satisfyingly from the shiny white kitchen. Little Magda is dozing on the sofa in the front room and if Maria had to fault anything, it would be the number of blankets piled up on top of the young child in an already too-warm house.

She's surprised to see Elena. *Why, where else would I be?* In bed, Maria thinks, or in church, anywhere but here, but she's pleased that she is all the same. She follows her into the kitchen and thinks she looks a little dishevelled. Her short limp hair is held back with a plastic grip and she's wearing a pair of Costa's faded blue and white pyjamas. She's tired, she blushes, when she catches Maria staring. She's not been sleeping well. Nightmares. She's been dreaming of little white coffins being lowered into the ground and bodies, riddled with bullet holes, tangled in the brush. She has no idea where they're coming from, the horrible dreams, but she doesn't relate this to Maria.

Maria gestures to the kettle and wonders if Elena would be so kind as to make her a chai. She's been at Mrs Koutsouli's funeral service daydreaming about bloody tea, and she thinks at one point she fell into a reverie because the next thing she knew, Pater Thanassi was standing next to her in his black dress looking most crow-like and he'd startled her. A neat segue into their conversation, she thinks, but Elena's hand flies to her mouth and she gasps at Maria's news.

I didn't know! The moment passes. It's OK, Maria replies. She's pretty inured to tragedy after enduring a mother's worst nightmare and Elena's face suddenly drains of all its colour. *You OK? Here, sit.* Maria gets up to pour the tea and Elena leans against the table and apologises. She doesn't know what came over her but something about those words made her blood run cold. A mother's worst nightmare. Her mother used to say that.

The very worst. After the child's funeral, Maria crawled into bed and stayed there for over five months, getting up only to feed the chickens, tend to the house, and cook a meal for Michali. With Costa at her sister's and Michali at the base, she was alone during the day, free to curl up into a ball and wait for the pain to pass. Her memories of the event were scattered and disorganised, like sheets of paper strewn across a class-room floor. She could remember the morning it happened, but not the date, and she could see a pink ribbon lying in the dust, but could no longer see her face. This had bothered her most of all because it felt like she was losing her all over again and she had blamed herself. She had blamed herself for months.

When she did eventually kick the bed sheets off and get out of bed, she found that the memories started to come back to her. Like flies initially, and then fists across the face and finally trains smashing into her body, and she couldn't get rid of them no matter how hard she tried. Some days the thoughts hurt her more than the tragedy itself, and that's when she had started to bake.

Elena's sorry about Mrs Koutsouli and Maria sips her tea and nods in agreement. She will be missed. Her and her stories about her handsome leventi. Elena couldn't understand why the woman spent so many years mourning a son she never lost. *How very strange* and Maria tells her that she's too young to understand, but old gojiakares such as themselves hail from a generation when things like that mattered. *You mean, like who you marry?* It's complicated, Maria replies. Much more complicated. And she drinks her tea and thinks that now might be a good time to bring up Pater Thanassi, but Elena gets up to tend to the sizzling onions and the moment, once again, passes.

What are you cooking? She's going to fry some steaks for Costa's lunch. Maria chuckles. *All this walking to deliver letters,* she says to Elena, *and the man is still shaped like a football!* And they laugh because ten years on, the thought of Costa dressed as a postman, heaving his sack around the streets, is still a source of amusement. Pushing letters through people's letterboxes instead of taking over the family business. What a peculiar choice, Maria thinks. Does he ring the bell and have a conversation with each and every recipient? she asks Elena. Or poke them through the flaps and run away?

She gets up to catch her bus home and she's had such a nice talk with her daughter-in-law that her discussion with the priest feels like it happened a hundred years ago. She decides that it will keep for another day, when Costa is on his own. On her way out she creeps into the front room to kiss Magda on the cheek. It's far too hot for the child, she thinks, as she tuts and peels back the blankets. Her hair is damp with sweat, and curls around her temples. Not that she'd dare to be critical, but if it were her daughter, she'd have used thinner sheets.

The book. She'd forgotten all about it but it's too heavy to carry home on the bus so she takes it out of her bag and places it carefully on the bottom step. Elena will know, she reasons. She'll know it was me who left it there. Who else could it possibly be?

Chapter 29

Cyprus – 1960

IT'S LATE IN November. Maria Petrakis climbs out of bed and pushes the wooden shutters open as far as they will bend on their hinges. She takes a breath of the cool fresh Cypriot air and feels her lungs inflating like a pair of red balloons. Her heart pumps in her ears, quietly at first, and then louder and louder. *I am here.*

She tears the sheets off the mattress and heaps them into a musty pile by the side of the bed. She pulls her damp nightdress over her head and tosses it over the top and walks naked into the bathroom. She feels more alive than she has done in months.

She runs a bath and immerses herself in the warm water, her long grey hair fanning out around her like a parasol. She lies there for an eternity, her bony arms wrapped around her emaciated chest, and she thinks of nothing.

When the water's grown cold, she stands up slowly and reaches for a towel. She climbs out of the bath and pads back into the bedroom, leaving a trail of damp footprints on the stone floor behind her.

She opens the wardrobe door and chooses a long

blue dress. She's not going to wear the black any more. She'll wear blue, to remember her. Or purple, but not the black. She pulls her wet hair back into a bun and fixes it behind her ears with a pair of pins. Then she picks up the dirty laundry from the floor, opens the back door and throws it into the yard. She'll wash it in her clay pot later, once she's had a chance to go to the shops for some detergent.

She boils herself a sweet kafe in the pot and sits on the back step to enjoy it like she used to in those red electric hours between night and day. The almond tree sways in the autumn breeze and the coffee and sugar fizzle on her tongue and wake her up anew. The chickens cluck at the far end of the yard and the smell of woodsmoke hangs in the air. It's time, she thinks. It's time to send for Costa.

When the child arrives home, he is much altered. His once plump face is pinched and grey and his eyes are bulging out of his skull like an insect's. He looks older than his eleven years. His round tummy has all but disappeared and his clothes hang from his limbs like the rags on a scarecrow. When he speaks, he rests his chin on his chest and refuses to look up from the floor. Sickly, she thinks. He looks sick. She blames herself. Another blame to add to the guilt that has been simmering inside of her. She has been gone far too long. A child needs his mother. She sweeps her grief to one side like the broken plates on the floor after an argument with Michali and rolls up her sleeves. It's time to get on with things.

My little changeling, she calls him at first. He smells like Thora. She treats him like a wounded chick. She feeds him. She bathes him. She holds him and sings to him. She strokes his face. It's not your fault, she whispers into his hair when he is sleeping at night, in case he's burdened by the things he's seen. It's not your fault. I was the one in charge that day, you are just a child.

Michali wants to call the doctor. He accuses her of neglect. First her, now him, he barks. Is there nothing she won't spoil? He'll be OK, she replies. The child just needs to be held. *He needs love.*

From who? You? Michali pretends to laugh in her face. *The worst mother in the world?*

The woman who emerged from her bed after five months of being curled up like a wounded animal is stronger than the woman who went shopping with two kids and came home with one. How can Michali hurt her now? She has endured more pain than she ever thought possible and she survived. Does he think he can break her now, with his spiteful insults or cruel blows to the face? *Fuck you.* He narrows his eyes and raises his fists. He's itching to hurt her, she can tell. He's been waiting for this moment. His wife, revitalised before him so he can knock her down again. It has been too long. *Hit me!* She screams in his face as she pounds at her chest, again and again, like a woman possessed and he backs away, thrown off guard by his loss of control and her lack of fear. She puts her face in his, close enough to smell his breath. He reeks of cigarettes and last night's brandy. A game of cards at the kafeneon, an all-night drinking session. Not that she cares. She screams at him to hit her and she showers him with her spittle. *You've lost your mind, woman.* He wipes his mouth with the back of his hand and smiles arrogantly as he walks out of the door.

Smile all you like, she thinks. She realises in that moment that she hates him and it scares her, makes her shudder. The apathy she can live with. You can coexist with apathy. You can make apathy a cup of tea and exchange pleasantries with it. Hate has no boundaries and when you truly hate another person, anything is possible.

Chapter 30

Cyprus – 1969

HE'S WAITING FOR her beneath the row of olive trees next to their school playground. *Kalimera.* He nods a hello. She takes the brown envelope out of her jacket pocket and places it in his extended hand. It's a fifteen-minute walk, he tells her. Give or take. His house is across town, in the posh part where the rich snobby people live. They head towards the bus stop and turn left onto Ayios Lazarus Street, the road leading to Brokobi's Beriptero and the opposite direction to the harbour. A secret adventure.

Have you told anyone?

No.

Have you?

Andoni shakes his head and picks up a stone. He's going to hurl it at Brokobi's ramshackle kiosk when they walk past, in revenge for the way he'd glared at her last week. They're all looking at her like that, she tells him. He shouldn't bother because it's not just Brokobi. *My mother says it's going to be a bastard. Your sister's baby.* It's what they call babies who don't have real fathers. Bastards. She shrugs. *Then I guess she's having a bastard.*

A Sunday morning and the neighbourhood is deserted. People are out at worship and front doors and shutters are closed. The white and pink houses look like sleeping faces with sad, drooping eyes, surrounded by dust and prickly yellow bushes. Even gojiakari Eleftherou has left her post and gone to pray.

There are no cars about and they walk in the middle of the street, passing old Mr Anastasi and his donkey. The animal is saddled with bundles of thick firewood and its spindly neck strains beneath the burden. Mr Anastasi tips his black cap at them and nods, and turns back to stare as they walk past. His clothes are loose and shabby and she wonders why he's not in church along with everyone else. He's a Communist, Andoni explains. Everybody knows that the Communists don't go to church. He reads books on Lenin and Stalin. *Do you know who they were?* Elena tuts. *Of course.*

She'd told her mother she was menstruating. You weren't allowed to kiss the icons or take Holy Communion if you were on your period and there was little point in going if you couldn't participate. Lenou's words. She'd been flustered this morning, pulling open drawers and searching for coins for the donations tray, and she'd barely noticed Elena standing in the doorway in her nightdress pretending to grab at her stomach. *Fine,* she'd snapped. *But don't stand around catching flies all day, shell some peas, hah?*

They stop outside Brokobi's so that Andoni can throw his stone at the Coca-Cola sign boarding up the front door, and they turn right again, onto Zinon

Street, and then left, onto Dimosteni Street. A wide, affluent road lined with eucalyptus and orange trees and two-storey houses crouching behind tall railings. She'd felt guilty about it, of course. She'd hated lying and especially to her mother but either way she was going to have to let somebody down and it may as well be Lenou.

They stop outside the biggest residence on the street. *It's that one, there, look.* An imposing house painted grey, with blue shutters and palm trees standing in red shiny pots by the front door. There's a black car parked outside and Elena recognises the sleeping headlights. Unwelcoming railings painted in white and gold circle the drive and warn those less fortunate to keep away. Andoni whistles through his teeth.

I wish we were this rich.

Me too.

Her Pappa used to sell fish at the Pantopoleio, the noisy and colourful public market that took place every morning outside the walls of the Old Town. Sometimes he'd take Elena with him, and she'd be excited by the sounds, sights and smells of the bazaar. The green water-melons and the bright red tomatoes picked from the farmers' own orchards , the newly baked breads, the rabbits and chickens dangling from hooks and the shiny silver fish splayed out on her father's stall, heaped over piles of crushed ice and smelling of the sea. So many fish it was a wonder he had the time to catch them all. She used to think that he must have emptied the oceans of them, her great Pappa.

When it was really busy, he'd sit her on his big broad shoulders for a better view and she'd call out to the customers in her loudest and most grown-up voice, come, come! Shouting enthusiastically over the cries of the other vendors and enticing them with a wave of her hand and a promise of the freshest fish at the lowest price. You're my lucky charm, he'd chuckle after he'd counted the shiny coins in his purse at the end of the day. He made more money when Elena was with him. *My little pixie girl.* It wasn't going to make them rich but they were luckier than most.

Would things have been different if they'd been wealthy, Elena wonders, and could afford a house like this with tall shiny railings and a car parked outside? Would it have made her mother any less bitter or her sister more obedient? Would Pappa still be alive?

They've been standing outside for too long and someone is going to notice them. *Give me the letter.* She's going to ring the bell and deliver it to him, like Valentina asked. He takes her hand and leads her across the street. Another secret mission, a better one. He winks at her. Much better.

Behind the houses on the left-hand side of the street is a small brown field strewn with weeds and prickly cacti, pregnant with fruit. He wants to kiss her, he croons in her ear. His lovely Elena with the shiny hair, the second prettiest girl in their class. His excitement makes her nervous despite her feelings for him, and she struggles to free her hand – desperate, suddenly, for him to let go. *I don't want to!* Her voice is filled with panic and she can hear him saying it's OK over and over. An idea, that's all. *It was just an idea.*

Get off me! She's screaming now and his face is clouded in confusion. He's not touching her. He holds his arms up in the air like a man surrendering to a gun and backs away slowly to prove the point. Her screams grow louder and she turns to run but she can feel something pulling at her clothes. Her jacket catches on the cactus plant and she tears it off and begins to run. *Elena?* He's calling for her to come back and she can hear him shouting about her coat and the letter but she no longer cares. What would her mother say, she thinks, if she could see her now? Both daughters tarnished by one sin. It was a mistake. All of it.

She runs as fast as she can, kicking up brown dust with her shoes as she flies past the rows of houses they've just ambled by until she recognises the bus stop and the schoolyard near their houses. She turns around to look behind her and he's no longer following her, but she charges home as if he is. She crashes through the front door, forgetting to close it behind her, and crawls into bed. She can hear herself gasping for breath, the panic and the exertion squeezing the air from her lungs and suffocating her. Ten, nine, eight. It's getting late. Seven, six, five. Somebody died. Four, three, two. A game of rope. Pound, pound, pound. The room grows dark and there's relief then as Elena is catapulted into oblivion. *Your turn, little angel.*

There are scratches on her arms but she doesn't know how they got there. Three on her right arm, extending from her wrist to her elbow, two on the left and one on the back of her calf. She lies in the small round tub and soaks them in the hot water. They're deep and red and when she places her fingertips on either side of them and gently parts the skin, she can see that the flesh underneath glistens orange like the centre of a plum. They hurt but she doesn't mind the pain.

She remembers the last time Lenou took Pappa's belt strap to her back. Elena, barely eleven, standing submissively in front of her waiting for the lashing to finish. She'd broken an ornament. By accident, of course, but it had belonged to her late grandmother, the formidable Xanthe, and Lenou had seen red. She was a charging bull that day, flying at them head first for trivial, inconsequential reasons. She'd shrugged at the end of the punishment and Valentina had sniggered from behind the bedroom doorway. She was getting old. Losing her touch. She'd almost taken a blow to the mouth in retaliation, but Elena was glad that she'd defended her. The two of them, standing in solidarity.

Later, she'd peeled off her T-shirt in front of the mirror. The right side of her back was red and swollen and there were welts where the belt buckle had connected with her skin. She'd realised, then, that she'd been hurt, but hadn't registered the pain. Valentina had been impressed. It's a superpower, she'd said. Not feeling things. Like being able to fly or making yourself invisible. It's not that she didn't feel the pain, she just processed it differently. What had bothered her the most, she'd confided to her afterwards, was that Lenou had used their dead Pappa's belt to hit her with.

She traces her scratches with her fingertips and then submerges them in the water. She feels strange, not remembering something she should, like forgetting the name of a favourite relative. But after a while, a new reality settles over the old one, like snowdrifts landing on top of dirty black ice, and she welcomes the chance to start over. A blank canvas, ready to receive a new set of footprints.

She must have delivered it because when she came round, the envelope wasn't in the pocket of her dress and she hadn't been wearing a jacket. She can recall the house and the imposing railings that surrounded it, painted in white with gold tips shaped like the blades of arrows, so she knows she was there and she must, therefore, have knocked on the door and handed it over. She means to speak to Andoni about it but he's not in class the following day or the day after that and then the news that Valentina is getting married hits the house like a tornado and she forgets all about the little brown envelope with the swirly black writing on the front, and Andoni Pavlou, because suddenly and after all these weeks, there's word from her beloved sister.

The young man's name is Taki and he lives in Edmonton, north London, a short distance from the cousin's house where Valentina is living. Edmonton, north London. Elena practises saying the words. They sound exotic, Elena thinks. A big and exciting place with bright lights and shiny cars. A place where things happen. A world away from her mundane existence in sleepy Ammochostos under Lenou's unrelenting tutelage.

They met on the bus, the cousin tells her. She'd sent Valentina out for a pint of milk and she'd returned home with a fiancé. Imagine that – and fair play to the girl. Not many women could manage that. *And does he know,* her mother stammers into the phone, *about her condition?* She rummages around for the right word lest the wrong one spoil her good fortune. Of course, the cousin replies. It would be very difficult not to notice the baby stuck in between them, doesn't she think? An audible sigh of relief.

Lenou is overcome by this unexpected change of luck and signals for Elena to bring her a chair so she can sit down without dropping the telephone. She pinches her forehead with her thumb and forefinger and decides that, for once, saying nothing might be better than saying the wrong thing and shooing happiness away. He is a few inches shorter than Valentina, the suitor, and a few years older, but what are inches and years in the grand scheme of things? Mere numbers. They certainly don't obstruct the path of young love. Lenou thinks that if a bastard doesn't, then nothing will. How many years were they talking here? Only five. And the wedding? Pretty much planned, the cousin continues. They just need her consent because of her age, and some money, if she can spare it.

Of course. She'd sell the clothes off her back if she had to and Elena didn't doubt it for a second.

Lenou replaces the receiver and turns around to face her. She claps her hands together.

She's getting married, thank God!

I heard.

She's lying on the couch behind her mother, staring at the marble mantelpiece where Valentina's school pictures used to stand in their glass frames. *What happened to all the photographs?* But her mother is in no great hurry to dredge up the past when, suddenly, there's a door to the future. Does she realise what this means?

Marriage. Valentina's bastard will have a father, her daughter no longer the talk of the town. She'll have a husband to take care of her. A husband to pick her up from the gutter and instate her in a decent home. Her daughter married. *My daughter is married!* Lenou practises saying this to herself, to Mrs Pavlou and Mrs Pappas and to anyone else who pretends to care as they sidle up to her in church, clutching at their bosoms and brimming with their insincerity. How is she, Kyria Lenou? She's married, thank you. The sneers wiped clean off their faces in an instant. Oh, I see? So soon? Who cares? Lenou thinks. As long as she can keep him. She says this to Elena. *As long as she can keep him happy, hah?* Elena sits up and tucks her hair behind her ears.

Why wouldn't she?

The baby, Lenou replies. Babies get in the way at the best of times but this one, this one is not even his. *I can't imagine he's going to forget that very quickly.* Still, she has a spring in her step and Elena can tell that she is happier than she was before the call from England.

In early January, there's a new photograph to place on top of the empty mantelpiece. It arrives from the mysterious Edmonton, north London, and it's a picture of Valentina and Taki on their wedding day. Lenou opens the large white envelope, careful not to tear its contents, and Elena snatches it greedily from her hands before she gets the chance to look at it. She takes it all in. Her sister is wearing a long lacy dress and a veil which touches the floor. Her long black hair is pinned up at the sides and fixed in place with dainty pearl clips. Elena's breath catches in her throat. *She looks beautiful, Mamma!* Taki stands behind her, a short man in a too-large suit. A deep frown is etched into his pale face and large black eyebrows dominate his forehead. His arms circle Valentina's waist awkwardly, as if he's unsure of where to put them. Elena can see that her belly is sticking out from beneath her dress. The baby, barely there, a whisper in the wind.

Lenou grabs the picture and props it up in the centre of the mantelpiece. Valentina, finally enjoying pride of place, long after she was banished. She takes a few steps back to make sure it's straight. *My daughter is married at last!*

Chapter 31

London – 1976

VALENTINA HAS A lover called O. A tall man with yellow hair and eyes the colour of the sky. He's English, she exclaims proudly. Not one of us. *A xenos.* Elena imagines Mrs Koutsouli standing in the corner of the room, wagging her finger and clicking her tongue. *Of all the men, she's gone and chosen a foreigner!* She won't tell Elena his name. Far better that she doesn't know, that she's kept out of it. She doesn't want to make her complicit, not like the last time. It wouldn't be fair. He's simply O. O for oh no. All right then, Elena can call him Tom if she'd prefer.

Why Tom?

Because I like Tom!

She blows a smoke ring into the air and pops it with the tip of her long red fingernail. She throws her head back and laughs, her long black hair touching the floor behind her.

Tom-O makes her happy. She shows Elena a photograph of him that she has hidden in her purse. He's the physical opposite of Taki. How funny. He takes her mind off things. Her marriage for a start. A marriage that entails sitting in their dingy old house all day smoking cigarettes and waiting for Taki to finish work. Or worse, hoovering the carpets in those ridiculous tarty boots. Elena knits her brow in confusion. He bought her the boots for her birthday. *They're hideous*, she explains. She sticks a leg in the air by way of demonstration. Long white plastic things with pointy heels and zips that fasten all the way up to the whatsit. He asked if she would wear them while she did the housework and if he could watch. *Don't you think that's weird?* Elena tries to imagine herself hoovering the carpets in provocative boots and wrinkles her nose in disgust. *Very*.

Best of all, the lover is a distraction from all the guilt. That five-letter word, suspended between them always like a shiny silver blade. So much guilt, she tells Elena, that some days she feels like she's going to burst with it. She blows another smoke ring into the air and Elena follows its trajectory until it pops by itself. But that's another story. Today is about darling Elena. *More champagne?*

They're sitting cross-legged in the front room of Elena and Costa's new house in Palmers Green, drinking fizzy wine from mugs they've rescued from the piles of unpacked boxes. So many boxes, boxes everywhere. Elena wonders how they managed to accumulate so many things in just a year and a half of marriage. The house is a small three-bedroomed terrace in Palmers Green, north London. There was a time when Elena would have given anything to live somewhere like that.

A house with three bedrooms in Palmers Green! It sounded like a place buzzing with possibilities, like Edmonton had done when her sister's photograph arrived in the post.

She looks around. So much space for just the two of them. The house itself is tired and old. The carpets are brown and worn at the edges and the kitchen is decorated in blue and white with missing tiles and mouldy black gaps in the walls where appliances have been torn out. The smile, she thinks, of a grinning and toothless old man. The third bedroom, she'd moaned to Costa when they'd gone round to view it the first time, was more of a cupboard than a room. But he'd had enough of listening to her ever-growing list of excuses by then and he'd put in a bid for it anyway.

He'd been right, about the list. They had been excuses. The truth is, she hadn't wanted to move out of Maria's warm cosy flat which smelled of freshly baked bread and cinnamon and rose water, and made her feel alive in a way she hadn't felt since Pappa died. The shop downstairs, packed with sticky golden pastries lined up in neat little rows. Some with nuts on the top, others sprinkled with icing sugar. A place where locals came to unburden themselves of their troubles and pick up a tasty treat or two. Maria, standing behind the till with her apron tied around her waist and her silver hair piled on top of her head. The pulsing heart of the centre of the world, ready to listen and comfort and make a tidy profit in between. Petrakis Bakery, a place like no other.

Valentina leans over and pokes her in the shoulder. *Don't tell me you're going to miss the mighty Maria Petrakis?* She stands up and pretends to ride a broomstick and Elena laughs in spite of herself. A naughty schoolgirl, giggling in class. *Of course not!* How could she admit that she'd rather live with her mother-in-law than with her own husband in their new home? Just the two of them, he'd said, when she'd gone off to sulk. Away from Maria's prying ears.

It's Pappa she misses the most. *Do you remember him?* Valentina shrugs. It's not that she didn't love him, Elena thinks, or that he didn't love her, but her sister had grown up so quickly that he hadn't quite known how to be himself around her. She didn't want to sit on his shoulders and accompany him to the market to sell pungent-smelling fish or wrap her arms around him in the sea and count the stars in the sky like Elena used to do. *Not really.*

He'd died of a stroke when Elena was eight and Valentina had just turned ten. He'd returned home from the Pantopoleio looking sweaty and pale and Lenou had ushered him into bed to take a siesta. She'd wake him up when it was time to prepare the nets for the next haul, she'd said. It was a hot day in July and she thought the heat must have overwhelmed him. She'd been worried, for a while. She'd left the bedroom door open and hovered around outside to make sure he was all right and after a while he'd grown still and quiet and she'd presumed he'd fallen asleep. A good thing, she'd said to the girls afterwards. He needed the rest.

Elena hadn't gone to the Pantopoleio with him that day because it was too hot even by Cypriot standards. A sun so intense it could blister your skin through your clothes. She'd been playing hide-and-seek beneath the olive trees with Valentina when someone had shouted at them to go home. Andoni Pavlou maybe, or his brother, Dimitri. Their father wouldn't wake up, he'd said breathlessly, and when they turned the corner Lenou was standing beneath the grapevine sobbing loudly into her hands. *I'm sorry for you,* Mrs Pavlou had come out to pay her respects. How trite and hollow those words had sounded when compared with what they had lost.

She's being morbid now, Valentina snaps. They should leave the dead to it. *Here, hold out your cup.* She pours them each another mug of sparkling wine and good times fizzle on Elena's tongue and lift her spirits despite the weight of her memories. Valentina stands up to imitate Maria again and Elena laughs at the impression. *Stop it!* It's a good day, after all.

Chapter 32

Cyprus – 1961

JUNE. IT'S A swelteringly hot day in Kyrenia. Maria Petrakis shovels the perfectly formed lump of dough into the clay oven with the ftiari and wipes the sweat off her creased forehead with the back of her hand. If it was any hotter, she thinks, she could crack eggs on the ground and watch them cook by themselves.

This heat! I think the good Lord means to suffocate us!

Mrs Kouli next door is hanging clothes on her washing line, her large colourful skirts sticking to the backs of her legs.

I think you are right, Mrs Kouli. I think you are right.

Maria unfastens the first two buttons of her long grey dress and tells her that at least the clothes will be dry in no time, but Mrs Kouli isn't thinking of her laundry.

The bread smells divine. Like manna sent from Heaven.

She points to the oven. She's always telling her husband that the smells which emanate from next door are worth dying for. Dying for! She should open her own bakery, she laughs. She'd make a tidy fortune. Folk around here would pay anything for a slice of one of her delectable cakes.

A hint for a freshly baked loaf of bread for Mr Kouli's supper. Most people are not well off and struggle to put food on their tables at night, but then, Maria doesn't have much either. She has to admit that the bread does smell good. Baking is the opposite of death, she thinks. You start off with nothing and you have something lovely at the end of it. You don't create something lovely and watch it turn to nothing in front of you. A pink ribbon lying in the dust. A bloodied knee. Maria closes her eyes to ward off the memories. She can't do this now. Not today. This is how she gets through her days. By swatting thoughts away as if they were flies come to plague her.

She leaves Mrs Kouli to her washing and walks across the yard to the old well, bending over to collect stray feathers discarded by the hens and groaning with the effort of carrying out chores beneath the midday sun.

They'd boarded up the well with long heavy planks a few years ago and it was already obscured by the thick insinuating weeds which thrived off the Cypriot heat. You could barely tell there was a well there at all unless, of course, you knew where to look.

There'd been no running water when they'd first moved into the house and she remembers getting up every morning to uncoil the wooden bucket from its trestle and lower it into the hole. It was a laborious task but she didn't mind it so much. It gave her a few precious minutes to herself when he wasn't standing over her shoulder and besides, she loved the way the water tasted. Like the dew which hung from the leaves on a fresh October morning.

By the time the children were tall and curious enough
to peer inside it, old Mr Christofides had started
charging the neighbours to fill up jugs from the spring
in his back garden. It would be a better idea, she'd said
to Michali, to buy their water from him and retire the
well in case the damned kids fell in. He'd been far too
grudging to agree to her request. Why would he line
Mr Christofides' pockets, he'd snarled angrily, when
they had a perfectly good supply of water in their own
yard? Did she think he was some sort of idiot? She'd
continued to use it until they'd had their taps fitted in
the summer of '58 and she'd spent every waking minute
worrying about the kids plunging into its murky
depths.

Maria walks back into the kitchen, throws the
feathers into the bin and switches on the fan. *Oof!* She
takes the fish out of the fridge, unwraps it and lays it
on the kitchen counter. She makes a cut in its side,
reaches in and pulls out the guts. She thinks of Michali.

He announced this morning that he had important
news to share with her. He wanted to speak with her
in private, he said, after the child had gone to bed. She
hopes he's going to ask her for a divorce. People rarely
get divorced. In the seventeen years she's been married
to Michali, she's only heard of one other person who's
left her husband. A former neighbour, Mrs Thanil. Mr
Thanil, it transpired, had another family with his
mistress and even gave the second set of children the
same names as the first so he wouldn't get confused.
Imagine that? Perhaps Michali has met someone else.

She wouldn't be that surprised. They haven't reached for each other in over a year and even then it wasn't to make love but to claw at each other's skin like two desperate people stranded in a hole and looking for a way out of the darkness. Another woman wouldn't surprise Maria. Good luck to anyone foolish enough to take him on, and good riddance to him.

She chops the head off the fish and it falls to the floor with a thud. It looks up at her with an open mouth, its small silver eyes staring into the past. She's going to barbecue the rest for their supper and with any luck, it will be their last.

~

They sit around the table beneath the almond tree, eating the fish and listening to the sound of the Kemals' dog barking at the moon. It's hard to imagine that just over a year ago, the five of them were sitting around this very table, laughing and joking with Mr Styliano about the colours of her tablecloth. So much has changed. Actual pieces of her are now missing and she's grown fixated on a man she hardly knows because he's filled the void, the husband-shaped void in her heart.

Mr Styliano. She thinks about him often. Every night if truth be told. In those dreamy hours between consciousness and sleep when nothing is out of bounds and anything is possible. His warm brown eyes looking into hers as he compliments her. Sometimes they are friends, and sometimes lovers, but mostly he is her

knight. Rescuing her from a life she can barely stand
to live.

He sends his regards, by the way. Your Mr Styliano.

He deliberately lingers over the name, forking the
last of the fish into his mouth and staring at her for
longer than is comfortable. She wonders, sometimes,
if he can read her mind. Don't they say that it happens,
after so many years of marriage? That two people are
able to read each other's thoughts? If he could, she
thinks, he'd be quite shocked at what else he would
find in there, hidden among the debris.

How kind, be sure to thank him from me.

She pushes her plate away and slips her sandals off.
Grateful to the darkness for masking her blushes. It's
late, she thinks, to be eating dinner. People around here
wake early, to sell fruit at markets or to go out on their
boats, and there's hardly anyone out tonight unless you
count the Kemals' dog and the cicadas, whose deafening
noise intensifies the silence and lends it structure.

He seems in a good mood, laughing and joking with
an animated Costa and offering to help him with his
schoolwork. It's about the Sahara, he tells his Pappa.
And how hot it is. Michali leans over and ruffles his
hair. *Ah, but is it as hot as Cyprus in June?* The illusion of
normality, she thinks. If Mrs Kouli were to poke her
head round her back door at this precise moment she
would see a family of three enjoying their supper. How
could she guess that in the time it had taken Maria to
gut the fish and barbecue it for them, she had planned
her life without him?

Now go, Michali tells his son. It's late and there's something he wants to speak to his mother about. *The sands of the Sahara will still be here tomorrow.* Costa, who's been waiting patiently for the appearance of the watermelon, is ready to burst into tears but Maria shoots him a look and nods in the direction of the house. You're in the lead, it says. Leave before your luck runs out. *Go. I'll save you some karpouzi for your breakfast.*

Michali insists on a toast and he sends her into the kitchen to fetch his bottle of ouzo from the fridge. *Bring two glasses.* A drink for her? A special occasion indeed. He arranges them side by side on the table in front of him and carefully pours the clear liquid into each one. He slides a glass across to her and picks up the other. *Yia mas!* He finishes his toast and tips his head back. He swallows the drink in one. He reaches for the bottle and pours himself another.

He picks at his large tar-stained teeth with his nail and smooths his fingers through his long grey hair. That dog, he begins, is barking because he is hungry. Mr Kemal has not been employed in years. Does she know why he can't find work? It's because he is Turkish. Of course, he continues, now she will tell him he's not the only Turkish man in Kyrenia and it's true, he's not, but how many Turkish people are gainfully employed in these parts. Does she know?

He wags his finger in her face.

The other day, in Nicosia, a Turkish taxi driver was dragged from his car and beaten half to death by three Greek yobs. He heard about it from Mr Styliano, although you'd think it had never happened at all given the coverage it had received. Did she know exactly how much coverage? None. There will be revenge, he warns her. It is inevitable. The Turks will form a group and they will attack a Greek taxi driver in retaliation, and maybe even kill his brother and his wife. They may attack a whole streetful of Greeks and then what? *Hah?*

Maria sips her ouzo and thinks that this is a curious prelude to divorce. It's what he wants, he says angrily.

Who?

Grivas!

If you poke enough baskets you will finally get one with a rattlesnake inside. There will be a civil war. He can assure her of that, although he can't tell her when. It might be tomorrow, it might be next year, or it might be when Costa is eighteen and in prime position for the front line. The bullseye. *Then what?* Always the same, she thinks. The same topic of conversation. He comes home from the base with politics on his mind and takes it out on her. She knows nothing of these things. What does she care about drunken brawls in the street and arguments about taxis? Men will be men. As long as her neighbours are pleasant and Mr Kemal bids her a kalimera every morning, it is good enough for her.

So? So, he replies, he's been thinking. And as coincidence would have it, last week marked his twentieth year at the air base in Nicosia. Twenty years, their star labourer! The Englesoi, he tells her. Everyone hates them, but they're not so bad at the end of the day. He'd rather climb into bed with Mr Smith and Mr Jones than

Grivas or any of those other enosis fanatics hell-bent
on killing them all. They've given him a gift, he says.
The English. A thank you present, really, or put another
way, a leaving gift.

Hah? She'd almost fallen asleep listening to his tirade
but the last part jolts her off her chair. *You're leaving the
base?* This is the news, he exclaims proudly, that he
wanted to share with her this evening. His gift from
the English, three British passports, and what better
time to leave than now? *Why wait?* Not this again. She'd
been thinking of Mrs Thanil, recently divorced and
living in her brand-new house up in the mountains of
Rizokarpaso where it was cooler, free from Mr Thanil's
controlling, philandering ways, and she wants to
scream now, as her hopes and dreams disappear faster
than spores in the wind.

She is back where she started. A wicked little circle.
He wants them to move to England, only this time he
has British passports and he has resigned from his job.
How could he? *What would we do in England?* She's
shrieking now, loud enough to wake the street, and
banging her glass on the table. *Tell me that?* They could
buy a bakery, he suggests. She's always loved to bake,
wouldn't that be the perfect thing for a consummate
baker to do? To buy a bakery? An attempt at flattery.
They don't speak English, she replies. How would they
get by? They could learn, he says. Besides, there are
apparently little communities in London where people
from Cyprus live together and they could move somewhere like that and mix with their own kind.

It's always raining in England, she moans. A friend
of a friend travelled there last year to visit her daughter
and she said it was an awful place. Grey and damp and
wet with these huge ugly buildings that loomed out
from the ground and almost touched the sky. *People
living in columns, one on top of the other, imagine that?* she
tells him. *Imagine living in a concrete column and never seeing
the sea again?*

He throws his head back and laughs at her. A loud
rasping laugh, thickened by years of tar. *Then we will buy
umbrellas and ladders!* She tells him that he's mad. Over
the years she has come to expect anything from Michali,
but this, this she didn't envisage. *And you are an ungrateful
bitch.* She begins to gather the plates before he can reach
over and start hurling them across the yard. *Like the
Turks' dog barking in the dark!* She bids him a kalinihta.
She's going to her room. She needs time and space to
think about the events which have just transpired and
besides, she doesn't want to give him the satisfaction
of seeing her cry.

Chapter 33

London – 1985

ELENA FINDS THE photograph while she is searching for a box of matches to light the censer. It's in a clear plastic folder, buried deep beneath a pile of forgotten papers and bills. She slips it out from beneath its cover and carefully holds it up to the window between her fingertips. She's seen it somewhere before, the picture. In the pocket of a dream, perhaps, or in somebody else's life. The little girl with long light brown hair and the bright blue eyes.

She knows it's her.

Now that she is out of her hiding place she has no idea what to do with her and she holds the picture as if it's burning her hand. It's too late now, to put her back in the drawer. She will only smother her and somehow strengthen the power of the curse. If she puts her in a frame and perches her on a shelf, she has conceded to her, given her dominion over the house.

Tell me, Mamma, what should I do?

Since the book appeared from nowhere she can't stop thinking about Katerina. Her mother used to say

that someone, somewhere was intending them harm.
A malevolent presence with no clear motive, but once
the evil eye had you in its sights there really was no
escape. Mrs Pavlou and her broomstick, darting in and
out of the shadows like a witch, wishing their demise
for no apparent reason. The scariest part of all. There
was never an apparent reason.

There's only one thing she can do now. Bless the
house with holy incense. She runs up and down the
stairs breathlessly with the censer, circling smoke from
the burning olive leaves around anything she can think
of. The girls' clothes, their beds, her own head. Round
and round it goes, three times for three prayers to ward
off the evil spirits. Finally, the photograph.

When they were younger, Pappa used to take them
to the beach down by the harbour. He preferred the
evenings, when the summer sun had turned its back
on the day and the heat was less intense. When there
was nobody else around. Elena and Valentina would
take off their clothes and fold them into neat little piles,
side by side on the pebbles, and run into the sea in
their underwear, giggling at the freedom of it. She
remembers how they laughed with pleasure as the cool
water embraced their sticky bodies and soothed their
burning skin. They would hold hands and look up at
the darkening sky, the two of them, swirling around
in the Mediterranean Sea like they were the last people
on the earth.

Pappa would join them when he'd finished untan-
gling his nets and he'd tell them stories about the stars.

This one, he would say, pointing up at the sky, died hundreds of thousands of years ago but its light is only just reaching us. Isn't that amazing? Elena thought that it was. The enormity of eternity would blow her mind, captivating and frightening her all at once and she would wrap her legs around his waist and bury her head in his neck to anchor herself to reality. She is reminded of her father's star now as she stares at the light in the little girl's eyes. It shines down at her from a distant past like a terrifying warning. A prophecy in reverse, captured in a photograph.

~

She's serving Mrs Iraklides when he walks into the shop in his postman's uniform and she nods to the little table at the back and tells him she'll be with him in a moment. There's nothing better than the smell of toasted sesame seeds, Mrs Iraklides concludes. Of course, freshly brewed coffee in the morning is nice and so is the smell of Cypriot jasmine in the summer, but toasted sesame seeds are something very special.

Mrs Iraklides looks around the bakery while Maria wraps up the bread, and she compliments her on her new paintings. New? Maria is confused. How are they new? How many years has it been since she was last in here? she asks her. Don't tell me that you have been buying your koulouri bread from somewhere else all this time, hah? She shakes her finger accusingly in her face and the poor woman winces in shame. Well, she replies, hesitantly, Mr and Mrs Papavasilakis sell koulouri which tastes almost identical to hers and although it is a little overpriced it does come wrapped in these convenient little bags which she can later recycle as food bags. They are very handy for covering up opened packets of ham, for instance. Or halloumi. And what she's overspent on the bread she then saves on the cost of clingfilm, so it all works perfectly. Maria narrows her eyes. *And to what do we owe the pleasure of your custom today, hah?* They're closed, Mrs Iraklides tells her. On a Tuesday afternoon. For stocktake. Well, she'll be sure to make a bloody note.

Maria waits until the door has closed behind her before flying into a tirade. For years, she tells Costa, those crooks have been reselling her koulouri and attempting to steal her customers and now they are branching out into the food packaging business? What's next, a van waiting outside with its engine running to empty her shop of baklava?

He's distant and distracted. She makes him a cup of tea with the kettle she keeps behind the counter and she sits down opposite him for a chat. She doesn't have much time, she tells him. It's the early summer rush and Maki is at the doctor's. *Or so he says. He's probably enjoying a few extra hours in bed on my nickel.* And there's no cinnamon either, not down here. She's had to learn to drink tea the English way as it brews more quickly, but it tastes like a pond. Nothing more, nothing less. Not that she's ever drunk water from a pond herself.

She knows what's bothering him before she's even asked the question. Elena's getting worse. Going to bed early is one thing, he tells her, but some days she barely makes sense and it's beginning to scare him. She found a book, he says, at the bottom of the stairs and she swore blind Katerina left it there as a message. *Katerina?* Maria is about to ask what sort of message and to finally take ownership of the book, but it doesn't seem right to interrupt him. Besides, it wouldn't do, to bring all that up again. She picks at the hem of her apron and sighs. A deep sorrowful sigh. She knew things were bad, but she didn't realise they were this bad. A doctor, she suggests. *Would she go?* Of course not, he tells her. In fact, she thinks he's the one with the problem because he doesn't believe that they're being taunted or haunted, or whatever.

Can you call that crazy sister of hers, tell her what's happened? It's been five years, he replies, since they stopped talking. Did she not know? Maria shakes her head and throws her hands up to the heavens. She had no idea. They fell out over the baby. Nina, not Valentina's baby, although to be honest, Elena was just looking for an excuse and she said as much herself once. She's more depressed, he admits. Since Valentina stopped talking to her. She's definitely more depressed.

Mamma, can I ask you a favour?

Oh, Costa.

She's said it before and she'll say it again. She would do anything for her Costa. Heaven and Hell know she's proved that in the past, but this, this is futile. She knows

what he's about to ask her and if she thought it would
make a difference she would get on the bus right now
and go and see her, traffic or no traffic, but honestly,
and from what she's heard, there is very little point.

Chapter 34

London – 1988

THERE WERE THREE tablets this morning. A red one, a green one and a white one. A woman she had never seen before handed them to her in a small white paper cup and watched while she swallowed them one by one and washed them down with water. They change things, the pills. They change the landscape of her mind. Things that once seemed so clear, like her beautiful child, are fading into the distance while other things, the colour of the sky and the grass outside, have grown so vivid that they make her head ache.

Somebody died but she doesn't remember who. Somebody died and that is why she is here.

She thought at first it was her child, but she's not even sure that the little boy with the blue eyes ever existed. Perhaps she mixed him up with someone else, or perhaps she was thinking of Andoni Pavlou or Giovanna Johnston, the Little Englesa of Ammochostos, when she walked into the police station to warn them that he was missing.

That word, she tells the woman, the word in the mist,

was always hanging between them like a shiny silver blade. A guillotine. Ready, at any moment, to slice her head off.

The woman with the blonde hair and the black-rimmed glasses is called Dr Nixon and Elena knows that she is in the place they sent Mrs Pantelis because it's stamped on the front of her cup. It's time, Maria had said to the husband as he'd half carried her to the car. To confront the inevitable and send her to a place where she can get the help she needs.

When you are ready, we can talk about it, Dr Nixon tells her. *But until then, take your time.* It's going to be difficult, she warns. Remembering will pull apart the tectonic plates of her life, like an earthquake rearranging the surface of the earth. It won't be the same as remembering Giovanna and Andoni, she warns. Everything will look different afterwards.

Guilt, she tells Dr Nixon. That's the word she drew in the mist. Guilt, because she has blood on her hands. Blood that can't be washed off with a bit of hot soapy water. She'd said that to her once, the last time she'd seen her.

It feels like she's been here for years, but Dr Nixon tells her that it's only been a few days and there's relief, then, that she hasn't missed seeing her daughters grow up. They are still little girls. You're making progress, she assures her. And progress means no more needles or arms that take her breath away. Progress affords freedom. Doors are closed in the middle of the day. There are walks, not just down corridors, but around

the hospital grounds. Finally, there is the time and space
to be alone.

She begins to notice things. It's summer. There are
wild flowers growing in the gardens. They're pink and
smell like Maria's bakery. The place where she was
happiest. Someone has left a change of clothes at the
end of her borrowed bed. Faded green tracksuit
bottoms and a white T-shirt which hangs loosely
around her concave chest. The woman in the room
nearest to hers has hacked off some of her hair and
cut herself in the process. There's a bloody red gash
running along the exposed part of her scalp. She's in
the garden sometimes, and seeing her staggering
towards the bench as if her life depended on it, as if
legs might not be able to carry her there, reminds Elena
that she doesn't want to be here any more.

She's there, of course, just beneath the surface.
Threatening to come out and confront her, but Elena
won't let her. She should have closed the door in her
face that day and then none of this would have
happened. Put her back in her box. It's like the dreams,
she tells Dr Nixon. The dreams she used to have about
the body buried in the garden.

Who was buried there?

Sometimes it was Andoni Pavlou. Because of the way
he died. She was scared he'd suffocated to death while
they shot at him and there was nothing worse than
choking to death in the dust. Sometimes she saw
Giovanna's coffin. Towards the end, she tells her, she'd
see a child swaddled in dirty blankets.

I want to go home now.
Are you ready to talk about it?
She takes a deep breath.
Yes, Dr Nixon, I think I am.

Chapter 35

Cyprus – 1970

MID JANUARY. IT'S still light, but the Ammochostos sky has acquired that temporary look which signals the end of a winter's day. The sun has dipped behind the row of houses and trees, and the lights from the school glow in the dusk as she hugs her school jumper to her chest and crosses the playground to go home.

She's late. She hung around in the cold after class in the hope of seeing Andoni, but she supposes he left without her. It's been months since they've spoken and Elena doesn't know why he's avoiding her. She wonders if she should write him a note asking for an explanation, an absolution even, but when she thinks about putting pen to paper, her stomach twists in pain.

She'd accosted Dimitri Pavlou. She'd stood in front of him with her arms outstretched, blocking his path to school until he'd been forced to stop and throw his satchel down in the dust. *What do you want?* his chins wobbling in frustration as he'd shouted in her face. To find out why his brother wasn't speaking to her any more. He'd sighed and told her he was going steady with Nicoletta Nicodemou and she was jealous of other girls. *Nicoletta?* She'd wrinkled her nose in confusion. *Since when?* A lie, she'd said, and a hurtful one at that and he'd almost spat in her face then. It would hurt much more if he was cruel enough to tell her the truth.

What truth? His silence felt childish and silly. Like the squabbles she used to have with Valentina. Sometimes they made up straight away and other times it took a few days, but they always came together in the end. Let him sulk, she thinks, as she walks down the driveway. Let him sulk all he wants.

Her mother is waiting for her outside the front door and her heart sinks. It's never a good sign, looking up and seeing her waiting on the step with her arms folded across her chest and her neck poking out of her cardigan like a cockerel's. Like the day that Pappa died. Something must have happened. *Mamma?* She ushers her furtively into the front room and closes the door behind them. She's turned off the lights and pulled the shutters closed to protect them from prying ears. She's placed lit candles in cups in every corner of the room. Candles on the shelf by the telephone. On the table in front of the couch and on the mantelpiece next to Valentina's wedding photograph.

Candles to memorialise the dead.

It's your sister, she tells her. She lost the baby yesterday. Valentina's baby, climbing out of her body and walking away. She didn't mean to imagine it that way, it was the way she'd said it. Lost. She sees an empty bassinet, Valentina looking for her baby beneath the covers, unsure of where it might have gone. A miscarriage, her mother clarifies. The cousin rang and told her that Valentina had suffered a miscarriage.

She's heard that word before. Mrs Jordano had lost many babies before she'd given birth to her son. *Another miscarriage, such a shame.* Her mother, crossing herself and tutting and gossiping about her in the street to anyone who had five minutes to spare. Mrs Jordano lost another baby. How terribly sad. Her wide eyes contradicting the sorrow in her words.

She thought these things happened earlier, she tells Lenou. In the first few months, not after the fifth. It's too late. *Sometimes it happens*, she replies. What more could she say?

Nothing. They sit next to each other on the couch and stare into the darkness. The candles burn brightly and remind them of what they have lost. A baby. Valentina's daughter. A grandchild. A niece. It was a girl, Lenou tells her, her eyes brimming with tears. The death blow, the final stab. The baby was a girl.

At ten, her mother gets up to light the foukou. She fans the flames until the coals glow red-hot and drags it back inside so they can warm their cold hands over its heat. She makes cinnamon tea with extra honey in it because the sweetness is good for shock and she kisses the cross around her neck and rubs Elena's back while she sips chai. She's grateful for the small comforts.

A knock at the door. It makes Elena jump. *Kyria Lenou. Everything OK?* It's Mrs Pavlou come to pick over what's left of the bones, a vulture circling carrion. This is all her fault, her mother spits into her ear. She's finally got what she wanted. *You can't blame Mrs Pavlou*, Elena whispers. She was miles away. Yes she can. If there's one thing she has learned in this life, she tells, her, it's that there is always someone to blame.

~

There is always someone to blame. Another of Xanthe's brutal lessons. Things didn't happen without good cause. We bring things on ourselves, she used to say. We pick them up and bring them crashing down onto our own heads. We trace them onto our backs with pointed arrows. The scars, indelible. Anger has displaced yesterday's sadness and Lenou is relieved. Sorrow is for the weak of mind, but she knows where she is with her anger.

She was turning into her, Pedro had remarked. As surely as the summer breeze turns into an autumn gale, and he couldn't be around her shouting and screaming at those poor girls. *Who's shouting?* she'd yelled at him that last time. *Hah?* So angry all the time. Just like her, the woman not fit to be called their mother. *Get out!* She had waved her arms around and shooed him to the doorway as if he were a trapped pigeon. The impertinence of it, of eating her sugared almonds and drinking her kafe and telling her how she should behave in her own home. He would be glad of it, he'd replied. Glad to leave and never come back, although it was the children he most felt sorry for and he would think of them often. *Don't bother.*

Of course she'd missed him for a short time and she'd wince when Elena asked after him but what use was regret? Far better to be angry. You could accomplish things with anger, you could pick things up and move them. Besides, as he grew older it became apparent to Lenou why their mother had picked on Pedro. He's one of them, her twin brothers who were only a year younger than her would snigger as they watched him skipping happily around the backyard. It's not natural, they would mock, the way the boy prances about the place as if he were a girl and she'd wondered, then, how much of it her mother had noticed and absorbed and if she'd been trying to beat it out of him all along.

The crack of dawn. The best part of any day. Fury propels her out of bed like a catapult. She shivers and drapes her gown around her shoulders to ward off the chill and God only knows what else that might be lurking between cold walls. She can't lie about all day wishing things had turned out differently. The house smells of burnt coal and stings the back of her throat and she opens the shutters in the front room for the cool fresh air.

She picks up Valentina's photograph, blurred with soot, and she wipes it clean with the back of her sleeve, wondering how she is still managing to put one foot in front of the other. A true martyr. Better than a martyr, even. Martyrs died a single death while she has endured a life of them.

She talks to her daughter as if she were here. *You're a stupid girl*, she tells her. *You know that? You almost had it all.* Things she didn't deserve in the first place, things that could have led to happiness and now she's gone and lost them all. They've vanished, like the wisps of smoke from last night's bonfire.

What would she have done? she wonders. Her mother? If the twins had been right about Pedro? Would she still have chased him around the streets with her cane? An old woman running after her grown-up son and telling him who he should love? She replaces the picture on the mantelpiece. Darker thoughts rush in like rapids and make her head spin. The inside of the next-door neighbour's washing machine and how nice for her that she has one while she herself kneels over a pot in the dust. Surreptitious whispers mingle with washing powders. Maybe it's for the best with the new husband on the scene. She could try again, start a family with him. That would be the right thing to do. Have a baby with the husband. Things happen for a reason. Xanthe used to say that as well. Everything happens for a reason and they were not worthy enough to understand His ways. *Not yet, my dear Magdalena. Not yet.*

She marches into the kitchen chest first, her large bent nose pointed at the ceiling and her grey curly hair bouncing furiously around her shoulders like Medusa's. She fills a pan with water so she can make tea. She reaches for the koulouri bread, forgetting what she usually puts in Elena's sandwiches. Halloumi, olives? *You see,* she spits under her breath. *What you've done?* And as if worrying about her wasn't enough, she's worrying about the soul of the child as well. She'll go and see

Pater Sotiri later, when Elena's in class. She needs to know if it will be OK. She can't bear to think of the babe lost somewhere, in the shadowy spaces of Xanthe's stories about goblins and devils and Purgatory. She smears butter onto the bread and shudders at the thought of it. *Now look what you made me do! There's butter everywhere!*

Elena pads into the kitchen in her nightdress, surprised that her mother is sending her to school. Of course she is, she replies. The world doesn't stop because Valentina has problems. Everyone has problems. She wraps the sandwiches in brown paper and ties them for her with string. *Here*, she tells her. *Halloumi. I remembered.*

She knows Elena's upset, but she doesn't have time for vulnerability this morning. Not hers and not anyone else's. She can go to school and cry there. Lenou has chores to do. Someone needs to strip the beds and wash the sheets and tonight's dinner won't cook itself. Has Elena ever seen a chicken pluck its own feathers and fry itself in lemon and salt? Then she has to go over to St Peter's Church and tell the Pater what has happened and put in a request for prayers to be recited because while there was certainly nothing to look forward to, there was always the possibility of things getting worse. Another important life lesson which Elena would do well to remember. Things can always get worse.

Then, of course, there's the gossip. The malicious tongues, momentarily silenced by news of Valentina's marriage, will now have other things to gloat about.

Oh, I'm sorry about the baby, Kyria Lenou, they'll say, dragging out their words and making two syllables sound like four. Professing their concern and empathy to her face and then whispering behind her back. She had it coming, she can hear them saying as they shake their heads at the back of the church. Did the stupid girl really expect to live happily ever after, given everything she'd done? Well, did she?

Chapter 36

London – 1978

SHE'S COME ROUND to admire the new kitchen. It's white and shiny with fake marble surfaces and a large kitchen table in the centre of the room and she whistles through her glossy red lips and makes all the right noises. It's very modern. *My compliments.*

She flits in and out of Elena's life like a beautiful butterfly, coming and going as she pleases. When the lover is at work she'll see her once or twice a week and then months can go by without a word. She's selfish, Costa tells her. She's using you. She's manipulative. He doesn't like her, never has. She reminds him of the dogs he encounters on his rounds. Little fluffy things. Perfectly sweet and friendly one minute and trying to bite your foot off the next. She drinks too much and she smokes too much and did she notice that she is cheating on her husband and that they were, in effect, condoning it? *We're collaborators. Co-conspirators.*

Elena dismisses his big words with a wave of her hand. She doesn't care. Perhaps her sister's visits were charged with ulterior motives, but she's far happier when Valentina is around. She gets under her skin, she tells Costa. She lifts her spirits like a warm sea breeze on a summer's day. Like the scent of Maria's cakes at the crack of dawn. V for vivacious. Or V, he mutters, for vampire.

When Valentina is too busy to visit, she'll ride the 329 bus to Wood Green station and wait for the 29 to take her up Green Lanes to Harringay. Her old haunt. Maria, standing behind her counter talking animatedly to her customers, her apron wrapped tightly around her waist and her eyes twinkling with mischief. Always mischievous and always happy to see her. Grabbing the kettle to make tea after they'd picked up their boxes and headed back to their cars, and gossiping behind their backs.

Sometimes, there'd be new customers to talk about. The defectors, Maria liked to call them. Customers who used to buy their pastries from other outlets on Green Lanes but had switched, more recently, to Petrakis. A vindication of all her hard work. All these years, she'd beam, Costa has nagged at her to use cheaper suppliers but this is why she never listened. If Mr Pappadopoulos, who owned half of the letting agencies on West Green Road, endorsed Petrakis, she knew she'd won the Oscar for cakes.

They'd chuckle together and drink tea for hours and before she knew it the sky outside would have grown dark and Maria would get up and turn the lights on. Home time. Time to ride the 329 bus back home to Costa, and her heart would plummet at the thought of it although she could never explain why. The reasons behind things eluded her. *You avoid things,* her mother had said to her after the baby died. She'd wanted to put the photograph away or at least turn it around, but Lenou had forbidden it. She was always running away from things. It wasn't healthy, she'd said. One of these days everything would catch up with her and there'd be no running away from things then.

They'd gone to church together, that Sunday. They'd sat at the back and held candles and prayed for the lost baby's soul. The little wooden church was packed with parishioners dressed in their finest clothes and she'd slid down in her seat as far as she could before her mother noticed, and tried to make herself inconspicuous among the crowd of worshippers.

She couldn't pray. She mouthed the psalms and breathed in the incense from Pater Sotiri's censer and crossed herself in all the right places during the service but all she could think about was Andoni Pavlou squeezing Nicoletta Nicodemou's bosoms. Why hadn't he said anything to her about it? she'd wondered. Why had he sent big fat Dimitri to spit in her face after so many years of being friends? Let him squeeze whomever he liked. Yet it had bothered her, and she'd thought about the pair of them necking behind the olive trees all the way through the service and through most of the sermon. In fact, by the time Mrs Pappas had crept over to their pew to tap her mother on the shoulder and mouth her deepest condolences, Elena had almost forgotten whose baby she was talking about.

Chapter 37

Cyprus – 1961

THE NEXT MORNING Costa wants to know what was so important that he had to miss out on his dessert. *Never you mind.* It's too soon, she thinks, to say anything. She needs to straighten things out in her own head before burdening the child with more worry.

She brushes past him and into the bathroom. She cleans her teeth and splashes water onto her face and pulls her hair back into a tight, silvery knot. She studies herself in the mirror. Turning first this way and then that, and then pinching her pointed cheeks to add some colour to her skin. She reaches for the cupboard above the sink and finds the little tube of lipstick that she keeps hidden from Michali behind the block of soap. She pops the lid off and twists it open and paints a pink smile on her lips, careful not to draw over the edges.

What are you doing? Costa is standing in the doorway scratching at his belly and watching her get ready. She fancies a change, she tells him. To cheer herself up. She puckers her lips together. *There!* Doesn't he sometimes do things just to cheer himself up? Like eating little snacks that he's squirrelled away in his room when he knows he's not supposed to and thinks that nobody is looking? She grabs at his cheeks and tickles him under the chin and he giggles playfully. She tells him to hurry up and get dressed otherwise he's going to be late for school. *Do I look nice at least?* she calls out after him. *After all this effort?* He tells her he prefers her old face.

Once he's left, she picks out a pale blue dress and slips on her brown leather sandals. She wants to do something to honour her today. Something special. She loved Kyrenia Castle by the harbour so perhaps she will head into town to sit in its great big shadow and watch the boats bobbing out to sea. Eight happy years she was fortunate enough to know her, and nothing could ever alter the fact. *You're lucky, Kyria Maria. That you had her for that long. My Simo died when he was just a baby and we never got the chance to know him.*

She'd begun collecting stories, over the past year. People suddenly relating to her pain and coming to share secret heartaches. A stillborn, a beloved parent gone too soon, a friend suffering from cancer. She's a magnet for their sorrow and soon discovers that she doesn't mind. She's good at it, even. Listening and commiserating and assuring people that they are not alone in trying to decipher the painful riddles of the world. She derives strength from it. It's not just us, she'd say to Michali afterwards. We're not the only ones experiencing hardship, but he didn't seem to care. To Michali, it was all wasted time and energy. Time that could be better spent furthering their own motives. She should charge, he'd bark, for all the hours she spent

listening to the neighbours moaning about their problems. *Then we'd have no problems at all.*

~

The midday sun is burning hot and she finds herself
scampering sideways to the castle like a bright red crab.
She sits in a cool dark alcove, out of the view of the
small groups of tourists wandering around, and she
stares out to sea at the swimmers and boats returning
from their hauls.

She used to bring the kids here when they were little.
They would play hide-and-seek between its stony
yellow walls or pretend to be warriors on the lookout
for mortal enemies crossing the water to capture the
island. *They're here, they're here!* Costa would pretend to
look through a telescope and point to the sea and shout
at the top of his voice while Katerina shrieked with
pleasure. She'd hush them, then, in case their loud
childish voices disrupted the paying customers. The
tourists who had come to Cyprus to see the great Castle
of Kyrenia. They underestimate the heat, she'd say to
Costa as they walked back towards the bus stop. The
Swedes and the Germans. Did he see how sunburnt
their pale freckly faces were beneath their sticky caps?
And they'd laugh, then, and Katerina would laugh with
them and she'd ruffle her hair and ask her what was so
funny in a silly voice when she was clearly too young
to keep up.

The colourful boats in the water begin to blur before

her eyes and her throat constricts in sadness. It was OK, Dr Pantazis had told her, to let it out sometimes. It was healthy to grieve. Plenty who thought crying was for the weak surely regretted it later when the lion inside of them broke free and began to maul their organs.

Mrs Petrakis?

She wipes her eyes and looks up.

Are you all right?

She doesn't recognise him immediately because there are tears in her eyes and his face is darkened by shadows. A handsome stranger, she thinks, come to save her from her memories at a most auspicious time. His skin is tanned and his hair is black and silver and his eyes, when he bends towards her, are the colour of honey.

It's Mr Styliano, from the base?

Of course. He gives her his hand and her heart skips a beat and later she will blame the summer heat and the events of the day for being so overcome with emotion, and not the fact that she was falling in love with a man she barely knew.

~

His car, he says, is parked right around the corner. Will she allow him to drive her home? She agrees, but for no other reason than it's too hot to wait for the bus, and by the time they arrive back at the house she's managed to pull herself together and apologise for inconveniencing him. *Please, there's no need.* Then he must come in, she insists. The very least she can do is pour him a cold drink for his troubles.

He follows her through the front door and into the kitchen. She pulls out a chair and beckons for him to sit while she fixes her hair, switches on the fan and opens the back door. She grabs two glasses and the rose syrup from the cupboard, pouring a measure into each and filling them to the brim with milk. Triantafyllo is his favourite, he says. Who can resist cold rose-flavoured milk on a hot summer's day? How did she know? *Mine too.*

He pulls out a string of shiny blue worry beads from the pocket of his white shirt and threads them between his long fingers. They listen to the humming of the fan and Maria wonders if her hot red cheeks betray her excitement at being in his presence. She points to the beads. Her father used to play with those, she tells him. He smiles. They were an old man's habit, it was quite true, but they kept him from smoking cigars.

He tells her that he is sorry for her loss. Most days she's OK, she admits. She can channel her grief into her baking or into Costa, but today she allowed herself to indulge in the pain of her memories. There is nothing wrong in that, he replies. Nothing at all.

There's a comfortable, familiar silence while they sip their drinks and listen to the soporific sound of the cicadas and then he asks her if Michali has been supportive. She kicks off her sandals and leans back in her chair. The breeze from the fan caresses her skin and makes her feel lighter than she has done in years.

She doesn't know the full extent of their friendship, so she is careful in choosing her words. Michali may be a loyal friend to him, she confides, tiptoeing around broken glass, but he is certainly not a good husband. They're not friends, Mr Styliano interjects. Whoever told her they were friends? He throws his head back and laughs. *Friends?* He's an employee, no more, no less. Truth be told, he was rather looking forward to seeing the back of the old goat. They all were. Though he would miss her cooking, of course. Maria Petrakis' tava. He winks at her and she smiles coyly into her lap.

You are too kind.

He laughs again in response to her compliment. She wouldn't say that if she knew him well. *Believe you me, Mrs Petrakis.* Even the moon has a dark side, he tells her. The side nobody can see. Although he would like it very much if she did become a friend. She sips her rose drink and assures him that he is kind. She should know. She's lived with a brute for seventeen years and she knows a gentleman when she sees one.

A brute? A violent man, she continues tentatively. A monster. A bully who hits and punches and bites and chokes the wind out of her until his face is replaced by little black stars. She's relieved, at last, to be confessing to someone and she's grateful that someone is him.

What a damned thing to do to a woman.

There's more besides, she tells him. Plenty more things that he's done to her when the two of them were alone in their bedroom, but it wouldn't be appropriate to divulge. She can see horror and shame reflected in his large golden-brown eyes and a part of her derives pleasure from his compassion. It spurs her on. She wants it to stop, she tells him. Last night, she thought he was going to ask her for a divorce and she was so excited at the prospect that she'd almost packed their bags in her head, but she was wrong.

He wants us to move to England, as I'm sure you've already heard.

He'd heard, of course, but the man was a dreamer. Michali, he scoffs, is one of life's losers. *Perhaps that's why he beats women, Mrs Petrakis.* He needs to feel big in a world where he is so very small and insignificant. A little ant beneath a rock in a jungle full of tigers. He sees tragedy when he searches her eyes, he tells her, but he also sees incredible strength and he knows that she will be OK. *Will I, Mr Styliano?* Yes, she will. She will be more than OK, he can promise her that and, if nothing else, he is always true to his word.

He gets up to leave and she begs him not to say anything to Michali at work. Not that she thinks for a moment that he would betray her, but she needs to be sure. For her sake and for Costa's.

I hope you can understand.

It goes without saying.

He kisses her on both cheeks and she leans against the door frame and watches him walk slowly back to his car. When he is halfway there he stops and turns around to retrace his steps to her front door. He leans in close and Maria wonders if he is going to kiss her on the mouth. Instead he turns his head, whispers in her ear.

Of course, there are ways.

Maria is confused.

Ways, Mr Styliano?

Yes. *Ways of making someone disappear.*

Chapter 38

London – 1986

IF COSTA COULD see her now, wobbling on her step-
ladder at the back of her bakery and dusting her Queen,
he'd berate her. Do you know, he would say, how long
it takes for a bone to heal in someone of your age? If
she needed things doing she should call him. He says
these things to her like she wants to break a leg and
spend three months recovering or that she wants to be
an old lady who is no longer able to do the things she's
always taken for granted. When she first bought the
bakery twenty-four years ago, she was up and down
ladders like a child's yo-yo. Painting this, decorating
that. Fitting shelves, fixing the bloody ovens if she had
to. She could do it all, once upon a time, be a man and
a woman. Whatever it took. Now, it's all she can do to
climb four little steps and dust her Queen.

She works carefully, methodically, rubbing a damp
cloth across her crown, her nose, her lips. There you
go, your Majesty. She nods her head in humility. She's
very grateful to the Queen for letting her live in England
and the least she can do is wipe her mouth. If it wasn't
for the Queen's England, she doesn't know what would

have become of her. She'd be back in Cyprus, married to Michali. Or perhaps she'd have run away with Mr Styliano, ignored the inevitable disgrace and caused a scene. Michali would have come looking for her, of course, but what could he have done? Mr Styliano was a powerful, well-connected man and Michali was nothing but an animal who, as luck would have it, owed a lot of money to some even bigger animals.

There were two conditions, he'd said, for his help. And he'd prefer it if she could call it that. He wanted her to go to England, as Michali had intended, and buy a bakery in his honour and forget that he ever existed. The first promise, she'd replied, would be easy enough to keep. She would even put up a white and blue sign to show him she was a true Greek patriot after all. The second, almost impossible. *Then keep me to yourself, Mrs Petrakis. Keep me to yourself as I will you.*

She'd succeeded in doing just that, and it hadn't been as difficult as she'd feared because silence, she quickly realised, invited all manner of confidences and people were much happier talking about their own lives and those of their neighbours than they were delving into her private affairs. Until yesterday, that was, when Mr Yiasoumi had come into the shop and his seemingly innocuous question had caught her by surprise.

Life had not been kind to Mr Yiasoumi. His mother had died when he was only five and her early demise had set the stage for an ever-growing catalogue of catastrophes. Two failed marriages, three brushes with cancer and a wife who never lifted a finger. And to add to his misery, Maria thought, the poor man looked like a garden gnome. Small and pale with protruding ears and a wispy grey beard. Still, he was one of her loyal regulars and never left the shop with less than three boxes of her finest pastries, so she had ample patience for his sorrows.

She'd grabbed her tongs as soon he'd entered the shop and stood poised to attention, her long tanned arm hovering over the pites, ready to serve. Kalimera! A smile and a nod. A large order today, he'd said. Mrs Yiasoumi had a delicate stomach and could hardly get out of bed, so he'd take five of her freshest spanakopites. The doctors, curiously, could never figure out what was wrong with her. Laziness, she'd thought, as she'd carefully placed the spinach puffs into a box, side by side. That's what was wrong with Mrs Yiasoumi, pure and simple. Laziness and an aversion to housework. *A few eliopites?* Of course. He must let her know, she'd urged, what they thought of today's olive rolls because she was trialling a new supplier. Leonidas and Son. Had he heard of them? They were becoming very fashionable. Very fashionable indeed.

She'd rung up the prices on the till and he'd fumbled around in his pockets for some coins, killing time. No, he hadn't, were they local? First this one, then that one, then the blazer pockets and she'd found herself counting the seconds and then the minutes while he searched his various crevices for change. When he'd finally managed to pay for his pastries, he couldn't work out which pocket he should drop his pennies into and she'd decided enough was enough, no customer was worth sacrificing an entire morning for when, unlike Mrs Yiasoumi, she had so many other things to be doing. She would chaperone him politely to the door to hurry proceedings along – and give him a little shove if needs be.

The problem was that he'd turned around at the most inopportune moment and the move, which usually worked well with most idle shoppers, backfired spectacularly. She'd found herself almost hugging him in the doorway of Petrakis and their close proximity apparently ignited his curiosity. He'd fixed her with his small grey eyes and asked her if she'd ever been married. *You never talk about yourself, Kyria Maria. Did your husband pass?* And she still doesn't know what came over her then, because for the first time in over two decades she couldn't help herself. *No, Mr Yiasoumi*, she'd whispered. *My husband vanished into thin air one evening after work. No one ever discovered what became of him.*

She'd done it for the reaction, of course, and it had worked because Mr Yiasoumi's face had lit up like an overloaded Christmas tree and he'd glanced furtively around the shop as if the mystery to her husband's disappearance might be hiding in the pastries. *Really? Tell me more.* But she'd said too much already and she'd opened the door and practically thrown him out onto the street.

She'd locked the door behind him and stood with her back to it for a few moments to compose herself, as the traffic roared behind the glass. She'd decided, when her breathing had steadied, that it was all right. She hadn't said very much and it would take a brave man to ask for any more detail after the way she'd thrown him to the pavement. But it was a lesson. A shot across her bows. Don't worry, Mr Styliano, she'd said to herself as she'd smoothed the creases in her apron and patted at her collarbone. That won't be happening again.

~

There is something Elena has to do today. Costa had reminded her of it before he'd left the house this morning. He'd kissed her on both cheeks and told her he would be late back and he'd pleaded with her not to forget. She wasn't going to forget, she'd replied, she would even write it down although she hadn't and the thing that she was supposed to do had slipped from her mind like sand falling through open fingers.

She blames the dreams. They fill her nights with horror and her days with confusion. Her mind is thick with fog and she's unable to remember simple things like where she is supposed to be and the thing she has to do today. She feels sorry for the child. For Magda. Playing by herself because she can't muster up the strength or the energy to take her out for a walk. If she wasn't so tired then of course she would, but it's all she can do to wait for Costa to come home so she can go back upstairs and try and snatch some sleep before the dreams start again.

Always one dream. The same dream. It's the middle of the night and she is standing outside in her long see-through nightdress holding a shovel. Someone is buried in their back garden. If only she can work out who it is who's lying there then the dreams will stop and she'll finally be able to sleep. She longs for the peace.

She begins to dig, her spade swinging back and forth and gleaming beneath a castigating moon and the earth piling up into a mound beside her. A tap. Metal on wood. She's exposed it. A small white coffin riddled with bullet holes. She can hear somebody urging her to go back inside, *this is no place for a child*, they're saying but it's too late because she's seen her and she drops the shovel and falls to her knees and begins to claw at the dirt with her hands.

She can't go back to sleep afterwards. She'll lie in bed and wait for the dawn and, when her pillow is soaked in her own sweat and too uncomfortable to sleep on, she'll get up and tiptoe downstairs into the kitchen to watch the new sun rising over the apple tree. It would seem to her, in those lonely moments, as if it rose not as a friend but to betray her. Another day to get through when she could barely get through the last.

She's woken by the sound of the doorbell and the child tugging at her sleeve. She must have dozed off at the kitchen table although she can't have been asleep for very long as she still feels tired and can't, for the life of her, remember the thing that she's supposed to do. She pushes her short hair back from her face and walks over to the front door with Magda in tow. *Maria. What a lovely surprise.* Maria is wearing her thick winter coat, her nose red with the cold, and she's holding Nina's hand. *Nina!* The little girl is dressed in her school uniform, her big curly hair twisted neatly into the plaits she'd braided this very morning and her scarf half covering her face. Elena's hand flies to her mouth when she sees her because, of course, that's the one thing she had promised to do today. Collect Nina from school. The thing he'd told her not to forget.

Maria barges past her and begins to unbutton her coat. She asks her if this happens a lot, because she's not doing that again. She had to walk ten whole minutes from Wood Green bus station to the Infants' School in the freezing cold and in the most unsuitable shoes and she was terrified of slipping over on the icy pavement and breaking her neck. And then where would they be, her and Costa? There'd be no more favours if she broke her neck! Why didn't she answer her phone when they rang? She was humiliated, she tells Elena, when she'd walked into the classroom to collect Nina. She'd felt smaller than the little tables and chairs arranged around the room and the teacher, the pretty one with the curly hair who looked like the poor astronaut who'd been blown up in that rocket, she'd been concerned and asked her if everything was all right at home. Of course, Maria continues, she'd told her that it was, but Elena really has to pull herself together because the situation is no longer tenable.

Elena's crying now, although she doesn't register the

hot salty tears until they are halfway down her cheeks, and she's not crying for the forgotten child. Not really. She's crying because all she's ever wanted is for Maria Petrakis to like her and these days, she can't even manage that.

Maria tells her it's OK, that no real harm has been done. She pulls a little parcel wrapped in tin foil from out of her bag and tells Elena that she's brought shamali from the shop and the girls squeal with excitement and climb up onto the table like a pair of monkeys and dig their fingers into the soft semolina cake and, at least where Nina is concerned, all is forgiven.

Maria is speaking to her kindly. She tells her that perhaps she should think about seeing someone. It was all getting too much and especially for Costa, but Elena can barely hear her over the whistling of the kettle and besides, out of the corner of her eye she can see that it's started to snow. She's always loved the snow! The way it looked when it first fell to the ground, like a child's nursery, freshly painted in white. A chance to wipe the slate clean and start all over again. Nina is licking syrup from her fingers, one by one – see, no harm done! And Maria suggests they start by calling Dr Johnny, but the events of the afternoon don't seem to matter as much as they did and they even start to diminish a little with the fading of the light.

Chapter 39

London – 1980

A BABY, DARLING, how wonderful! Costa picks her up and twirls her around the front room, her feet narrowly missing the spider plants perched on the shelves. *Just marvellous!* Has she just been to the doctor? *Just now,* she lies. The appointment was, in fact, hours ago but she couldn't face coming home to his excitement when she couldn't muster any for herself. She'd crossed the road afterwards and sat on a bench opposite the surgery and she'd stared at the cars and buses rushing up and down Green Lanes until the noise of the traffic had started to sound more like waves crashing onto the shore and had almost sent her to sleep.

They'd stop every time the lights turned red and they'd form a long colourful queue, and she'd have a clearer view of the drivers sitting behind their wheels. Some of them were listening to music and nodding along in time with the beat or drumming their fingers on their steering wheels. One or two of them turned to stare at her as they waited for the lights to turn green and she'd blushed at their attention.

Mostly, though, they'd ignored her and been as

oblivious to her presence as the warm May breeze which rustled the leaves of the trees. She'd wondered where they were all hurrying to, these people who somehow seemed busier and happier than her. Were they heading up to Harringay to buy cakes from Maria's bakery, or were they heading off to interesting places to live interesting lives?

She'd got up from the bench after a few hours, and she'd buttoned up her cream cardigan and smoothed it over her tummy and she'd ambled over to the little park a few streets along from the doctors' practice. She'd stopped by the playground to watch the young kids swinging from the various shiny apparatuses and thought about Valentina's daughter who would be ten years old if she had lived to be born.

She'd tried to imagine what she might have looked like. She'd be tall, she's somehow certain of that, and she'd have long black hair, which would trail behind her as she skipped off to school. Her eyes would be black, just like her mother's. Big and black and brimming with sorrow.

Valentina. The doctor had been effusive in her congratulations, but all she could think about was Valentina and how she would take the news. She wanted to be the one to tell her, to break it to her gently, and she implores Costa to keep the announcement from Maria until she's had a chance to speak with her. *Do you promise?* It's been years, he replies, surely she will be happy for them after all this time, but she knows her sister best of all and she knows that Elena's happiness will be the last thing on her mind. Especially, she tells Costa, if she finds out from someone else.

She means to tell her the very next day, but she doesn't feel too well and she doesn't feel well the day after that either. She waits a week and then two, and by then she's almost three months pregnant so she decides it's better to tell her face to face. She's too nauseous to take the bus to Edmonton so she asks Costa for a lift, but he tells her he's too busy. *Just call her, get it over with.*

She doesn't call her and she wishes she had because, of course, he's already told his mother so it's only a matter of time before the whole of north London finds out and, at the end of June, Costa comes home white as a sheet and she knows, then, that he's done the one thing she asked him not to and blurted it out to the wrong person.

In his defence, Costa stammers, Taki practically walked into him on Green Lanes and he'd asked after Elena. He'd circumvented the subject for a full fifteen minutes, he explains. Swerving this way and that, like a car on thin ice, and just to fill the silences he'd even boasted that she was learning English and Taki had laughed at this and said something ridiculous about the English needing to learn Greek and not the other way round and Costa had grown more and more uncomfortable because, he tells her, the man really is quite obnoxious. A real fool, shouting and gesticulating in the street on subjects he knows nothing about. Eventually, he had told him because he'd needed to pop a cork into his mouth and their news, as it turned out, was the perfect cork. *I'm sorry, darling.*

He assures her that it will be all right, that Valentina will get used to the idea in the end, but Elena knows otherwise. For years her sister has been looking for something to pour her pain and anger into and now she has her baby. She'll never forgive me, she tells Costa, never. *And I'll never forgive you.*

Chapter 40

Cyprus – 1974

THE THREAT OF war hangs in the air like a fine mist. You can't see it, but you can feel it prickling the skin. People who know about these things can speak of nothing else. They pack the churches of Ammochostos and pray for enosis with Greece, for a united Hellenic Republic and for a good outcome for Cyprus. Nobody, it seems, is praying for peace except her mother. Think of those boys, she whispers, as they sit beneath the vine during the long sultry evenings and drink chilled apricot juice to cool themselves down. Like lambs to the slaughter.

She mutters warnings to the cross around her chest, unaware, it seems, of the excitement growing around them. Andoni Pavlou is in the army and when he returns home at the weekends he lets Dimitri try on his boots. He runs up and down the driveway shouting *exo oi Tourkoi* and the chants make Elena shudder. Mrs Pavlou is shuddering, too. She's stopped hanging out of her windows to air her laundry and doesn't talk to anyone when she goes out shopping for her groceries.

See how she likes it, Lenou sneers. Now that the evil

eye is on her and her family. How things have changed! Elena doesn't understand how she can pray for the lambs and, in the same heartbeat, wish harm on Andoni Pavlou. She's not wishing harm on the boy, she retorts. Just on his dreadful mother.

When Lenou isn't gloating about Mrs Pavlou's misfortunes, she channels her anxiety into making preserves out of walnuts and watermelons and whatever else comes to hand. She works silently, manically, her chest heaving with the effort of it and her cross swinging back and forth over the sweets as if to bless them. The kitchen is full of little pots and jars and Elena dollops syrup into her mouth with her fingers as she walks past the table. Lenou slaps her on the back and tells her they're for an emergency. *What emergency?* Elena mocks. Does she think the Turks will jump out of the bushes and barricade them all in their houses, starve them all to death? Anything is possible, Lenou tells her. Absolutely anything.

If the Turks did indeed jump out of the nearby bushes, then they could do worse than nailing their doors and windows shut and eating Lenou's gliko. She's heard stories, terrible stories, about the things soldiers do to women in wartime. She pulls at Elena's arms and spits these things in her ears as if they were not alone in the house and hadn't been for years. *There's no one here to hear you ranting. There's nobody here except me.*

She thinks about Andoni Pavlou. He stopped talking to her a long time ago and she still has no idea why. *It's because he thinks you're crazy*, Dimitri tells her as they stand next to each other at the bus stop in the morning. He says he tried to kiss her once, when they went to deliver some stupid letter, and she went mad and scratched at his arms like a wild cat. She laughs, then, because it's such a ridiculous story to spin, even for Dimitri. She preferred it, she tells him, when he was lying about Nicoletta. That was just to protect her, he sniggers. He'd felt sorry for her despite the things his brother was saying behind her back. He taps his finger to the side of his head. *Crazy, like a wild cat.* She doesn't believe a word of his tale and, besides, she's too hot to care. The unforgiving rays of the July sun lash at her skin and she prays that the bus is on time so she can escape the heat and Dimitri's vile, hurtful tongue.

She's heading to her job at Aleko's Biblia, a small dusty bookshop in town that sells academic textbooks specialising in politics. Mr Aleko is a neighbour of theirs and one of the few people in Ammochostos that her mother actually approves of. He was kind, she maintains, when Savva died, but Elena knows it's because he writes for the local paper on matters that impress people.

He'd approached her in the courtyard of St Peter's Church one Sunday morning a few months after she'd finished school. He'd offered her a job in his shop while she was eating koliva, to commemorate her Pappa, beneath the fig and lemon trees. He was a tall wiry man, with receding grey hair and large owl-like eyes perched peremptorily over a hooked nose. He knew more about politics than anyone she'd ever met and she wondered why he'd chosen to sell dusty old books instead of lecturing at a university with Makarios or running the country. He couldn't pay her a fortune, regretfully, but she could borrow anything from the second-hand section and help herself to chai while the shop was closed for the siesta.

She'd almost broken his arm off when she'd shaken it in acceptance. She would have done anything, by then, for an escape from the house. The job meant coins in her purse and a stepping stone to some sort of a future, and she loved the way the books smelled. Like dusty school libraries and secret promises. Most of all, it kept her from thinking about Valentina. What she was doing and how she was feeling and whether she was as lonely as Elena. It's the soul of that baby she should be worrying about, her mother would say when she caught her sulking. *And where it's gone.* Although she never said more than that.

They'd adopted a cat, just after Pappa had died. A black and white stray barely bigger than a kitten. They'd named him Panteloni because his paws were a different colour to his legs and he looked like he was wearing trousers. When Valentina bent over to stroke him, her long girlish hair would tickle his back and the cat would purr in satisfaction. He's so silly, she'd exclaim, wrinkling her nose in delight. *Panteloni. A silly name for a silly cat!*

He'd shown up a few weeks after the funeral. They'd been sitting beneath the grapevine talking about Pappa when he'd jumped up onto the table in front of them and demanded to be fed. Valentina had gone inside to fetch a saucer of milk and they'd watched him drink, grateful for the distraction his appearance afforded and for the change in conversation at last. He'd started coming every night after that, and it had been exciting waiting for his little shadow to appear at the top of the driveway. *There he is! There he is!* He was tentative, in the beginning, his movements growing ever bolder as he got to know them. *Look at him jump!* Valentina would squeal. *He's not scared of us at all.*

Even Lenou and Mrs Pavlou got into the spirit of things after a while, wrapping up bits of bones and chicken fat in tea towels and saving them for Panteloni's visit. But then Valentina had said what she had said and the thought of it had spoiled everything.

She'd thought that perhaps Pappa had sent the cat to keep them company, or to let them know that he was OK. Her words had been a comfort at first, but the closer Elena looked into the cat's eyes, the more convinced she became that Pappa was trapped inside him. Panteloni's meows for milk took on a different meaning after that. He wasn't jumping into their laps for a stroke, he was pleading with them to help him. What if his soul is stuck, she'd thought, and couldn't get out?

It had haunted her for months, this idea of her Pappa being caught inside Panteloni, until finally, she'd had enough and shooed the poor thing away. Both Valentina and Lenou had shouted at her for being so mean and her sister had even slapped her across the face, but she didn't care. Better to release poor Pappa from Purgatory, she'd thought, than to have a pet to feed.

It won't last, Mr Aleko warns impatiently. This fragile peace built on lies. She's late to arrive and he's already unpacked the new boxes and drunk three cups of kafe. The fanatical puppet they've put in power in place of President Makarios is going to say the wrong thing to the wrong person at any moment and Turkey will invade us. *Mark my words.* He was right, of course, like he was right about everything political, and three weeks into July there's a sudden burst of war, like fire from a cannon, and it sends her mother into a fit of hysteria.

It's swelteringly hot, even in the late afternoon, and she seeks temporary relief in the shadows of the olive trees by the school as she walks backs from the bus stop. The neighbouring houses swim in the haze of the heat and she thinks of Andoni in his khaki green uniform. Marching around with his gun like he'd always dreamed and dying to be a hero.

When she arrives home, her mother is pacing around nervously, fiddling with her cross.

You're going to wear it out, and then what?

Have you heard?

Of course, you think Aleko talks about anything else?

Elena takes her sandals off and wipes the sand from the bottoms of her feet.

What are we going to do, Elena?

She pushes past her mother and lowers her head into the kitchen sink, turning the tap on and allowing the cold water to work the dust from her hair and the back of her neck and soothe her burning scalp. Lenou hands her a towel and hovers around her like a fruit fly and Elena trips over her feet. *What are we going to do?*

She suggests they eat the gliko she's spent months making for this very moment and Lenou nods like an obedient child waiting to be led to her mother. She fetches a little pot of karydaki from the cupboard and twists the lid off it. She spoons a walnut onto each of their plates and they eat the sticky sweet with their fingers beneath the vine, while their island goes to war.

~

The fighting ends almost as soon as it begins. A new government is hastily assembled in place of the old one and Mr Aleko tells her to think of the reprieve as a stay of execution. There will be another war, he warns her, and this one will have consequences. It's only a matter of time.

He says the same thing to the customers who come in to buy books for the new school year, popping up behind them and frightening them half to death with his ominous predictions while they browse the shelves for maps. Why bother? he says, as he hands them their packages, when they'll all need new maps in a few months anyway? Thank God that he's been blessed with four daughters as he'd be crying right now for his sons. Those with sons are crying and the rest avoid his business.

He's glad of the peace, he tells her. The fewer idiots

he has to talk to the better. He turns the radio up so he can discredit the pundits. Extolling the merits of Clerides? Where, he asks her, did these so-called experts acquire their qualifications, because a mosquito could make more intelligent statements. Here they all were, thanking their lucky stars and barbecuing pigs in celebration while the typewriters were glowing red-hot in Ankara.

She relates these things to her mother when she returns home from work. Lenou chews the inside of her cheek, her brown eyes darting from side to side, as she takes it all in. The man, she tells her, is always right, it's almost uncanny how right he is and perhaps it is time for her to go. *Go?* Go somewhere safe. Go to the only other place besides Cyprus her mother knew existed. London. Better than staying here, eating walnut jam and waiting for the Turks to kick down the door and do God knows what to them. She's already lost one daughter, she cries, and she's not losing the other one too.

Elena's heart begins to knock in her chest at the thought of seeing Valentina again. The war of the lambs, she thinks, has suddenly become the gateway to her long-awaited freedom.

Chapter 41

Cyprus – 1961

HE MEETS MARIA at Kyrenia Castle. Between the crumbling walls of the old Venetian fortress. A fitting place, she thinks, for a secret rendezvous. He takes her by the hand and leads her to an alcove so they can sit together in the shadows and watch the suntanned fishermen in the harbour toiling with their nets. The blue sea extends for miles before them and she sighs as the salty air fills her lungs and revives her soul. There is so much beauty to behold that she's not sure she'll be able to leave it all behind. Think of it as an exchange, he tells her. The island for her freedom.

She'd been terrified, that first night, that her husband would suspect something. That his lingering scent would give her away or that Mrs Kouli would knock on her door at the wrong moment to gossip about the mysterious handsome stranger who had spent the afternoon with her. She'd scoured the kitchen for things he might have dropped, parts of himself he might have left behind to inadvertently incriminate her. His worry beads, an initialled pen, a handkerchief which smelled of his aftershave.

He'd prowled around behind her like a lion stalking meat when he'd returned home from work. Why was she so nervous, what had she been doing all day and where was his son? His questions made her jump and her heart knocked furiously against the buttons of her dress.

Costa is in his room, she'd replied, working on the Sahara, and as for her, she'd spent the day sweeping sand from every nook and cranny in the house. So much sand, she'd joked, that she could fill Costa's desert twice over and wouldn't that impress his teacher? She'd washed laundry in the clay pot outside after lunch and she'd hung it out to dry beneath the scorching sun and it was a wonder that it hadn't burned holes in the bed sheets it was that hot. She'd walked around the kitchen banging pots and pans together with great alacrity, hoping to convince him of her whereabouts through excess noise and embellished detail.

He'd silenced her with a flick of his hand but she could tell he was far from convinced. The tone of her voice, she'd thought, must be betraying her. Like it did the day her mother had come to visit. It had been a year or so after their wedding and she'd already endured many beatings, but she was desperate to maintain a semblance of happiness and she'd practically squealed into her kafe. Her mother had guessed, of course, and there had been marks on her arms and a bruise around her eye to attest to Michali's temper, but she'd talked so quickly, and with such forced excitement, that alluding to anything being wrong would have been embarrassing for the both of them.

She'd poured him an ouzo then, to calm her own nerves more than his, and she'd unwrapped the louka-nika and dropped them into her pan in the hope that the sizzling sausages and the smell of spicy pork would lift his spirits. Were they millionaires, he'd growled, eating overpriced sausages on a Wednesday night when there were perfectly good chickens in the garden? And she'd lied for an easy life and told him that Mrs Kouli had given them to her in return for a loaf of fresh bread. The words had flown out of her mouth before she'd had the chance to stop them and she'd regretted it instantly because another lie meant another person caught in their web of deceit and why would Mrs Kouli swap a bag of expensive loukanika for a loaf of bread which had cost a bean to make?

He'd watched her for hours, it had seemed like, until his eyelids had grown heavy with the boredom and the drink and he'd gone outside into the yard to smoke his cigar. She'd rubbed at her chest and reduced the heat beneath the pan and wondered if she'd ever make it to fifty with all the stress, but then Mr Styliano had come to mind. Mr Styliano with the big strong hands and honey-coloured eyes, and the beginnings of happiness had stirred within her. How lovely, she'd thought, as she'd fingered the bruises on her arms, to wake up every day and feel like this and she'd resolved, then, to hear the man out. There was no crime in listening.

He tells her things about Michali as they stare out to

sea. Things she didn't know. He owes money, he tells her, to some nasty people. Enough money that he would want to leave and never come back and the pieces begin to fit together like a child's puzzle. His reason for leaving, self-preservation and not a political mission. *So you see*, he continues, *his disappearance would come as no great surprise.* A man like Michali could vanish for any number of reasons and none of those, he points out, would lead back to her. *None.*

These people, she asks hesitantly, that he's in debt to, could they be capable of the unthinkable? Anyone is capable of unspeakable things if they really put their minds to it. Absolutely anyone, he replies. He pulls out his worry beads and twirls them around his fingers. *I think I understand now, Mr Styliano.* She doesn't want him to say any more. At least, not out loud. She looks down at her wedding ring, wedged into her skin like a stamp of ownership, and wonders if it would come off with a drop of olive oil.

He asks her about the well in her backyard and whether she still uses it and she tells him they boarded it up when the water came like everybody else. What would be of real interest to him, he whispers, is how deep the thing was, perhaps she could take a look and let him know the next time, and her heart soars like a balloon on a summer's day at the thought of seeing him again. Next time. She guesses it is fifty feet deep, maybe even more, but she'll pull the boards off the top and try to measure it somehow and she'll be sure to let him know. He brings his finger to his lips and smiles

and the lapping of the waves against the sea shore fills
the silence which falls between them.

~

She's careful to get back from the castle before Costa
arrives home from school. She changes out of her best
dress, wipes the lipstick from her face on the back of
her hand and ties her apron around her waist. She even
has time to fry the child a pita and let it soak in a bowl
of syrup so he has something nice to eat when he gets
in.

   She waits for him by the front door and waves enthusiastically when she sees him coming round the corner
like it's a normal day. She plants a kiss on both of his
cheeks and she sits with him at the kitchen table and
asks him about his classes and his project on the desert
and if she continues to do the things she's always done,
she thinks, she might still suppress the feelings
exploding within her.

   He's telling her about dust storms. Huge great
swirling things that can suffocate you in an instant and
she gets up from her chair, suddenly unable to breathe
herself. She leaves him to his melopita and walks into
the yard, rubbing at her neck. A normal day, despite
the sound of her heart knocking against her chest. She
picks up feathers from the ground and wanders over
to the well and fingers the little wooden bucket perched
on the top of it and then she carefully removes the
heavy planks from its mouth, one by one, because it's

an ordinary day just like he said and here she is, doing something quite ordinary. Although she does turn around to make sure Mrs Kouli isn't spying from her back door. What are you doing, Mrs Petrakis?

What is she doing, indeed? That is the question. She picks up the bucket by the rope tied to the handle and she lowers it slowly into the exposed well. Down and down it goes. Everyone has a secret if you dig deep enough. She wonders what else she doesn't know about her husband, about people in general. You see them walking here and there but you never really know what's going on inside the mind of another. Down, down, down. The bucket hits the bottom with a soft thud just before the rope runs out. Maria leans over as far as she can and comes face to face with the darkness.

Chapter 42

London – 1986

A SUNDAY MORNING in July. Elena marks the date in the calendar by the kitchen sink. A circle in bold black ink. A circle so black and bold, in fact, that it stands out in their now too-white kitchen and hurts her eyes. She writes herself little notes on sticky bits of paper and leaves them all over the house. She puts them on the fridge and the walls and shelves, and anywhere else Magda can't reach. The notes remind her to do things, to clean things, to buy things and to collect Nina from school when Costa is working late. Some of the notes have addresses and numbers on them. The address for the school and the office where Costa works and the number for Petrakis Bakery. *Just in case*, he says.

He's taken the girls to the park so she can enjoy a few hours of peace and quiet. She makes herself a chai and opens the back door to stare dreamily at the apple tree as she sips, envious of its ability to adapt to the seasons and withstand its burdens gracefully. She wishes they could swap places, her and the tree. She could stand outside in the garden with her arms in the air, obediently bearing fruit and shedding her leaves, while the tree came inside and lived in her mind.

It's a beautiful warm day. The English summer, pleasing rather than punishing. She leaves the back door open so she can hear the leaves rustling in the breeze. She pads up the stairs in her dressing gown and slippers and pushes open the bedroom doors, making the children's beds and putting their toys and books back into their boxes in an effort to tidy them away. How lovely to have children when they are not here. When they are just a nice idea floating around in her imagination.

She runs herself a bath. She sits on the edge of the tub and stirs the hot soapy water with her fingers, waiting for it to fill almost to the brim so it can better support her weight. She loves these mornings when nobody is home. When she doesn't have a million things to do and a million places to be. When she can escape from expectation and float in the bath like the pad of a lily.

She steps out of her robe and sinks into the hot water. A sigh of relief. The bath cream smells of jasmine and she thinks of Valentina, stepping out of his car into their old school playground and into a life she didn't deserve. *She deserved it all right,* her mother had cried. *There is always someone to blame.* She can feel her muscles melting into the bubbles and the distant sound of tweeting birds has a welcome soporific effect. She closes her eyes and remembers a time when it had all been going so well. When the flowers had poked their heads out from beneath the soil in response to the warmth and she'd thought there might be a chance that her life could start over again.

She's almost asleep when she notices them. The scratches. Three on her right arm and two on her left and one just by her calf. They're long and deep and when she touches them, they feel sore and tender. Where did they come from, all these scratches? She sees him clearly then. Andoni Pavlou. He's standing by a cactus plant and he's telling her that she's pretty, the second prettiest in their class after Nicoletta Nicodemou. He wants to kiss her but she's shouting at him to let her go. He puts his arms up in the air and he looks confused, and the pain of it, the pain of hurting him like that, makes her cry. Suddenly, there are bullets. Three of them. They're fired from the house with the white and gold railings and they strike him through the chest, one after the other. He falls to the ground and he tries to get up again, to run away from the gunfire, but his jacket has become impaled, somehow, in the spikes of the cactus and there is blood running out of his mouth and his nose, and he starts to scream. She screams, too, with the fear of what she's just seen and what is about to happen to Andoni Pavlou. The noise is deafening and when Costa wakes her up she's sitting in a bath full of cold water and half drowning in her tears.

There is something important that she has to do today, she tells him. She has to deliver a letter. *Will you help me?* He lifts her out of the tub as if she were a small

child and he wraps her in a soft fluffy towel. *Wait here.*
He leaves her sitting on the bathroom floor shivering,
her hair dripping with soapy water, and wondering
what day it is because the calendar is downstairs and
things slip from her mind if they are not written down
and presented to her like a slap. She can hear him
ushering the girls into the kitchen and pouring them
each a glass of milk. Cupboard doors open and close
and Nina is casually asking after her and she wants to
know why they could hear screaming when they
arrived home from the park and she feels sad, for a
while. For an instant really, and then the feeling that
she should be a better mother to them swirls down the
plughole with the last of the soapy water.

She can hear him running back up the stairs and she
smiles at a comment Maria once made. How did Costa
manage to stay fat while burning off all that energy?
Her smile turns into a laugh and before she can help
herself she's shaking hysterically on his shoulder and
the look on his face is priceless. He should stand in the
mirror, she tells him, and see the priceless look on his
face because he seems so frightened and he picks her
up and carries her into the bedroom because she's
laughing so hard that she can hardly walk and he lowers
her onto the bed and tells her that she should get some
rest. *For goodness' sake, Costa!* She doesn't want to rest
and there is no need to stare at her like that.

Fear. He's afraid of her, and she misses her suddenly.
There's an ache in her heart where her sister should be
and she gets up from the bed and tosses the wet towel

onto the floor and flings open the wardrobe door with
such force that she almost takes it off its hinges. She's
looking for a pair of jeans to wear, she tells him,
because she's going to go and see her right now. It's
been far too long and she can't even remember why
they stopped talking to one another but somebody has
to put a stop to the madness and she guesses it's her
responsibility.

Six years. It's been six years since she last saw her and
today is not the day for it, or so he claims, and the truth
of it is she doesn't believe him because half of the things
he tells her these days don't make any sense. Like why
she can't take care of the girls on her own, and why
Maria comes round to see Magda every morning and
why Valentina hates her. The baby, he tells her. It's to
do with the baby, but she doesn't remember which baby
as there have been three babies over the years. Three
babies, she tells him, and a letter, and one very terrible
mistake.

Chapter 43

London – 1980

AUTUMN. ELENA RUBS her swollen belly, billowing out beneath her pale pink dress, and stares gloomily out of the window of their front room. All around her, it seems, is death. Brown leaves fall aimlessly from the trees outside, whispering ominously to her on their way down. Like little graves, she thinks. Littering the pavements. She points this out to Maria who is sitting on the sofa opposite her eating tahini cake and dropping crumbs into her lap. The leaves on the ground look like graves, she tells her, doesn't she think? And Maria raises her eyebrows in confusion.

Tahini cakes are my favourite. Costa hates them, she tells Elena. He says they taste like sand. Truth be told, it was a relief to finally discover something the boy didn't want to eat. Elena had forgiven him, of course. After a while. It was hard to stay angry at someone you lived with, walking past them every day, sharing a bathroom sink, bearing a grudge. It was more Valentina's style than hers. He'd apologised profusely and then, once the dust had settled, he'd blamed Valentina. Her reaction to their news was bordering on hysterical, he'd said, but then again, what did he expect from a woman like her sister?

It was the way she'd found out, she'd screamed at Elena. From Taki of all people. A careless, clumsy word in the street, as if Costa was announcing the time of day or talking about the football. *How fucking insensitive.* She'd refused to let her speak, blocked her every attempt; she didn't care to listen to her defending herself. Elena had called back, many times, but she'd persisted in her rancour and after a while she'd been too afraid to go anywhere near the phone and so the days had turned into weeks and the weeks into months and here she was with a big rounded belly and still no word from her sister.

She felt sorry for her, Valentina had said finally. Elena had had the life sucked out of her just like she had and they were no different. Not really. *I wish only good things for you, Elena, I really do,* only she didn't, of course. It was the very last thing she wished on her and Elena had been heartbroken. It was like losing her all over again.

The colour is draining out of the world in preparation for the winter and the arrival of the child. Did she know, Maria says, that she'd given birth to Costa beneath the almond tree in their backyard at home? She'd pulled her underwear down to her ankles and waited for the midwife to appear on the back of the Mrs Kouli's son's bicycle. She wondered if the pushes were going to kill her before she got there because the agony of it was truly unbearable, like being pulled apart. *How far can a person go before they snap,* she asks her. *Do you know?* She'd certainly found out that day.

Then, of course, Maria continues, there was the perennial problem of the milk. Not like nowadays, she tells her, when you can buy powders in tins; then, you had to hope your milk came through or the poor child would starve to death. Mrs Kemal had taken her baby to a local woman who had given birth to her own child only days before and she'd fed the hungry little mite for her. Imagine that, she tells Elena, as she finishes the last of her cake and noisily slurps her tea. Another woman feeding your child in front of you?

She's changed, Maria thinks. In the past few months. She's not happy, anyone can see that, but there's something else. It's as if a light has gone out from behind her eyes. *This about your sister?* He'd asked her not to talk about it, when he'd summoned her to the house to sit with Elena. Cheer her up, talk about anything but the bloody sister, and yet here she was, unable to resist because it was as plain as the tahinopita crumbs at the sides of her mouth that the girl was aching for her. Someone of a similar age to delight in the pregnancy news, shop for things for the baby. She didn't want to sit with an old lady and hear horror stories about starving infants and placentas wrapped around trees.

It's normal, she tells her, to be missing her and especially at a time like this. *It's not just that.* She's not ready to be a mother, Elena explains, and she fears she's made a dreadful mistake and Maria laughs, then, *because, my darling, who does feel ready?* Did she think a woman got up one morning and decided she wanted to put her life on hold and have a baby and then worry herself senseless for the next twenty years and that's if she's lucky? Motherhood comes naturally, she tells her, like the gradual blossoming of a flower. Costa was tiny when he was born, although you wouldn't think it now. She chuckles. A little red bundle and there physically wasn't very much to love. Not at first.

He'd come early, and Michali had blamed her for it, of course. She couldn't sit still for a minute, he'd shouted, always fussing over this and that and it was no wonder that the child had arrived prematurely with all the bending and lifting. It's the first time, Elena thinks, that she's mentioned her husband and she lets the curtain drop back to its former position so she can turn around and face her.

He doesn't sound very nice, Costa's father.

He wasn't. And there was plenty more besides.

Costa had let it slip once. That his father used to beat his mother, and she'd been broken-hearted at the thought of anyone hurting the mighty Maria. She belonged in her bakery, surrounded by cakes that smelled of cinnamon and brought joy to people's lives. She was someone to be exalted, not beaten and humiliated. *How awful.* She doesn't want to talk about it, she replies, it was a sorry situation which she righted many years ago but the point is that Elena will love her child regardless of how gloomy she's feeling now and, furthermore, she will do anything to protect them from harm.

Chapter 44

Cyprus – 1961

OCTOBER IN KYRENIA, and a stay from the exhausting summer inferno. The weather has turned and the evenings, mercifully, are cooler. They've arrived. He proudly arranges them on the table in front of him. His gold bullion. British passports. She reaches out to touch one, but he slaps angrily at her hand. He slides the passports back towards him and shuffles them like playing cards before slipping them into the pocket of his shirt. His actions are taunting, slow and deliberate. Maria shrugs her shoulders and does her best to appear uninterested. *Please yourself.*

He pulls his thin grey hair out of his face and leans back in his chair, daring her to take the bait. He hasn't hit her in ages. Those long dirty fingernails must be itching to tear at her skin, to gouge at an eye and then claim ownership of it. Gazing at her injuries from behind shadowy doorways like a pervert admiring the pain he's inflicted. *I did that.*

She gets up and goes back to her stove and carries on stirring the trahana soup. She wonders what Mr Styliano will be eating this evening. Perhaps she'll put some of the soup aside and take it to him tomorrow. It would be a shame to waste it all on Michali. *What are you smirking at?* Maria walks over to the fridge and peers inside, looking for halloumi. The soup on its own is too insubstantial and won't touch the hungry sides. She's thinking about his farewell gathering at the base, she replies. It will be a big party, no doubt. Perhaps he should sleep the alcohol off in the back seat of the car afterwards. She wouldn't want him getting stopped by the British on his way home and imprisoned for driving whilst inebriated. *The British are strict about these things, not like us Cypriots, hah?* The last thing he would want, she thinks, is a delay to his escape.

Maybe I will, maybe I won't. She straightens herself and grabs two bowls and a couple of spoons from the cupboard to ladle the trahana into. She places Michali's in front of him, a master feeding an angry dog and needing to remove her fingers from the vicinity of his mouth as quickly as possible. She unties her apron from around her waist and sits down opposite him at the table in the kitchen. His hair is almost hanging into his soup as he bends over to blow at it. They slurp their meal in silence. There's always time, she thinks. Time to unspeak things spoken in dark shadowy places. Wheels set into motion can be halted.

You look old. Or then again, maybe not. Men, he sneers, grow old with grace and style. Their ageing faces commanding authority and respect, but once a woman loses her youth and beauty she has nothing but creases and wrinkles. *Like you!* He's pleased to have found another weapon, another way to hurt her.

Some men grow old better than others. Maria dabs at the corners of her mouth with a tea towel. *Like Mr Styliano, for an example.* Michali glances up from his spoon. His dark eyes fixing her beneath the unconvincing lights of the kitchen. Mr Styliano, he retorts, doesn't have a wife henpecking him to death. *Peck, peck.* He can come and go as he pleases, free as an eagle soaring in the sky. He dances to his own tune. He's hardly at work these past months, always needing to be somewhere else. How nice for life's bosses and managers. The same the world over. *Oh?* she asks. What did she care, he wonders aloud, about the comings and goings of Mr Styliano? She couldn't give a damn, she replies. Merely making conversation over the soup.

Costa meanders into the kitchen in his pyjamas and bare feet foraging for food, his belly protruding over his waistband and his unruly dark hair half covering his eyes. Michali jabs at him roughly in the stomach. He's getting fat and unkempt! The boy's eyes grow wide with hurt and the colour of his cheeks deepens and Maria tactically changes the subject. She fills a bowl of soup for Costa and asks Michali about London.

Tell us, she implores, *about this bakery we are supposedly buying.* She can't imagine that they will leave the airport and walk into a bakery that's for sale.

Of course, he can't help but brag, but they are to wait obediently until he finishes his soup and pushes his bowl away. Michali, leaning back in his chair and fiddling with his toothpick. The end of dinner. It's easy enough, he says, waving his stick in the air. When you know somebody who is selling one. A relative of a friend of a colleague and he even has a telephone number for the owner in London. The shop, he says, has a flat above it with two bedrooms – what could be more fortuitous? What indeed? And she congratulates him, then, on being so very clever and resourceful. Very organised and he really has excelled himself this time, she tells him. He really has excelled himself.

~

There is always a final straw. The moment that changes everything. It should have come right after they were married, when he'd charged over to her like an angry bull and hit her in the face while she was daydreaming about her new life by the well. That should have been the end of it. It should have been, but it wasn't, and there were so many opportunities to leave after that but somehow she'd stayed because the idea of running away terrified her more than being beaten half to death. She'd learned to hide the bruises over time, with sleeves and face powders and long dresses and a loud, high-pitched voice which could only stem from a happy place.

Did the neighbours know he beat her? Probably, but people had their own troubles and after a while even they'd grown inured to the wailing and screaming from behind closed shutters. Times were tough and her domestic issues were not their problem to resolve.

Everybody has their breaking point, though, and yesterday, when he'd insisted they exhume Katerina so they could bury her all over again in London, England, he'd found hers. After all the years and everything she'd endured, it was this that had tipped the balance. Finally, the last straw, and Maria had placed her head on Mr Styliano's shoulder as they sat between the curved walls of the fortress and she'd whispered dark things into his ear and the thing was done.

He returns to the house one last time. He is looking for something by the well in the backyard. She watches him circle it like a bird of prey, his head bowed and his worry beads threaded between his fingers while she stands at the kitchen sink and washes okra for lunch. He moves slowly, deliberately, stopping at one point to place his large outstretched palms on the grey stones and push his weight against them, his back flexing with the effort. When he's found what he's been searching for, he comes back inside and wipes his feet on the mat by the door. She moves away from the sink so he can rinse the dirt from his hands beneath the cool running water and she pulls the plug afterwards to get rid of the stains as he searches her eyes for doubt.

He suggests that she go away, the night of the party. Perhaps she and Costa could stay with a friend and she thinks it's a good idea. It's been over a year since she's seen her sister, Thora, she tells him and it would be nice to catch up with her. Costa, especially, would enjoy playing with his cousins. A welcome distraction. He stands behind her and she can feel his warm breath on the back of her long exposed neck. The sound of his worry beads clicking in his hand punctuate the silence. She should come home the following afternoon and report her husband missing. The okra, she tells him, is especially fresh; she bought it this morning from Pampo in town and she would very much like it if he stayed for a bite to eat. She puts it into a pot along with potatoes and tomatoes and leaves the stew to simmer. He tells her he can stay a while and they sip hot sweet coffee at the kitchen table and talk about the future while the smell of okra and onions wafts around the room.

You found your bakery? She's already in touch with the owner, she explains proudly. In London. She even has an appointment to go and see the place when they get there. He makes her promise, then, to buy a blue and white sign for the front of the shop so the world knows that she is a true patriot and she laughs at this allusion to her tablecloth and the night they first met and promises him that she will. *Well, I hope you will be very happy, Mrs Petrakis, running your bakery in London. Truly, I do.*

There's another promise he wants her to make. The last one. He insists that she never speak of him to anyone or try to contact him again. And, of course, he didn't really know Michali. He was just another employee at the base, one in a line of many, a fool indebted to some dangerous men. She tells him that she knows just what to say and that she will think of him often and most probably for the rest of her life. They kiss passionately for the first time, but when he leans across to pull her towards him she stops him. She doesn't want it to be about that. It would change everything. Taint it. He understands, he says, and his restraint stings her heart.

He stays until it is almost time for Costa to return from school and when he finally gets up to leave she's already missing him. He pulls her close and whispers in her ear. *Board it up properly, Mrs Petrakis, before you sell the house.* And the weeds can grow as high and as thick as they like. It's dangerous, otherwise. For children. He kisses her again and tells her that he will think of her often in her bakery in London, England.

Thank you, Mr Styliano. He tells her that it's an honour to help a woman such as herself. The mighty Maria Petrakis, he calls her, and she smiles at the accolade. She will adopt the title from now on. She will be Maria the Mighty.

She stands by the front door for a long while after he has driven away. The sky is changing colour and she rubs at her arms to ward off a chill. People turn on the lights in their front rooms and prepare for late afternoon and the smell of food mingles with a distant laughter.

Chapter 45

London – 1987

THE GIRLS CHASE a blue butterfly around the back garden with a watering can, squealing with pleasure as they watch it dance from flower to flower, eluding them. A Valentina-shaped butterfly, dropping in only when it suited her.

Elena watches from behind the open kitchen door, hugging her mug, worried that if she lets it go, even for a second, she'll have nothing else to be present for. She's envious of her daughters' ignorance, their ability to experience joy. Strange, really, to think that these tall, alien children with the spindly legs and jagged elbows protruding from fluorescent summer clothes once belonged inside her.

She drinks the last of her coffee. She yawns and puts the kettle on to make herself another, the jisveh long abandoned as inconvenient. She's wearing her night clothes and scoffs at the irony. It's been years since she slept. Years and years. Since the dreams began spooling behind her eyelids like a terrible film. But there's something else now. A ghost. The ghost of a little girl whose name she can no longer remember. She first met her in a photograph and she's come and gone since but she's here now. Standing beside her while she waits for the kettle to boil and hissing in her ear.

Maria used to have a customer who claimed she could see ghosts. Her name was Mrs Louca. She would come into the bakery to buy tiropites and she'd tell Maria that they were following her. They're here, she would say, looking furtively over her shoulder. They'd taken the bus down with her. *This one likes daktyla and that one likes bourekia and they don't leave me alone for a second!*

When she'd gone, Maria would wink at Elena and ask Mrs Louca's ghosts if they wanted to stay a while and drink tea. The bourekia are fresh, she would chuckle. Please pull up a chair, you can take a later bus home. They would giggle for hours, then, knowing that they shouldn't. Eventually, Mrs Louca's heart gave in and she went off to join her spirits. Poor Mrs Louca and her haunt of hungry ghosts.

Elena's ghost is different. It doesn't follow her around the shops looking for tea. It exists in the margins of her life. In the shadowy spaces in her head. In the pit of her stomach. Some days it even makes her afraid of residing inside her own skin. Leave me alone, she says to her when nobody is around. Leave me alone, I know who you are.

Then there are the early mornings when she's standing alone by the kitchen door, watching the sun rise over the apple tree as her family stirs upstairs, and wondering, in those sad, solitary moments, if it is she who is the ghost. The shrill of Costa's alarm clock, the floorboards creaking with the weight of him as he pads towards the girls' rooms and shouts at them to get out of bed and get ready for school. Costa, inured to his responsibilities.

Muffled, girlish voices added to the cacophony of running taps and banging doors, their laughter growing louder and louder as they bounce down the stairs in unconstrained excitement. The three of them together, off to live another day, oblivious to her whereabouts.

Time is no longer an accurate delineator of her days. Dreams fill her waking moments and waking moments fill her nights and if she was being truthful she would admit that reality was no longer a truth. *Are you sick, Mamma?* Nina had asked this yesterday and Costa had answered for her and she'd cried, then, because first there was the gloom and then the unhappiness and now, she thinks, now he's taken away her voice and left her with nothing but terrifying shadows.

The doorbell rings and interrupts her jumbled thoughts. A loud insistent ringing followed by knocking. *Are you there?* She places her cup back down on the counter and waits for it to stop. *Are you there?* The knocking intensifies and she walks over to the door and opens it an inch at a time. She must have fallen asleep, she thinks. In the kitchen just now, listening to the sound of the girls' laughter. She can't be real. She can't be standing on the doorstep after all these years.

~

Well, aren't you going to ask me in?

She looks older. Of course she does, she thinks, it's been years. Too many to count. There are creases etched around her eyes, at the corners of her mouth. She's cut her hair short and Elena gasps at the incongruity of it. Valentina, with no hair. What did she do with it? she wonders. All that thick shiny hair?

She forces her way in and barks at her to close the door. She stands facing her in the hallway, her hands on her hips and her sticky red lips pursed into a scratch. *Your hair.* Valentina laughs at her then. Never mind the hair.

She has a horrible laugh, Elena thinks. Loud and cruel, like the cackle of a beautiful witch. It's a wonder she's never noticed it before, all those years of living together. *We need to talk.* Of course they do, it's been so long. She asks her if she wants to sit down. She can put the kettle on and make chai or coffee. Does she remember teasing her about it at Maria's flat? Since when did her sister drink coffee like an American? she'd joked. Those were good days. The only good days, really, if she's honest. There haven't been that many since. She can meet her daughters, if she'd like? They're in the garden and Elena would enjoy introducing them. They didn't hear the bell or Nina would be here now, peering curiously at her from behind her big bush of bouncy curls.

Valentina's wide black eyes stop her in her tracks and Elena tightens her dressing gown around her waist. Perhaps today is not the day to introduce her to her daughters, although she's glad she came all the same. Someone had to make the first move, Costa used to say, and Valentina slaps her hard across the cheek.

The first move.

The letter, she begins. All these years and she's been lying to her because she didn't deliver it at all. Elena's hand flies to her stinging cheek in hurt and confusion. *What did you do that for?* The envelope she was supposed to deliver with Andoni Pavlou. She knows that Elena is lying about everything because he'd called her, he'd finally called, and do you know what he said? *Who?* The father, she shrieks. The father of the baby. Little spots of spittle appear at the corners of her lips and remind Elena of the lemon-flavoured arguments they used to have with their mother. His wife had confessed that a young man had slipped a note beneath their door and he'd had no idea that she was pregnant because she hadn't handed him the letter like she'd promised. The wife had kept the news to herself.

The malevolent swan, Elena thinks. Cutting through the frozen water with a pair of shiny diamonds. Does she realise what she's done? Valentina tells her that she killed her own baby. A dagger to Elena's stomach. Thick black blood sliding out of her side and filling her sister's empty bassinet. Taki, she cries, didn't want a bastard and neither did his bitch of a mother, but they'd waited until after the wedding to tell her so that she would be well and truly trapped. He'd given her an ultimatum. Abortion or divorce after three weeks of marriage and do you realise, she asks, what that would have meant?

The scandal of a divorce after a few short weeks. *What would she have said then, our darling mother that you love so much?* Did Elena know? Because Valentina does. A putana, she would have screamed. She would have called her a whore and so she'd waited until the last possible moment for the father to rescue her. All the while feeling her growing bigger and bigger and tickling her insides and when no word came from the one person who could have saved her, she did as he bid. At the end of the day, what choice did she have? What choices had she ever had?

I killed my own child, Elena. Only I didn't kill her, did I? You did!

She has blood on her hands and it won't come out with a bit of hot soapy water and it's far too late for sorry. She pulls at her short hair and in that moment Elena can see Mrs Pavlou, moaning in agony until there were no more tears left inside her. Does Valentina know, she wonders, that Andoni Pavlou died in the war? They found his body beneath the brush, blackened by the sun. Such a shame, someone had once said to her, but at least he'd been wearing his tags and it had really hurt her to imagine it. The great life that was Andoni Pavlou, lying dead in the dust.

Elena wonders if her sister might strike her again but she sees in her eyes that she's afraid of something and it's the same look she saw on Costa's face the day she passed out in the bath. He puts his arms around her again and drags her into the kitchen.

Get out, he's shouting. Valentina tells him to fuck off,

he doesn't know what he's talking about. *You've no idea what she's done!* The voices are accusatory and distant, like the memory of the scratches on her arms and the house with the white and gold railings perched peremptorily at the top of an imaginary hill. He'd called her a wild cat, Dimitri had said. Why would he say something like that when she had loved him, despite herself, for all those years?

Elena is sick, he says. She's not been well for a long time and any fool can see that. *Take your dirty laundry and get out of my house.* She's glad he came running down the stairs when he did, her knight in shining armour. Just like that first night when she'd been worried about her mother and the war, and he'd put his arm around her shoulder and stroked her hair. She'd only married him because she was lonely. Silly, really. To marry someone she hardly knew because she'd hated living with her sister.

She should have married Andoni Pavlou and hidden his black shiny boots so he couldn't go to war. *Oh she's sick all right. And so am I.* Someone is laughing again. Apples and trees, she is saying. *The apple doesn't fall far from the tree, hah, Costa?* She laughs and laughs and then there's crying, a terrible high-pitched cry, like the sound of an animal being tortured to its death. He's always liked to save people, her Costa. He was such a good man and she really didn't deserve him.

Chapter 46

London – 1961

MARIA IS STANDING by the window watching the English rain come down in sheets. She has never seen so much water, it's as if God means to drown the world. She pulls the navy blue cardigan she's borrowed from Mrs Iacovou's lost property drawer tightly around her shoulders and shivers. Her own clothes, it seems, too insubstantial for the climate. For the first time in her life, the winter cold cuts her to the core.

She is renting a small cheap room on the third floor of Mrs Iacovou's house, on a road called Elgar near Green Lanes in Harringay. A long colourful road, full of Greek Cypriot bakalies selling fruit and vegetables and fish and meat and there's even the type of kafeneon that Michali used to frequent back home. He was right, she thinks, about there being a little community of Greeks in north London and she's relieved that she can blend seamlessly into her carefully chosen setting without eliciting attention.

The room is the least expensive place she could find at short notice. The house itself is falling apart. There is black mould growing on the walls and ceilings and the windowsills crumble to the touch. The pernicious smell of damp hangs in the air and pervades the dark red curtains and the stained green carpets and there is barely enough space in her room for their two beds. Her bed and Costa's.

At night, Maria pulls her scratchy blankets over her head and tosses and turns uncomfortably as the pointed springs dig into her hips and the cold draught makes her tremble. The angry sound of cars and buses rushing up and down the nearby high street keeps her awake. So much noise on a road which never sleeps and, despite all this, she has never been happier.

The landlady is a tall frail woman in her early sixties who lost her husband to cancer a decade earlier. Her black hair is thinning at the front and her teeth are held together by decay. She's partial to a drink after dark. At night, once Costa has gone up to bed, Mrs Iacovou winks at her and takes a rusty key out of her apron pocket to unlock the cabinet at the far end of the room. *It's time.* Her movements are slow and deliberate and Maria wonders how many times she has reached for that key over the years. The key as worn as her liver.

Zivania? Her father used to call zivania the truth serum. It's what they deploy in war, he'd joke. To make the enemy talk. *Force some of this down their throats and they'll sell their own children down the river.* Maria can well believe it. A few sips of the clear liquid that sent her father to his grave early and she can feel her jaw loosening and her tongue relaxing in her head. She slumps back in her chair, mesmerised by the spirit and the heat from Mrs Iacovou's crackling fire.

Be careful, he'd said the last time she'd seen him. Be careful who you talk to and what you say. Don't incriminate yourself. It's a novice's mistake. I've done nothing wrong, she'd replied. Exactly. Then there would be nothing to say.

I'm sorry about your husband, Mrs Petrakis.

They sit in armchairs blackened by damp and mould in the front room with the worn green carpets and the television box in the corner. She stares at the fire in front of them and thinks of Mr Styliano. Mrs Iacovou has an ear for a story and more time to fill, it would seem, than rooms. She reads her mind. The house was busy once. People came for a while and then left. On their way to someplace better. Bags were piled high in the passageways and coins filled the tins in Mrs Iacovou's cupboards. Now it's rare she'll take in a lodger: the mortgage is paid and the bills are bearable. She's after the company, now, more than anything else.

Someone to drink with and the tales they tell, she tuts. You've never heard such things. She leans in close, turns her glass around in front of her wrinkled face. Another woman, perhaps? *I think so, Mrs Iacovou, but who knows?* Mrs Iacovou smiles and bares her camel-like teeth. Men want one thing, she laments, and if you don't give it to them they will find a woman who will. Maria agrees and wishes her luck, whoever she may be.

He was not an easy man to live with.

Was?

She corrects her mistake, stumbling over her words as she finds new footing and Mrs Iacovou shakes her head sympathetically. She has heard it all over the years. Cheating lovers and much, much, worse. There was once a lodger, she whispers in excitement, who killed his wife and brought her with him in his bags. Her head was in one suitcase and her torso in the other and she should have suspected something wasn't right when he'd insisted on dragging the great big cases up to his room by himself.

She slips her stockinged feet out of her slippers and warms them by the fire. The room had started to stink after a while. Such a terrible smell, like the inside of a person's stomach and then a dark red patch had opened in the ceiling above her like a gash and she'd gone up, she says, and rapped on the bedroom door and asked him if he was all right. There'd been no response. The other guests noticed it too, the foul odour, and after a few days it had become so unbearable that she'd been forced to call the police.

They found his corpse hanging by its neck from the light fixture and the dismembered body of his wife beneath his feet. She can imagine the stench and once you smell rotting flesh you never forget it. Maria declares the story truly terrible. She can feel herself uncoiling after centuries of fear. The flames of the fire flicker around the logs like little forked tongues. Mrs Iacovou places her hand over hers and pats it reassuringly. Men are never easy, she complains, and of course, she and the child can stay as long as they like.

She gets up to pour herself another drink, completely untouched by the first, and she offers to refresh Maria's glass. *I'd better not*, she replies. Or she might be seduced into selling her soul in exchange for the heat and the charm.

She asks why the man had brought his wife with him to the house. Couldn't he have chosen a more suitable place to hide her? A field, a river, a cave? Who knows, says Mrs Iacovou, returning to her chair, why people do things. If there's one thing she has learned over the years it's to stop looking for answers in a world where there are only questions.

Wouldn't you agree, Mrs Petrakis?

Maria couldn't agree with her more.

~

With her large bosoms and tiny feet, Mrs Chrysostomou looks more like a chicken than a shop owner and it's a mystery, Maria thinks, how the woman manages to stay upright. She marches around the bakery with her small head in the air, flapping her arms and clucking under her breath. This changes things, she snaps cantankerously, because what if the foolish husband were to have a change of heart and come running back to her with his tail between his legs and Maria decided halfway through the sale that she didn't want a bakery on Green Lanes after all? No, what she really wanted was to go back to Cyprus and play house with the newly pardoned husband. *Then what, hah?*

Maria nervously fiddles with the buttons of her long black coat and assures Mrs Chrysostomou that Michali is long gone. They parted ways, said their farewells, and the money for the shop is hers to invest entirely. In fact, Michali has already received his share from the sale of their house in Cyprus. He got what was coming to him that's for sure, so Mrs Chrysostomou can rest easy in her bed tonight that there is nobody else to stake a claim on the bakery but her.

Still, it's a bloody inconvenience, Mrs Petrakis. A bloody inconvenience.

According to Mrs Chrysostomou, there are only two types of women. Wives and widows. And a woman who does not fall neatly into these categories is to be regarded with suspicion. She claims she's separated. The husband left her and what does that mean, exactly? Is she married, is she single, is he living down the road from her with a family of his own? How ridiculous! Patience. These things required patience and to bail the minute the boat started leaking seemed to be the fashion. You wouldn't have dared to step out of line when she was a young girl. Wouldn't have dared! Where would she be if she had walked out on Mr Chrysostomou every time they'd exchanged a cross word or argued over the change in weather, or come to blows for that matter?

She tells her this, now, and despite the woman's presumptuousness, Maria knows that a discourteous tone will buy her nothing but a permanent room in Mrs Iacovou's house. She changes tactic and tells Mrs

Chrysostomou that of course, if she'd rather sell to another buyer then she should go ahead because, at the end of the day, it is her business to do as she pleases with, and she knows that there is no other interest because the shop is quieter than an abandoned cemetery and at eleven o'clock on a Saturday morning, that is certainly not good news.

Mrs Chrysostomou follows her gaze and tells a few lies that are emptier than her tills. The truth is, Maria thinks, looking around at the plain white walls and dirty glass counters partially filled with pastries that have seen better days, the woman knows as much about running a bakery as she does about other people's marriages. Absolutely nothing.

Mrs Chrysostomou relents. Life's far too short for the likes of Mrs Petrakis and her misfortune and besides, if she stands around the shop arguing for much longer, her retirement will have been and gone and she'll be just about ready for the grave. She agrees to show Maria the rooms. She opens a door at the back of the shop and leads her up a short staircase culminating in a front room decorated boldly in red and orange colours. Maria runs her fingers along the banister on the way up and thinks that there are three things she would like to do immediately upon taking ownership of the property. Clean the place thoroughly, because God knows it hasn't seen a sponge in years, rename the shop in white and blue letters in honour of Mr Styliano, and learn how to make a pyramid out of kourabiethes to sit in the bakery window. An attractive window display is most definitely what she needs to lure the customers back in.

We have a deal, but if she reunites with the philandering husband and tries to pull out of the sale at the last minute then Heaven help the both of them and Maria promises Mrs Chrysostomou that the next time she'll likely see Michali is when they meet in Hell. Mrs Chrysostomou tuts to herself in disgust and thinks that Greek women are not like they used to be. No wonder the silly woman is in this predicament and couldn't keep her marriage intact.

Chapter 47

London – 1987

FINALLY, A BREAKTHROUGH. Maki has mastered the art of the butter biscuit pyramid, no small feat for a clumsy man with big hands. The pyramid stands proudly in the bakery window and is, therefore, literally and metaphorically speaking, at the centre of Petrakis' fortunes. To attract bees you needed alluring flowers.

Now that he has mastered the pyramid, Maria is one step closer to retirement, or at least retirement as she sees it. She imagines herself sitting at the back of the shop, her feet up on the chair opposite, administering orders over the downturned pages of the local Greek Cypriot newspaper. Of course, she'd have to get up occasionally, to serve the customers who refused to deal with Maki. Mrs Vasili with the faint moustache and Mrs Kyriacou, a tall, fastidious woman with a giant purse who came into the shop every Saturday to buy just one kouba. It may have seemed to an outsider like a paltry spend but Mrs Kyriacou had, in fact, been coming into the bakery since 1968 and if you added up the pennies over the years, the woman was practically a shareholder.

Why, Maki would ask, does she travel all the way
from Finsbury Park on the most laborious bus route
in north London to purchase only one kouba, and she
tells him it's a habit and that he should never underestimate the allure of a ritual.

Take Mrs Solomonides, for instance. Unlike Mrs
Kyriacou, Mrs Solomonides didn't have a preference
for a particular pastry but she would only ever order
three of a kind in a box that was designed for four.
Now why, one might think, did the woman simply not
fill her box and eat the remaining pastry later and the
answer was simple. She had grown accustomed to
doing things in a certain manner and like many of the
others who came into the shop to order the things
they had always ordered, there was no persuading her
otherwise.

Mrs Solomonides had been Maria's first customer.
That very first day in sixty-two, when she'd stood nervously behind the counter pulling at her large silvery-grey
bun and smoothing the creases in her apron and hoping
that her instincts about the business had been trust-
worthy, Mrs Solomonides had poked her head around
the door and asked after Mrs Chrysostomou. Maria had
announced in her most confident voice that she was
now the new owner. *Please, do come in!*

Mrs Solomonides had sighed with relief and crossed
herself three times because the woman, she'd exclaimed,
used to cut more corners than Pythagoras and were
her galatobourekia fresh? As fresh, Maria had replied,
as early-morning dew on grass, and she'd come in then,

and looked tentatively around the shop and noticed that the pastries were colour coordinated in neat sticky columns and that the glass counters were shiny and clean and the place smelled temptingly of rose water and vanilla and she'd nodded in approval and sat down at the table.

Maria had poured her a cup of tea with the new kettle she'd acquired for this very, imagined, scenario and Mrs Solomonides had accepted her offer gratefully and eaten the galatoboureko in front of her and declared it very nice indeed. Better than nice, even. She'd even spoken of her daughter's new baby and her husband's predilection for teenage girls and in that moment, Maria knew that she was fulfilling a calling that had always been waiting for her. Baking joy, selling happiness and offering a sympathetic ear with a nice cup of chai.

Of course, she'd almost expected him to walk into the shop in those early days. Wearing the face she'd glimpse before he struck her. Only this time, he'd have no fingernails to scratch at her with because, he'd shout, he'd had to claw his way out of a long black hole to get to her. She'd be afraid, then, but it was a different sort of fear. A fear of losing her new life and there were no tears for Michali whatsoever. Think of it as a trade, Mr Styliano had said. The island in exchange for her freedom. His life in exchange for hers.

She'd reported him missing the next day just like Mr Styliano had asked. She and Costa had arrived home from Thora's house in Paphos late in the afternoon and they'd put their bags down and she'd looked around

the house and called out to him and she'd declared it
quite strange that he wasn't at home yet. It was all for
the boy's benefit, of course, and she'd waited a few more
hours just to be sure that there was something wrong
and when the light had faded and stars began to appear
in the early night sky, she'd called the police.

They had sent someone round to take down some
details. A tall thin man barely older than a child, with
olive skin and a shaven head and a cap which didn't
quite fit. She'd invited him in and he'd scribbled down
notes. She'd last seen him yesterday morning before
he'd left for work. Yes, she's sure that was the last time.
It was to be his last day at the base and he was planning
to have a few celebratory drinks with his colleagues
last night, although she was expecting him to be at
home today when she returned from her sister's.

Perhaps, the officer volunteered, he was still drunk
and sleeping the ouzo off somewhere else? *Is that likely,
Mrs Petrakis?* And she'd conceded that it was a definite
possibility and she felt silly for worrying and wasting
their time when that was most probably it. She'd call
tomorrow to let them know that he was safe and she'd
be sure to reprimand him for his drinking.

The following afternoon, she'd called the station in
a panic and they assured her they would send someone
down to the base in Nicosia to speak with his super-
visor and she'd hovered nervously by the telephone
just in case they called. A few days later, the same
young man with the too-big cap returned to the house
and told her to send the boy to his room and to sit

herself down because he had learned some troubling information about her missing husband. It appeared that Michali may have left the country entirely of his own accord.

Left the country? They'd spoken with a Mr Styliano, he'd explained, looking down at his notepad, and he'd told them a few interesting things about her husband. Mr Petrakis owed a lot of money to a loan shark named Mr Pericles, a notorious gangster who had even served time in prison for attempting to snap an associate's neck in two. It looked like he may have owed Mr Pericles more money than he could repay and Mr Styliano, and indeed, several other of Mr Petrakis' colleagues, had seen him brandishing a British passport in the days leading up to his disappearance. *So it seems, Mrs Petrakis, you might stand a better chance of seeing your husband again if you looked for him in England,* and after that they'd been as interested in finding him as she was.

She'd conceded to the young police officer that their marriage was on the rocks and had been for a while and she's not sure he would want her to join him, and the young man had yawned disrespectfully in her face because the case was starting to irritate him and he didn't give two figs about the state of Maria's marriage to Michali. She'd thanked him profusely for his time and watched his cap wobble all the way back to his car and she'd closed the door behind him and told Costa that it would all be OK. *You'll see.* His life, she'd thought, would be infinitely happier without his father in it. At the very least his mother no longer had to worry about her son growing up to become the kind of man who brutalised women.

She'd been right, it had been infinitely better. Costa had loved living upstairs in the bakery with her, so much so that she'd had to find a wife for him and kick him out in the end, and up until a few years ago when Elena had deteriorated almost beyond recognition, he seemed to be living a very nice life indeed.

Elena. Now there was a problem encapsulated in five letters. Did she know? Costa had asked her over the telephone the other day, that Taki had paid for Valentina to have an abortion when she'd first arrived in England and that she was blaming Elena for it? Maria had crossed herself repeatedly when she heard this, God give them all strength, and she'd told him in no uncertain terms that the poor girl couldn't hurt a fly, never mind a baby. If Valentina was looking for someone to condemn for her decisions, she needed only look as far as Lenou, her husband and his mother.

He'd heard it all, he'd told her. He'd been standing at the top of the stairs listening to Valentina's accusations and he'd had to half throw her out of the house in the end because poor Elena was growing agitated, although she'd barely understood a word of it. And that was the worst part about the whole thing. Her grasp on reality was weakening. *She's really sick, Mamma.* She's not been herself, he'd cried, for years and Maria had sighed and told him that she could see that. It was as plain as the nose on the end of her face that something was wrong with Elena. Forget about the doctor. She needed to be in a place where they could help her. He'd hung up on her, again, just like all the other times, because when push came to shove, neither of them wanted to believe that they were approaching the end of the road.

Chapter 48

London – 1988

MY SISTER WAS really beautiful.

Another day and three more tablets. Elena wonders what would happen if she decided to take the pills in reverse order and swallow the white one before the green one and the red one. Perhaps she would find herself hanging upside down and talking to the doctor from the ceiling. Better not find out, Dr Nixon replies, they like routine in hospitals, it's part of the shtick. She winks at her and Elena can see it for the first time. A silky gossamer of trust suspended between them.

She was tall and elegant, with long black hair which reached all the way down to her waist and if the light caught it at the right angle, it shone like silk. She had big dark eyes and when she looked at you, you knew she felt fortunate. She was blessed to have looked the way she did in a world that valued beauty. She could have been anybody she wanted to be, her mother used to say, with a face like that. She'd secretly hoped she would catch the eye of the mayor of Ammochostos and that they'd live happily ever after in a great big house. Exalted on a hill and surrounded by orange blossoms.

Valentina had different ideas. She wanted to sew herself some fashionable clothes and move to Italy or France. She wanted to meet a famous photographer and have her pictures published in magazines. Sometimes they'd pretend they were already there, in Paris or Milan. Valentina would twirl around the room and pose for Elena's imaginary camera, *kiss, kiss,* and there'd be so much laughter then. Dreams, she tells her. She had so many dreams. All before she met him. The downside of good looks, her mother used to say. Being beautiful has its upsides and its downsides so she'd better watch her step.

Dr Nixon is not sitting behind her desk this morning and Elena is surprised to see that she has legs, knees and shiny black shoes which twinkle in the sunlight. They sit on chairs by the window and it's a privilege, she tells her, to allow her to do so.

You've reached a milestone.

She wants Elena to talk about the last time. The Day of the Butterfly, Elena calls it, because she'd been standing by the back door in her dressing gown watching her daughters chase a butterfly around the garden and she'd been so jealous of their joy. So very envious. It had been years since she'd felt even the faintest flutter of happiness. Years and years.

The sound of the doorbell had startled her from a reverie because she was always falling asleep on her elbows in those days. Forgetting where she was and what she was supposed to be doing. She'd forgotten to pick her daughter up from school so many times that

Costa had changed his hours at work. He didn't trust
her any more.

She'd opened the door and noticed that she had cut
off her hair and it was such a shock, she tells Dr Nixon,
to see her like that. A slap in the face. Another part of
her was missing. First the baby and then her hair. It was
as if she was disappearing before her in little pieces.

She wants to know about the conversation they had,
but Elena can't remember it. She looks outside the
window and the sky has changed colour again, only
this time it's streaked with pink and a blood-red sun
sets behind a row of white houses. It's cool outside and
Elena rubs at her arms to keep warm. She is wearing
her school uniform. She can see the playground and
the dark green olive trees lined up next to each other,
little old ladies stooped over their canes. When she
turns the corner and walks towards home, her mother
is standing on the doorstep with an empty bassinet in
her hands. *It's gone, the baby has gone!* She reaches out to
touch the basket.

What do you remember?

She doesn't want to remember anything. To recollect
is to leave oneself open to the possibility of pain and
she wants to hide these thoughts somewhere, along
with all the others, where no one will be able to find
them. It's what she does. What she's always done.

But she is here because somebody died. A baby died
and Elena has blood on her hands and it won't come
out with a bit of hot soapy water. That's what she said
to her, the last time she saw her. The Day of the Butterfly.

She pulls up the sleeves of her top and holds them out in front of her for the doctor to inspect.

Dr Nixon, I think I killed my sister's baby and then I killed my sister.

Chapter 49

London – 1988

SHE'S TURNED OVER a new leaf. The start of May.
The phone rings in the middle of the night. A harsh
unrelenting noise which pierces the silence of the dark
bedroom. *Ring, ring, ring.* Costa sits up and fumbles for
the lamp beside the bed. This can't be good news. If
the phone rings at this hour, something bad must have
happened. *Mamma.* The room is suddenly illuminated.

He races down the stairs so fast that she's worried
he might trip and roll to the floor, a falling rock gathering pace down a hillside. She can hear his voice,
strained and muffled, coming from someplace else.
Mamma? Oh. What do you want? It's not Maria. She sits
up against her pillows and wonders if she's awake or
asleep and why Costa has left his slippers by the bed
when it's so very cold outside. She thinks she might
take them to him in case his feet freeze on the January
ice but her attention is drawn, in that moment, to the
moon shining through a chink in the curtains and she
forgets about the slippers.

The moon beckons her over to the window. *Hello,*
moon. She has something important to tell her. Elena

gathers up her nightdress and climbs slowly out of the bed. She walks unsteadily towards the window. There is a baby asleep in the corner of the room in a little Perspex box and despite the light of the moon, it is the blackest night she has ever seen. She shivers at the memory of it.

Come, Elena. She pulls back the curtain and stares at her cold, hard, indifferent face. *Come closer,* she whispers. She presses her nose against the glass. *Good.* Now fetch a pair of scissors, she's saying, from downstairs and cut the strings that anchor me to this world. She wants to leave. It's what she's wanted for a long while and it's time, now, for her to float away and leave the sky bereft.

She shouts for Costa to come back up the stairs because she's afraid, now, of the ominous whisperings of the moon. *How?* he's asking. *Why?* A silence as he absorbs the enormity of what's just happened and she imagines him sitting on the bottom step and rubbing his forehead with his thumb like her mother used to do. *Let me tell her in my own way. She's not well.* Somebody must be sick, she thinks, for Costa to be talking like that. It's you, Dimitri Pavlou is saying. *You're the one who's sick.* She lets the curtain drop from her hands and she can hear him walking back up the stairs, only this time he's not running. There is a heaviness in his step and the wood creaks respectfully beneath his feet.

She covers her ears with her hands and she turns around to face him, but it's not Costa who's standing before her, or Dimitri Pavlou, but Pappa. Dear, kind Pappa. *Pappa!* She exclaims. *Where have you been all these years?* She's so very happy he's come back for her. He takes her into his arms and she buries her face in his chest and she tells him that she misses him, oh how she misses him, and he strokes her hair and kisses her cheek and everything is like it used to be when she was a little girl and Uncle Pedro used to turn her upside down and twirl her round and round. Tomorrow, he murmurs to her, when they return from the Pantopoleio, he has some sad news to share with her, some very sad news and she must be prepared. She asks him, then, if he is dying and he tells her that he's already dead. *I'm so sorry, Elena.*

Oh Pappa. He is crying and he looks at her with such pity and sadness that her heart breaks for him and she tells him that she's only sad because she's missed him and not to worry about her so much. *You do like to worry!* When he left, she explains, he took all the light with him and her whole world fell apart piece by piece, but she is glad that he's come back. Sweet Pappa. Come back from her memories to save her from herself.

~

Something has happened. Something truly terrible. Elena can tell from the mournful way the disembodied faces from her past look down at her. It's the way Mrs Mavrides had looked at Mrs Pavlou the day she'd read her coffee cup. *I'm so sorry, Elena.*

Someone has died. He tries to tell her who it is, but she struggles to comprehend the events he's describing.

His giant, enormous words float around like unscrambled letters on a silver screen in a language she doesn't have a code for. She remembers the day, back in time when they'd first met, that he'd taken her to the cinema to watch a film and she'd had no idea what was going on because it was all in English. She'd thought afterwards how easy it was to become lost in the moment and to pretend that you weren't, until one day, it wasn't possible to pretend any more and everyone knew you were lost except you.

She's not suffering any more. He says this to her again and again but she doesn't understand what it means. A baby born beneath an almond tree. How far, someone had once asked her, can a person stretch before they finally snap? She doesn't remember who it was now but she had looked for death that day and she had found it growing inside her. How far, she wonders, can a troubled mind stretch before the elastic snaps and the lights are turned off for good?

Chapter 50

London – 1988

IT'S TIME TO talk about her. There is nowhere left to hide.

The word which was always hanging between them like a knife, she'd infected her with it that day. Guilt. The word in the mist. Valentina's disease. She'd carried the burden by herself for too long, she'd said, and it was time for Elena to share the blame. They were sisters, weren't they, and isn't that what sisters did? Share the bad times as well as revel in the good?

There was a letter. A brown envelope with his name on the front, written in large swirly letters. The hand of a girl with long black hair, dabbling in things she knew nothing about. She'd given it to Elena before her exile and she'd begged her to deliver it. It was a confession, of a kind, about the baby, and it was a childish plea for help. Come and save me, Elena presumes it read. *I'm a shiny, black spider caught in a web.* Her sister had naïvely believed that it was his ignorance keeping them apart. If only he'd known, she'd screamed that day, none of this would have happened. If Elena had delivered the letter like she'd asked they'd be living happily ever after

with their child. But she hadn't. Instead, her friend
Andoni Pavlou had shoved it beneath his door and the
letter had found its way into the wrong hands.

Do you still think that, Elena? That this was your fault?

The man was an adult, Dr Nixon points out. And you
were two young girls with no experience of the world.
Prey, Elena thinks. He was a predator and Valentina his
prey, and she realises now that even if she had handed
him the letter it wouldn't have changed a thing.

Excuses. The life raft of the culpable.

There were ghosts, she explains. When she'd first
arrived at Valentina's house. Perhaps Valentina wasn't
living in Paris or Milan, but she'd expected to find her
living in a bubble of bliss, happily married to Taki. At
the very least, she'd be pleased to see her little sister, but
she wasn't. She was dwelling in the darkness. There were
shadows everywhere. Across the walls and ceilings and
the carpets and they flittered across her sister's face like
wretched souls when Taki walked into a room. She
should have known, then, that something was wrong
with her, but she was hurt by the reception she'd received
and was too self-absorbed to care. If only she'd looked
beyond the shadows. If only she'd seen more. If only
they'd all seen more.

Dr Nixon asks Elena what happened the day the lights
went out. *Can you tell me?* She couldn't live with herself
any more. She traded her life, that night. So her pain
might stop and the baby might have another chance at
existing because, at the end of the day, she thought her
daughter deserved it more than she did.

My beautiful sister killed herself.

Someone is crying now, a long low horrible moan and she knows that it's emanating from her and it doesn't matter any more because her tears have been hard-fought. Finally, she has earned the right to cry like this.

Let them come.

The cries are loud and visceral and it's as if someone is reaching deep into her chest and tearing out her beating heart and holding it before her. Look, they are saying. This is what it means to be human.

Let them come.

She cries for Giovanna Johnston, the Little Englesa of Ammochostos who died too soon, and for a little girl exposed to the cruelty of a child's funeral beneath an ominous crimson sky. She cries for Andoni Pavlou, who went off to war to become a hero and came home to his mother in blackened pieces. She mourns her Pappa, who died without warning and took all the kindness with him, and she mourns her sister's empty bassinet, its blankets wrapped around a broken promise. Most of all, she cries for her sister. Valentina. She had so many paths laid out before her but she slipped, instead, on sliding stones and plunged into oblivion.

Chapter 51

London – 2007

YOU'RE LATE. MARIA sits dressed and ready on the edge of her bed and shakes her long bony finger at the darkness. He's kept her waiting a good long while. She thought he would come for her on her ninetieth birthday, but he's begrudged her three more years. It was typical of her, Costa would joke, to hang around way past her welcome, although he suspected she was only there to make sure he was running things properly. *Perhaps,* she'd chuckle. *Perhaps.*

She's already wearing her coat but she asks the stranger if she'll need a bag where she is going. *I'd hate to leave without one.* It was a great fear of hers, embarking on a long journey without possessions. Like forgetting her apron or her welcoming smile. She felt exposed without her handbag. He assures her she won't need her belongings where she's going. A relief. The damn thing was like an anchor and she's been carrying it on her shoulders for seventy-five odd years. A long time to carry a bag, she tells him. A long time to be alive, come to think of it.

She called him a stranger but he wasn't a stranger. Not

really. She's seen him plenty of times before. He'd been lurking beneath the almond tree in her back garden when she'd given birth to Costa and she'd seen him at the graveside of many a friend's funeral. And he'd been there, of course. Standing among the crowd gathered in the middle of the road on the day her daughter had died.

She'll take her photograph. She must do that! She's been hiding in her pockets for almost half a century and Maria is not about to leave her behind. She won't need that either, he assures her. She'll be there waiting for her when they arrive, so there's little use for a worn picture, and her soul almost screams out of her body when she hears this. She has longed to see her again with every ounce of her being, but has never been sure if she deserves it.

She'd retired upstairs to her flat fifteen years ago, almost to the day, and Costa and Elena had taken over Petrakis Bakery. Costa had agreed, eventually, and only because the timing of the thing had been so fortuitous. Or so he'd claimed. In reality, he'd grown too fat and weary to walk his rounds with his sack on his back and bakery life suited him far better. *Just think of all the bourekia you'll get to scoff now*, Maria had laughed, as he'd finally hung up his uniform, and he'd pretended to sulk at the insinuation. That uniform! She could never get used to him wearing it. To her, he was always just a little boy playing make-believe with a box of dressing-up clothes.

She'd insisted they keep Maki on as assistant manager and how Costa had mocked her. *Maki?* he'd teased. *The delusional fantasist who didn't know his arm from his elbow?* And she'd conceded that she may have become accustomed to him, but only in the manner that a person learns to live with a spot or a scar and not in a good way at all. *A likely story,* Costa would laugh. *A very likely story.* He'd died in '95 from brain injuries he'd sustained in the Cypriot war and she'd cried for him, in the end, as if he had been her own flesh and blood. She'd cried like a baby for the poor man and it had almost broken her heart when she'd put his apron away for the last time a day after his funeral.

Petrakis had been a godsend to Elena. Maria remembers almost gasping at the sight of her after they'd discharged her from St Katherine's. She was frail and thin and her eyes were large and sunken, like two big lumps of coal. She would hug her clothes around her shoulders as if she were afraid of the air and Maria would wonder if her skeleton would crumble if she let herself go.

They'd given her a bag of pills to take home that was bigger than she was and Maria had been scared for them in those early days. For Elena, Costa and the girls. For what it would mean for their family to have a mother who was sick and had to swallow so many pills. This tablet for that and that pill for this. *What have they done to her?* she'd whispered to Costa. Why did she look like that? She was healing, he'd replied, and it would take time. It was a long slow process, not like putting bread in the oven and turning the timer on. She was lost and needed to find herself again. *Her sister committed suicide, Mamma. Give her a chance.*

That's when she'd decided. It was the comment about the bread rising in the oven and her sister's suicide and second chances and she knew, then, that it was time for her to relinquish the keys and let Costa and Elena take over Petrakis. It was exactly what the woman needed, she'd resolved. To rescue her from her grief. There was something restorative about the act of kneading and baking bread and it was impossible, in those moments, to feel sad. The shop saved me, she'd told Costa, and now it was time for it to save Elena.

She'd flourished. Slowly, at first, and it was Costa who came in the mornings to fire up the Champion and the Apprentice and greet the grumpy wholesalers unloading their vans and even deal with most of the customers. But she'd gradually grown interested in her surroundings like a twitchy mouse emerging from a hole in the wall.

After a while, and in a reversal of roles, it would be Maria sitting at the back of the shop sipping tea, her hair now whiter than the newly painted walls, while Elena served Anna-Maria Loizou. She could tell from her demeanour that she was starting to get better. Her cheeks had filled out, the dark circles around her eyes had begun to fade along with her nightmares and there was a palpable joy in her face, now, when the girls walked in looking for shamali after school. *See,* she'd joked to Costa, *it's the curative power of pastries. And the smell of cinnamon, of course.* Who could resist?

There was something else she'd come to realise as she sat at the back of the bakery and watched Elena serving the customers. Almost everybody she knew had passed away and it was their children who came into the shop to buy bread. Mrs Vasili and her big hair had succumbed to pneumonia five years previously and Mr Yiasoumi and Mrs Kyriacou had passed away last summer. George next door had died of cancer a few months ago and the shop next to theirs stood empty, waiting for a new owner. Costa, she'd like to hope. If he could pluck up the courage to borrow some money and knock through the walls dividing them.

The people she remembered from long ago felt more real to her than the people standing in their own flesh and she knew that the world was forging forwards without her because she was not a part of its future. *It's OK*, she'd say to Costa when he consoled her. She'd seen her reflection in the mirror, her smile now almost toothless and her face creased beyond recognition, and there was really no need to convince her of anything. She was dying, but she was happy to have achieved what she'd set out to do when she'd first set foot in London, England. To leave Green Lanes a little happier than she had found it, and it was time for the new generation to take over.

Nearly time, but not quite.

There's something else. Something that happened a long time ago. She unburdens herself to the darkness and it's a relief to say the words out loud after almost half a century of keeping their secret. She wasn't there for the execution of the thing, she tells the stranger. And she'd asked him to keep her out of it for the most part, but she can guess at the outcome because of the types of people Mr Styliano knew and because he never came back to bother her again.

It had saved her, this thing that they had done together. An exchange, Mr Styliano had whispered in her ear as they'd held each other between the walls of Kyrenia Castle. And, at the end of the day, her choices as a woman were limited. She could wait until he beat her to death, he'd said. Her son, cowering in the doorway, fearing he would be next. Or she could run and spend the rest of her life waiting for him to find her and mete out her ultimate punishment. *You choose.*

She had, and the choice she'd made had afforded her a second chance at life, but she'd carried a heaviness around in her chest all the same. She sighs and nods her head up and down. At the end of a man's life there must be a reckoning and it is time for hers. She covers her eyes, suddenly afraid of what might appear before her in the darkness. Her husband's face, perhaps, dancing in the embers of Mrs Iacovou's fire.

Instead, there is nothing and she weeps softly into her hands in gratitude. An absolution of a kind, she hopes. For trying to live a life worthy of it afterwards. Baking her breads, selling her cinnamon pastries and lending a sympathetic ear to those that needed her.

Tell me this, have I atoned?

She's growing tired now, so tired, and it comes just in time. The vision of the well. Standing at the bottom of the yard, just beyond the almond tree. Someone has taken the boards off the top of it so she can start using it again. To draw water, maybe, or to bury a secret. A little girl with big blue eyes stands beside it and she extends her hand towards her. She's overcome, and she falls to her knees and kisses the dust. Time hasn't changed her as she feared it would and she's exactly as she remembers her. She's been waiting for this moment for so long that it's now too much for her to bear and she wonders if she'll be able to get up again or if they'll find her on the floor. *Come*, she is saying. I'm ready, Maria thinks. To go. To see the well and face the truth.

She notices that someone else is standing with Katerina. A young woman. She's seen her before, in her bakery, many years ago. Or back in Kyrenia, perhaps, where everybody knew everybody and the neighbour was likely a cousin. She walks towards her and the outline of her pale round face becomes clearer and she smiles and nods a yia sas. Of course. How could she have not known that it was her all along? The girl with the sorrowful eyes and the rain-soaked hair.

She's not as sad as she used to be. She can't stay very long, she tells Maria, because it's growing light and the ovens need firing up, but she couldn't not come to bid farewell to the mighty Maria Petrakis and to thank her for bringing her back from the darkness. The girl laughs, then, because the name suited her so well and they all said as much. It's how she'd like to be remembered, Maria replies. The mighty Maria Petrakis.

Now run along, dear Elena. Katerina and I are heading upstairs to enjoy the last slice of shamali and with any luck, Mr Styliano from the base will join us.

Glossary

THE MAKING OF Mrs Petrakis is peppered with the Greek words and phrases which defined my childhood. I could almost hear them as I typed. The names of the pastries and sweets and delicious dishes my sisters and I grew up relishing. Each connoting something tantalisingly rich and flavoursome. I wanted to share them as they sounded to me, these words, to bring them to life through writing and consequently lend a layer of authenticity to the speech and actions of the characters.

In doing so, I appreciate that I may have aroused curiosities. What is this mysterious, polysyllabic dish? What does it consist of, what does it smell like? Is it sweet or savoury and what sensual, gastronomic journey do the characters experience when bringing the first forkful to their lips? I have tried to answer these questions by translating the words literally, in this glossary, and where possible, imaginatively. My motive: to extend a welcoming hand and a sense of belonging which I hope will endure beyond the pages of the book.

Afelia – pork fried in red wine and coriander

Anari – whey cheese

Avga – eggs

Avgolemoni – egg and lemon soup

Bakali – traditional grocery and deli

Baklava – filo and nut pastries soaked in honey

Beriptero – kiosk

Biblia – books

Bourekia – fried pastries filled with either sweet or savoury fillings, Anari cheese, custard or mince

Bouzouki – long-necked lute popular in Greece and Cyprus

Boxamati – breadstick

Chai – tea, usually brewed with cinnamon sticks

Christos Anesti – Christ is risen

Glafcos Clerides – fourth President of Cyprus 1993–2003. Also temporary President July 1974–December 1974 during the Cypriot civil war

Daktyla – ladies' fingers, filo pastry wrapped around crushed almonds, sugar and cinnamon

Eliopita – savoury olive pastry

Englesa – English lady

Englesoi – the English (pl)

Enosis – apolitical union (with Greece)

EOKA – Ethniki Organosis Kyprion Agoniston, a Greek Cypriot nationalist guerrilla organisation which fought to end British rule in Cyprus and campaigned for a union with Greece

Exo oi Tourkoi! – out with the Turks!

Faji (or *fakes*) – lentils

Ftiari – a type of shovel used to place bread into clay ovens

Flaounes – traditional cheese, raisin and egg scones eaten during Greek Easter

Foukou – barbecue

Galatobourekia – custard pies soaked in syrup

Giorgos Dalaras – popular Greek singer (b.1949)

Glika (or *glyka*) – sweets or preserves (singular, *gliko*)

Gojiakari – (colloq) old woman

Georgios Grivas – leader of the guerrilla EOKA organisation, campaigner for enosis with Greece until his death in 1974

Gymnasio – high school

Hade – come on

Halva – sweet semolina pudding soaked in syrup (also a sweet made from sesame)

Jisveh – (colloq) small metal saucepan used for cooking traditional coffee

Kafe – Greek coffee

Kafeneon – traditional, male-only café serving coffee, spirits, Greek delight and meze

Kaimaki – froth

Kalimera – good morning

Kalinihta – good night

Kalispera – good evening

Karydaki – preserved walnuts

Kita – look

Kleftiko – traditional slow-roasted meat

Koliva – dish made from boiled wheat and pomegranate, usually eaten in commemoration of the dead

Kolokotes – slightly sweetened Cypriot pumpkin pies

Koubes (also *koupes*) – bulgar croquettes filled with mince and spices

Koulouri – traditional white loaf with sesame seeds

Kourabiethes – butter biscuits filled with nuts and dusted with icing sugar, traditionally given as favours at weddings or christenings

Kyria – madam

Kyrie – sir

Kyrie eleison – an important prayer of Christian liturgy, but also used colloquially to express disbelief

Lambatha – large traditional candle

Leventi – beautiful young man

Liturgia – the Liturgy

Loukanika – semi-cured pork sausages seasoned with spices

Loukoumades – fried pastry balls soaked in honey

Macaronia – macaroni

Mahalebi (or *mahalepi*) – traditional Cypriot pudding made with water, milk and cornflour and traditionally served with rose syrup

Makarios – President Makarios III, served as the first President of Cyprus (1960–1977), surviving four assassination attempts and a coup d'état. Also Archbishop of Cyprus (1950–1977)

Marketler – Turkish grocery shops

Mashallah – Arabic phrase meaning 'God has willed it' but used colloquially as a term of appreciation

Melomakarona – crumbly honey cookies soaked in orange juice and brandy and traditionally served at Christmas

Melopita – honey pancake

Mou – my

Nana Mouskouri – popular Greek singer (b.1934)

Nyphi – bride

Pantopoleio – traditional farmers' market

Pastichio – Greek lasagne made with bucatini pasta

Pastirma – air-dried cured beef sausage

Pastitsia – almond cookies

Patates – potatoes

Pites – generic term for pastries, pancakes, pies or pitta breads

Portokalopites – orange cakes

Proxenia (or *broxenia*) – traditional matchmaking 'date' arranged by the families of the prospective couple

Putana – (colloq) whore

Ravioles – Cypriot ravioli

Shamali – syrupy semolina cake baked with yoghurt and mastic

Shamishi – fried semolina pie dusted in icing sugar

Simbethera – the mother of your daughter-in-law or son-in-law

Souvlakia – kebabs

Spanakopita – spinach pastry

Stifado – Greek stew, usually made with beef

Tahinopita – tahini cake

Tava – meat casserole cooked with vegetables, potatoes, tomatoes and spices

Thea – aunt, but also a polite form of address for an older woman

Tiropites – puff pastries filled with cheese

Trahana – fermented milk soup

Triantafyllo – rose cordial, usually blended with water or milk

Tsipa – sheep's buttermilk

Tsipopites – sweet cakes made from sheep's buttermilk and filo pastry

Xeni – (f) foreigner

Xenos – (m) foreigner

Xenoi – (pl) foreigners

Yia sas – hello

Zimari – dough

Acknowledgements

TO THE FIRST daisy in my chain, my dear friend and fellow alum, Sandra White. You always said I had a story to tell and you challenged me many times to write it. This is for you.

To my parents. Thank you for delving into your own jasmine-scented childhoods and sharing all the magical details which brought this book to life.

A heartfelt thanks to my husband, Jim, for sitting on our back step and listening to me read aloud. I enjoyed hearing your comments at first and then I came to rely on them.

A huge debt of gratitude to John Sutherland and Sarah Lee for reading an early draft of the manuscript and implanting two invaluable seeds. Confidence and possibility. Those seeds and a little water meant everything.

To my agent, Eleanor Birne at PEW Literary, my publisher, Lisa Highton at Two Roads, and my editor, Cari Rosen. Thank you for hearing the hum of the Cypriot cicadas from the very outset. Your belief both in me and Maria Petrakis made this book possible.

Last in my chain, but certainly not least. A special thank you to Luli and her daughter, Nikola, of Nick's fame. I'm grateful for the helpful hints, the wonderful cakes and the little table at the back of the shop with plenty of room for a pram. Your bakery on Green Lanes was an irresistible light at the end of a wintery road.

Author's Note

AN EARLY MEMORY. London in the late '80s. I'm standing in a bakery on Green Lanes with my dad. It's gloomy outside and the pavement is wet but the shop is warm and welcoming. Colourful pastries line the counters and a pair of silver tongs stands poised and ready to serve. The woman behind the cakes greets me with a smile but I reciprocate with a frown. I'm grumpy. I scrape my shoes against the floor, annoyed to have been dragged away from the allure of friends and weekend television to run errands for my mum in the cold.

Fast forward more decades than I'd like to admit and the transience of these moments leaves an indelible impression in reverse. If I could live again for the second time, I would go back and smile at the woman in the shop. Return her *'yia sas'* and absorb the scene greedily. And so to the next best thing. Reliving memories here, in the pages of this book. Memories made in little bakeries. To share the sounds, smells and tastes of my childhood. Honey, cinnamon, mastic, rose-water. Flavours to excite and delight.

In the background, the summer sun rises in the clear, blue sky to scorch the island of Cyprus. Dreamy holidays to the place of my parents' birth mingle with ubiquitous, yellow sands, parched soil, and the feeling of sun-burned shoulders. The smells of jasmine and chai pervade the evening air and they inspire, these scents. It's time to tell a story.

The voice belongs to a sixty-year old matriarch named Maria Petrakis and it is a surprise at first, this storytelling voice. I wasn't expecting it and wonder where it came from. Perhaps, looking back, she was always there. The head of her family, Maria is the mouthpiece of generations, of wisdom and hard-fought experiences woven into edible tapestries. She stands behind her own counter as one woman and yet she is every woman. It is through her formidable legacy that these recollections now flow. I hope you will enjoy getting to know Maria Petrakis as much as I enjoyed creating her. Above all, I hope that she will bring laughter, comfort and promise for the future in sticky, golden slices.